The Village in the Jungle

The Village in the Jungle

A Novel

LEONARD WOOLF

With an afterword by Christopher Ondaatje

ELAND

London

First published by Edward Arnold Limited 1913

This edition published by Eland Publishing Limited
61 Exmouth Market, London EC1R 4QL in 2008

The Village in the Jungle © 1913 The University of Sussex
'Pearls and Swine' from Stories from the East
© 1924 The University of Sussex

ISBN 978 0907871 29 3

Cover image: The Snake Charmer, 1907
(La Charmeuse des serpents), Rousseau, Henri J.F. (Le Douanier)
(1844-1910)/Musee d'Orsay, Paris, France, Lauros/Giraudon/
The Bridgeman Art Library

Text set in Great Britain by Anthony Gray
Printed in Spain by GraphyCems, Navarra

To V. W.

I've given you all the little, that I've to give;
You've given me all, that for me is all there is;
So now I just give back what you have given –
If there is anything to give in this.

Contents

Chapter 1

THE VILLAGE was called Beddagama, which means the village in the jungle. It lay in the low country or plains, midway between the sea and the great mountains which seem, far away to the north, to rise like a long wall straight up from the sea of trees. It was in, and of, the jungle; the air and smell of the jungle lay heavy upon it – the smell of hot air, of dust, and of dry and powdered leaves and sticks. Its beginning and its end was in the jungle, which stretched away from it on all sides unbroken, north and south and east and west, to the blue line of the hills and to the sea. The jungle surrounded it, overhung it, continually pressed in upon it. It stood at the door of the houses, always ready to press in upon the compounds and open spaces, to break through the mud huts, and to choke up the tracks and paths. It was only by yearly clearing with axe and katty that it could be kept out. It was a living wall about the village, a wall which, if the axe were spared, would creep in and smother and blot out the village itself.

There are people who will tell you that they have no fear of the jungle, that they know it as well as the streets of Maha Nuwara or their own compounds. Such people are either liars and boasters, or they are fools, without understanding or feeling for things as they really are. I knew such a man once, a hunter and tracker of game, a little man with hunched up shoulders and peering, cunning little eyes, and a small dark face all pinched and lined, for he spent his life crouching, slinking, and peering through the undergrowth and the trees. He was more silent than the leopard and more cunning than the jackal: he knew the tracks better than the doe who leads the herd. He would boast that he could see a buck down wind before it could scent him, and a leopard through the thick undergrowth before it could see him. 'Why should I fear the jungle?' he would say. 'I know it better than my own compound. A few trees and

9

bushes and leaves, and some foolish beasts. There is nothing to fear there.' One day he took his axe in his hand, and the sandals of deer-hide to wear in thorny places, and he went out to search for the shed horns of deer, which he used to sell to traders from the towns. He never returned to the village again, and months afterwards in thick jungle I found his bones scattered upon the ground, beneath some thorn bushes, gnawed by the wild pig and the jackal, and crushed and broken by the trampling of elephants. And among his bones lay a bunch of peacock feathers that he had collected and tied together with a piece of creeper, and his betel-case, and the key of his house, and the tattered fragments of his red cloth. In the fork of one of the thorn bushes hung his axe: the massive wooden handle had been snapped in two. I do not know how he died; but I know that he had boasted that there was no fear in the jungle, and in the end the jungle took him.

All jungles are evil, but no jungle is more evil than that which lay about the village of Beddagama. If you climb one of the bare rocks that jut up out of it, you will see the jungle stretched out below you for mile upon mile on all sides. It looks like a great sea, over which the pitiless hot wind perpetually sends waves unbroken, except where the bare rocks, rising above it, show like dark smudges against the grey-green of the leaves. For ten months of the year the sun beats down and scorches it; and the hot wind in a whirl of dust tears over it, tossing the branches and scattering the leaves. The trees are stunted and twisted by the drought, by the thin and sandy soil, by the dry wind. They are scabrous, thorny trees, with grey leaves whitened by the clouds of dust which the wind perpetually sweeps over them: their trunks are grey with hanging, stringy lichen. And there are enormous cactuses, evil-looking and obscene, with their great fleshy green slabs, which put out immense needle-like spines. More evil-looking still are the great leafless trees, which look like a tangle of gigantic spiders' legs – smooth, bright green, jointed together – from which, when they are broken, oozes out a milky, viscous fluid.

And between the trees are the bushes which often knit the whole jungle together into an impenetrable tangle of thorns. On the ground beneath the trees it is very still and very hot; for the sterile earth is covered with this thorny matted undergrowth, through which the wind cannot force its way. The sound of the great wind rushing over the tree-tops makes the silence below seem more heavy. The air is heavy with the heat beating up from the earth, and with the smell of dead leaves. All the bushes and trees seem to be perpetually dying for ten months of the year, the leaves withering, and the twigs and branches decaying and dropping off, to be powdered over the ground among the coarse withered grass and the dead and blackened shrubs. And yet every year, when the rains come, the whole jungle bursts out again into green; and it forces its way forward into any open space, upon the tracks, into villages and compounds, striving to blot out everything in its path.

If you walk all day through the jungle along its tangled tracks, you will probably see no living thing. It is so silent and still there that you might well believe that nothing lives in it. You might perhaps in the early morning hear the trumpeting and squealing of a herd of elephants, or the frightened bark of the spotted deer, or the deeper bark of the sambur, or the blaring call of the peacock. But as the day wore on, and the heat settled down upon the trees, you would hear no sound but the rush of the wind overhead, and the grating of dry branches against one another. Yet the shadows are full of living things, moving very silently, themselves like shadows, between the trees, slinking, under the bushes and peering through the leaves.

For the rule of the jungle is first fear, and then hunger and thirst. There is fear everywhere: in the silence and in the shrill calls and the wild cries, in the stir of the leaves and the grating of branches, in the gloom, in the startled, slinking, peering beasts. And behind the fear is always the hunger and the thirst, and behind the hunger and the thirst fear again. The herd of deer must come down to drink at the water-hole. They come down driven by their thirst, very silently through the deep shadows of the trees to the water lying white under the moon. They glide like shadows out of the shadows, into the moonlight, hesitating, tiptoeing, throwing up their heads to stare again into the darkness, leaping back only to be goaded on again by their thirst, ears twitching to catch a sound, and nostrils quivering to catch a scent of danger. And when the black muzzles go down into the water, it is only for a moment; and then with a rush the herd scatters back again terror-stricken into the darkness. And behind the herd comes the leopard, slinking through the undergrowth. Whom has he to fear? Yet there is fear in his eyes and in his slinking feet, fear in his pricked ears and in the bound with which he vanishes into the shadows at the least suspicious sound.

In the time of the rains the jungle might seem to be a pleasant place. The trees are green, and the grass stands high in the open spaces. Water lies in pools everywhere; there is no need to go stealthily by night to drink at rivers or water-holes. The deer and the pig roam away, growing fat on the grass and the young leaves and the roots; the elephant travels far from the river bank. The time of plenty lasts, however, but a little while. The wind from the north-east drops, the rain fails; for a month a great stillness lies over the jungle; the sun looks down from a cloudless sky; the burning air is untempered by a breath of wind. It is spring in the jungle, a short and fiery spring, when in a day the trees burst out into great masses of yellow or white flowers, which in a day wither and die away.

The pools and small water-holes begin to dry up under the great heat; the earth becomes caked and hard. Then the wind begins to blow from the south-west, fitfully at first, but growing steadier and stronger every day. A little rain falls, the last before the long drought sets in. The hot, dry wind sweeps over the trees. The grass and the shrubs die down; the leaves on the small trees shrivel up, and grow black and fall. The grey earth crumbles into dust, and splits beneath the sun. The little streams run dry; the great rivers shrink, until only a thin stream of water trickles slowly along in the middle of their immense beds of yellow sand. The water-holes are dry; only here and there in the very deepest of them, on the rocks, a little muddy water still remains.

Then the real nature of the jungle shows itself. Over great tracts there is no water for the animals to drink. Only the elephants remember the great rivers, which lie far away, and whose banks they left when the rains came; as soon as the south-west wind begins to blow, they make for the rivers again. But the deer and the pig have forgotten the rivers. In the water-holes the water has sunk too low for them to reach it on the slippery rocks; for days and nights they wander round and round the holes, stretching down their heads to the water, which they cannot touch. Many die of thirst and weakness around the water-holes. From time to time one, in his efforts to reach the water, slips, and falls into the muddy pool, and in the evening the leopard finds him an easy prey. The great herds of deer roam away, tortured by thirst, through the parched jungle. They smell the scent of water in the great wind that blows in from the sea. Day after day they wander away from the rivers into the wind, south towards the sea, stopping from time to time to raise their heads and snuff in the scent of water, which draws them on. Again many die of thirst and weakness on the way; and the jackals follow the herds, and pull down in the open the fawns that their mothers are too weak to protect. And the herds wander on until at last they stand upon the barren, waterless shore of the sea.

Such is the jungle which lay about the village of Beddagama. The village consisted of ten scattered houses, mean huts made of mud plastered upon rough jungle sticks. Only one of the huts had a roof of tiles, that of the village headman Babehami; the others were covered with a thatch of cadjans, the dried leaves of the coconut palm. Below the huts to the east of the village lay the tank, a large shallow depression in the jungle. Where the depression was deepest the villagers had raised a long narrow bund or mound of earth, so that when the rain fell the tank served as a large pond in which to store the water. Below the bund lay the stretch of rice-fields, about thirty acres, which the villagers cultivated, if the tank filled with water, by cutting a hole in the bund, through which the water from the tank ran into the fields. The jungle rose high and dense around the fields and the tank; it stretched away unbroken, covering all the country except the fields, the tank, and the little piece of ground upon which the houses and compounds stood.

The villagers all belonged to the *goiya* caste, which is the caste of cultivators. If you had asked them what their occupation was, they would have replied the cultivation of rice; but in reality they only cultivated rice about once in ten years. Rice requires water in plenty; it must stand in water for weeks before it grows ripe for the reaping. It could only be cultivated if the village tank filled with water, and much rain had to fall before the tank filled. If the rains from the north-east in November were good, and the people could borrow seed, then the rice-fields in January and February were green, and the year brought the village health and strength; for rice gives strength as does no other food. But this happened very rarely. Usually the village lived entirely by cultivating *chenas*. In August every man took a katty and went out into the jungle and cut down the undergrowth, over an acre or two. Then he returned home. In September he went out again and set fire to the dead undergrowth, and at night the jungle would be lit up by points of fire scattered around the village for miles; for so sterile is the earth, that a *chena*, burnt and sown for one year, will yield no crop again for ten years. Thus the villagers must each year find fresh jungle to burn. In October the land is cleared of ash and rubbish, and when the rains fall in November the ground is sown broadcast with millet or *kurakkan*[1] or maize, with pumpkins, chillies, and a few vegetables. In February the grain is reaped, and on it the village must live until the next February. No man will ever do any other work, nor will he leave the village in search of work. But even in a good year the grain from the *chenas* was scarcely sufficient for the villagers. And just as in the jungle fear and hunger for ever crouch, slink, and peer with every beast, so hunger and the fear of hunger always lay upon the village. It was only for a few months each year after the crop was reaped that the villagers knew the daily comfort of a full belly. And the grain sown in *chenas* is an evil food, heating the blood, and bringing fever and the foulest of all diseases, *parangi*. There were few in the village without the filthy sores of *parangi*, their legs eaten out to the bone with the yellow, sweating ulcers, upon which the flies settle in swarms. The naked children, soon after their birth, crawled about with immense pale yellow bellies, swollen with fever, their faces puffed with dropsy, their arms and legs thin, twisted little sticks.

The spirit of the jungle is in the village, and in the people who live in it. They are simple, sullen, silent men. In their faces you can see plainly the fear and hardship of their lives. They are very near to the animals which

1 *Kurakkan*, a grain, *Eleusine coracana*.

live in the jungle around them. They look at you with the melancholy and patient stupidity of the buffalo in their eyes, or the cunning of the jackal. And there is in them the blind anger of the jungle, the ferocity of the leopard, and the sudden fury of the bear.

In Beddagama there lived a man called Silindu, with his wife Dingihami. They formed one of the ten families which made up the village, and all the families were connected more or less closely by marriage. Silindu was a cousin of the wife of Babehami, the headman, who lived in the adjoining compound. Babehami had been made a headman because he was the only man in the village who could write his name. He was a very small man, and was known as *Punchi Arachchi* (the little *Arachchi*[1]). Years ago, when a young man, he had gone on a pilgrimage to the *vihare*[2] at Medamahanuwara. He had fallen ill there, and had stayed for a month or two in the priest's *pansala*. The priest had taught him his letters, and he had learnt enough to be able to write his own name.

Silindu was a cultivator like the other villagers. The village called him *tikak pissu* (slightly mad). Even in working in the *chena* he was the laziest man in the village. His real occupation was hunting; that is to say he shot deer and pig, with a long muzzle-loading gas-pipe gun, whenever he could creep up to one in the thick jungle; or, lying by the side of a waterhole at night, shoot down some beast who had come there to drink. Why this silent little man, with the pinched-up face of a grey monkey and the long, silent, sliding step, should be thought slightly mad, was not immediately apparent. He seemed only at first sight a little more taciturn and inert than the other villagers.

But the village had its reasons. Silindu slept with his eyes open like some animals, and very often he would moan, whine, and twitch in his sleep like a dog; he slept as lightly as a deer, and would start up from the heaviest sleep in an instant fully awake. When not in the jungle he squatted all day long in the shadow of his hut, staring before him, and no one could tell whether he was asleep or awake. Often you would have

1   The lowest rank of headman, the headman over a village
2   A Buddhist temple containing an image of Buddha.

to shout at him and touch him before he would attend to what you had to say.

But the strangest thing about him was this, that although he knew the jungle better than any man in the whole district, and although he was always wandering through it, his fear of it was great. He never attempted to explain or to deny this fear. When other hunters laughed at him about it, all he would say was, 'I am not afraid of any animal in the jungle, no, not even of the bear or of the solitary elephant (whom all of you really fear), but I am afraid of the jungle.' But though he feared it, he loved it in a strange, unconscious way, in the same unconscious way in which the wild buffalo loves the wallow, and the leopard his lair among the rocks. Silent, inert, and sullen he worked in the *chena* or squatted about his compound, but when he started for the jungle he became a different man. With slightly bent knees and toes turned out, he glided through the impenetrable scrub with a long, slinking stride, which seemed to show at once both the fear and the joy in his heart.

And Silindu's passions, his anger, and his desire were strange and violent even for the jungle. It was not easy to rouse his anger; he was a quiet man, who did not easily recognise the hand which wronged him. But if he were roused he would sit for hours or days motionless in his compound, his mind moving vaguely with hatred; and then suddenly he would rise and search out his enemy, and fall upon him like a wild beast. And sometimes at night a long-drawn howl would come from Silindu's hut, and the villagers would laugh and say, 'Hark! The leopard is with his mate,' and the women next morning when they saw Dingihami drawing water from the tank would jeer at her.

At length Dingihami bore twins, two girls, of whom one was called Punchi Menika and the other Hinnihami. When the women told Silindu that his wife was delivered of two girls, he rushed into the hut and began to beat his wife on the head and breasts as she lay on the mat, crying, '*Vesi! Vesi mau!* Where is the son who is to carry my gun into the jungle, and who will clear the *chena* for me? Do you bear me *vesi* for me to feed and clothe and provide dowries? Curse you!' And this was the beginning of Silindu's quarrel with Babehami, the headman; for Babehami, hearing the cries of Dingihami and the other women, rushed up from the adjoining compound and dragged Silindu from the house.

Dingihami died two days after giving birth to the twins. Silindu had a sister called Karlinahami, who lived in a house at the other end of the village. Misfortune had fallen upon her, the misfortune so common in the life of a jungle village. Her husband had died of fever two months before: a month later she bore a child which lived but two weeks. When Dingihami died, Silindu brought her to his hut to bring up his two children. Her hut was abandoned to the jungle. When the next rains fell the mud walls crumbled away, the tattered roof fell in, the jungle crept forward into the compound and over the ruined walls; and when Punchi Menika was two years old, only a little mound in the jungle marked the place where Karlinahami's house had stood.

Karlinahami was a short, dark, stumpy woman, with large impassive eyes set far apart from one another, flat broad cheeks, big breasts, and thick legs. Unlike her brother she was always busy, sweeping the house and compound, fetching water from the tank, cooking, and attending to the children. Very soon after she came to Silindu's house she began to talk and think of the children as though she had borne them herself. Like her brother she was slow and sparing of speech; and her eyes often had in them the look, so often in his, as if she were watching something far away in the distance. She very rarely took much part in the interminable gossip of the other village women when they met at the tank or outside their huts. This gossip is always connected with their husbands and children, food and quarrels.

But Karlinahami was noted for her storytelling: she was never very willing to begin, but often, after the evening meal had been eaten, the women and many of the men would gather in Silindu's compound to listen to one of her stories. They sat round the one room or outside round the door, very still and silent, listening to her droning voice as she squatted by the fire and stared out into the darkness. Outside lay Silindu, apparently paying no attention to the tale. The stories were either old tales which she had learnt from her mother, or were stories usually about Buddha, which she had heard told by pilgrims round the campfire on their way to pilgrimages, or in the *madamas* or pilgrims' resting-places at festivals. These tales, and a curious droning chant with which she used to sing them to sleep, were the first things that the two children remembered. This chant was peculiar to Karlinahami, and no other woman of the village used it. She had learnt it from her mother. The words ran thus:

> Sleep, child, sleep against my side,
> *Aiyo! Aiyo!* The weary way you've cried;
> Hush, child, hush, pressed close against my side.
>
> *Aiyo! Aiyo!* Will the trees never end?
> Our women's feet are weary; O Great One, send
> Night on us, that our wanderings may end.
>
> Hush, child, hush, thy father leads the way,
> Thy mother's feet are weary, but the day
> Will end somewhere for the followers in the way.
>
> *Aiyo! Aiyo!* The way is rough and steep,
> *Aiyo!* The thorns are sharp, the rivers deep,
> But the night comes at last. So sleep, child, sleep.

Until Punchi Menika and Hinnihami were three years old Silindu appeared not even to be aware of their existence. He took no notice of them in the house or compound, and never spoke about them. But one day he was sitting in front of his hut staring into the jungle, when Punchi Menika crawled up to him and put her hand on his knee, and looked solemnly up into his face. Silindu looked down at her, took her by her hands, and stood her up between his two knees.

He stared vacantly into her eyes for some time, and then suddenly he began to speak to her in a low voice:'Little toad! Why have you left the pond? Isn't there food there for your little belly? Rice and coconuts and mangoes and little cakes of *kurakkan*? Is the belly full, that you have left the pond for the jungle? Foolish little toad! The water is good, but the trees are evil. You have come to a bad place of dangers and devils. Yesterday, little toad, I lay under a *domba* tree by the side of a track, my gun in my hand, waiting for what might pass. The devils are very angry in the jungle, for there has been no rain now for these three months. The water-holes are dry; the leaves and grass are brown; the deer are very thin; and the fawns, dropped this year, are dying of weakness and hunger and thirst. Therefore, the devils are hungry, and there is nothing more terrible than a hungry devil. Well, there I lay, flat on the ground, with my gun in my hand; and I saw on the opposite side of the track, lying under a *domba* tree, a leopardess waiting for what might pass. I put down my gun, and, "Sister," I said, "is the belly empty?" For her coat was mangy, and the belly caught up below, as though with pain. "*Yakko*, he-devil," she answered, "three days now I have killed but one thin grey monkey, and there are two cubs in the cave to be fed." "*Yakkini*, she-devil," I said, "there are two little toads at home to be fed. But I still have a handful of *kurakkan* in my hut, from which my sister can make cakes. It remains from last year's *chena*, and after it is eaten there will be nothing. The headman, too, is pressing for the three shillings[1] body tax. 'How,' I say to him, 'can there be money where there is not even food?' But the *kurakkan* will last until next *poya*[2] day. Therefore, your hunger is greater than mine. The first kill is yours." So we lay still a long time, and at last I heard far away the sound of a hoof upon a dry stick. "Sister," I whispered, "I hear a deer coming this way." "*Yakko*, have you no ears?" she said. "A long while now I have been listening to a herd of wild pig coming down wind. Can you not even now hear their strong breathing, and their rooting in the dry earth, and the patter of the young ones' feet on the dry leaves?" "*Yakkini*," I said, for I heard her teeth clicking in the darkness, "the ear of the hungry is in the belly: the sound of your teeth can be heard a *hoo*[3] cry's distance away." So we lay still again, and at last the herd of pigs came down the track. First came an old boar, very black, his tusks shining white in the shadows; then many sows and young boars; and here and there the little pigs running in

1   Shilling used colloquially for the half *rupee* or fifty cents = 5p
2   A *poya* day is the day of the change of the moon, which is kept as a sacred day by the Buddhists, answering in some ways to the Christian Sunday.
3   A common method of measuring distance – the distance being that at which it is possible to hear a man cry '*hoo*'.

and out among the sows. And as they passed, one of the little pigs ran out near the *domba* bush, and *Yakkini* sprang and caught it in her teeth, and leapt with it into the branch of a *palu* tree which overhung the path. There she sat, and the little pig in her mouth screamed to its mother. Then all the little pigs ran together screaming, and stood on one side, near the bush where I lay; and the great boars and the young boars and sows ran round the *palu* tree, looking up at *Yakkini*, and making a great noise. And the old sow, who had borne the little pig in *Yakkini*'s mouth, put her forefeet against the trunk of the tree, and looked up, and said, "Come down, *Yakkini*; she-devil, thief. Are you afraid of an old, tuskless sow? Come down." But the leopardess laughed, and bit the little pig in the back behind the head until it died, and she called down to the old sow, "Go your way, mother. There are two cubs at home in the cave, and they are very hungry. Every year I drop but one or two cubs in the cave, but the whole jungle swarms with your spawn. I see eight brothers and sisters of your child there by the *domba* bush. Go your way, lest I choose another for my mate. Also, I do not like your man's teeth." The old boar and the sows were very angry, and for a long while they ran round the tree, and tore at it with their tusks, and looked up and cursed *Yakkini*. But *Yakkini* sat and watched them, and licked the blood which dripped from the little pig's back. I too lay very still under my *domba* bush, for there is danger in an angry herd. At last the old boar became tired, and he gathered the little pigs together in the middle of the herd, and led them away down the track. Then *Yakkini* dropped to the ground, and bounded away into the jungle, carrying the little pig in her mouth. So you see, little crow, it is a bad place to which you have come. Be careful, or some other devil will drop on you out of a bush, and carry you off in his mouth.'

While Silindu had been speaking, Hinnihami had crawled and tottered across the compound to join her sister. At the end of his long story she was leaning against his shoulder. From that day he seemed to regard the two children differently from the rest of the world in which he lived. He was never tired of pouring out to them in a low, monotonous drone his thoughts, opinions, and doings. That they did not understand a word of what he said did not trouble him in the least; but when they grew old enough to understand and to speak and to question him, he began to take a new pleasure in explaining to them the world in which he lived.

It was a strange world, a world of bare and brutal facts, of superstition, of grotesque imagination; a world of trees and the perpetual twilight of their shade; a world of hunger and fear and devils, where a man was helpless before the unseen and unintelligible powers surrounding him. He would go over to them again and again in the season of drought the reckoning of his small store of grain, and the near approach of the time when it would be exhausted; his perpetual fear of hunger; his means and plans for obtaining just enough for existence until the next *chena* season. But, above all, his pleasure seemed to be to tell them of the jungle, of his wanderings in search of game, of his watchings by the water-holes at night, of the animals and devils which lived among its shadows.

Chapter 2

SO PUNCHI MENIKA and Hinnihami grew up to be somewhat different from the other village children, who crawl and play about the compounds, always with the women and always listening to women's gossip. Long before they had grown strong and big enough to go down in the morning and evening with Karlinahami to the tank, and to carry back on their heads the red earthenware waterpots, they had learnt from Silindu to sit by his side for hour upon hour through the hot afternoons, very still and very silent, while he stared silently before him, or droned out his interminable tales. They grew up to be strange and silent children, sitting one on either side of him in a long, thoughtless trance. And they learnt to believe all he told them about the strange world of jungle which surrounded them, the world of devils, animals, and trees. But above all they learnt to love him, blindly, as a dog loves his master.

When they grew old enough to trot along by his side, Silindu used to take them out with him into the jungle. The villagers were astonished and shocked, but Silindu went his own way. He showed them the water-holes upon the rocks; the thick jungle where the elephant hides himself from the heat of the day, strolling leisurely among the trees and breaking off great branches to feed upon the leaves as he strolls; the wallow of the buffalo, and the caves where the bear and the leopard make their lairs. He showed them the sambur lying during the day in the other great caves; they dashed out, tens and tens of them, like enormous bats from the shadow of the overhanging rocks, to disappear with a crash into the jungle below. He taught them to walk so that no leaf rustled or twig snapped under their feet, to creep up close to the deer and the sambur and the pig. They were surprised at first that the animals in the jungle did not speak to them as they always did to Silindu when he was alone. But Silindu explained it to them. 'You are very young,' he said. 'You do not know the tracks. You are strange to the beasts. But they know me. I have grown old among the tracks. A man must live many years in the jungle before the beasts speak to him, or he can understand what they say.'

Punchi Menika and Hinnihami were also unlike the other village children in appearance. They, like Silindu, never had fever, and even in the days of greatest scarcity Karlinahami had seen that they got food. Karlinahami was far more careful to wash them than most mothers are: she used to quote the saying, 'Dirt is bad and children are trouble, but a dirty child is the worst of troubles.' The result was that they never got *parangi*, or the swollen belly and pale skin of fever. Their skin was smooth and blooming; it shone with a golden colour, like the coat of a fawn when the sun shines on it. Their eyes were large and melancholy; like the eyes of Buddha in the Jataka, 'they were like two windows made of sapphire shining in a golden palace.' Their limbs were strong and straight, for their wanderings with Silindu had made their muscles firm as a man's, not soft like the women's who sit about in the compound, cooking and gossiping and sleeping all day.

There was therefore considerable jealousy among the women, and ill-feeling against Karlinahami, when they saw how her foster children were growing up. When they were ten or eleven years old, it often burst out against her in angry taunts at the tank.

'O Karlinahami! Nanchohami, the headman's wife, would say, 'you are growing an old woman and, alas, childless! But you have done much for your brother's children. Shameless they must be to leave it to you to fetch the water from the tank and not to help you. This is the fourth chatty full you are carrying today. I have seen it with these eyes. The lot of the childless woman is a hard one. See how my little one of eight years helps me!'

'Nanchohami, your tongue is still as sharp as chillies. Punchi Menika has gone with my brother, and Hinnihami is busy in the house.'

'Punchi Menika wants but three things to make her a man. I pity you, Karlinahami, to live in the house of a madman, and to bring up his children shameless, having no children of your own. They are *vedda*[1] children, and will be *vedda* women, wandering in the jungle like men.'

The other women laughed, and Angohami, a dirty shrivelled woman, with thin shrivelled breasts, called out in a shrill voice: 'Why should we suffer these *veddas* in the village? Their compound smells of their own droppings, and of the offal and rotten meat on which they feed. I have borne six children, and the last died but yesterday. In the morning he was well: then Silindu cast the evil eye upon him as he passed our door, and in the evening he was dead. They wither our children that their own may thrive.'

'You lie,' said Karlinahami, roused for the moment by this abuse; 'you lie, mother of dirt. Yesterday at this hour I saw your Podi Sinho here in the tank, pale and shivering with fever, and pouring the cold tank water over himself. How should such a mother keep her children? All know that you have borne six, and that all are dead. What did you ever give them but foul words?'

'Go and lie with your brother, the madman, the *vedda*, the pariah,' shrieked Angohami as Karlinahami turned to go. 'Go to your brother of the evil eye. You blighter of others' children, eater of offal, *vesi, vesige mau*! Go to him of the evil eye, *belli, bellige duwa*; go to your brother. *Aiyo! Aiyo!* My little Podi Sinho! I am a mother only of the dead, a mother of six dead children. Look at my breasts, shrivelled and milkless. I say to the father of my child,[2] "Father of Podi Sinho," I say, "there is no *kurakkan* in the house, there is no millet and no pumpkin, not even a pinch of salt. Three days now I have eaten nothing but jungle leaves. There is no milk in my breasts for the child." Then I get foul words and blows. "Does the rain come in August?" he says. "Can I make the *kurakkan* flower in July? Hold your tongue, you fool. August is the month in which the children die. What can I do?" Then comes fever and

---

1   The *veddas* are the aborigines of Ceylon, and are or were hunters. They are often identified with *Yakkas* or devils.

2   A Sinhalese woman will not speak to or refer to her husband by name. She always speaks of or to him as 'The father of my child,' or 'The father of Podi Sinho,' etc., or simply 'He'.

Silindu's evil eye, curse him, and the little ones die. *Aiyo! Aiyo!*'

'Your man is right,' said Nanchohami. 'This is the month when the children die. Last year in this month I buried one and my brother's wife another. Good rain never falls now, and there is always hunger and fever. The old die and the little ones with them. The father of my children has but nine houses under him, and makes but five shillings a year from his headmanship. His father's father, who was headman before him, had thirty houses in his headmanship, and twenty shillings were paid him by the Government every year, besides twenty-four *kurunies*[1] of paddy from the fields below the tank. I have not seen rice these five years. The headman now gives all and receives nothing.' Here one of the women laughed. 'You may well laugh, Podi Nona,' she continued. 'Did not he[2] lend your man last year twenty *kurunies* of *kurakkan*, and has a grain of it come back to our house? And Silindu owes another thirty, and came but yesterday for more. And Angohami there, who whines about her Podi Sinho, her man has had twenty-five *kurunies* since the reaping of the last crop.'

These words of Nanchohami were not without effect. An uneasy movement began among the little group of women at the mention of debts: clothes were gathered up, the *chatties* of water placed on their heads, and they began to move away out of reach of the sharp tongue of the headman's wife. And as they moved away up the small path, which led from the tank to the compounds, they murmured together that Nanchohami did not seem to remember that they had to repay two *kurunies* of *kurakkan* for every *kuruni* lent to them.

Nanchohami had touched the mainspring upon which the life of the village worked – debt. The villagers lived upon debt, and their debts were the main topic of their conversation. A good *kurakkan* crop, from two to four acres of *chena*, would be sufficient to support a family for a year. But no one, not even the headman, ever enjoyed the full crop which he had reaped. At the time of reaping a band of strangers from the little town of

1 *Kuruni* is a measure employed in the measurement of grain.
2 *Vide* note *supra*.

Kamburupitiya, thirty miles away, would come into the village. Mohamadu Lebbe Ahamadu Cassim, the Moorman boutique-keeper, had supplied clothes to be paid for in grain, with a hundred per cent interest, at the time of reaping; the fat Sinhalese *Mudalali*,[1] Kodikarage Allis Appu, had supplied grain and curry stuffs on the same terms; and among a crowd of smaller men the sly-faced low-caste man, who called himself Achchige Don Andris (his real name Andrissa would have revealed his caste), who, dressed in dirty white European trousers and a coat, was the agent of the tavern-keeper in Kamburupitiya, from whom the villagers had taken on credit the native spirit, made from the juice of the coconut flowers, to be drunk at the time of marriages. The villagers neither obtained nor expected any pity from this horde. With the reaping of the *chenas* came the settlement of debts. With their little greasy notebooks, full of unintelligible letters and figures, they descended upon the *chenas*; and after calculations, wranglings, and abuse, which lasted for hour after hour, the accounts were settled, and the strangers left the village, their carts loaded with pumpkins, sacks of grain, and not unfrequently the stalks of Indian hemp,[2] which by Government order no man may grow or possess, for the man that smokes it becomes mad. And when the strangers had gone, the settlement with the headman began; for the headman, on a small scale, lent grain on the same terms in times of scarcity, or when seed was wanted to sow the *chenas*.

In the end the villager carried but little grain from his *chena* to his hut. Very soon after the reaping of the crop he was again at the headman's door, begging for a little *kurakkan* to be repaid at the next harvest, or tramping the thirty miles to Kamburupitiya to hang about the bazaar, until the *Mudalali* agreed once more to enter his name in the greasy notebook.

With the traders in Kamburupitiya the transactions were purely matters of business, but with the headman the whole village recognised that they were something more. It was a very good thing for Babehami, the

1 Term applied usually to a rich trader.
2 Called *bhang, ganja*, or hashish

Arachchi, to feel that Silindu owed him many *kurunies* of *kurakkan* which he could not repay. When Babehami wanted someone to clear a *chena* for him, he asked Silindu to do it; and Silindu, remembering the debt, dared not refuse. When Silindu shot a deer – for which offence the *Arachchi* should have brought him before the police court at Kamburupitiya – he remembered his debt, and the first thing he did was to carry the best piece of meat as an offering to the headman's house. And Babehami was a quiet, cunning man in the village: he never threatened, and rarely talked of his loans to his debtors, but there were few in the village who dared to cross him, and who did not feel hanging over them the power of the little man.

The power which they felt hanging over them was by no means imaginary; it could make the life of the man who offended the headman extremely unpleasant. It was not only by his loans that Babehami had his hand upon the villagers; their daily life could be made smooth or difficult by him at every turn.

The life of the village and of every man in it depended upon the cultivation of *chenas*. A *chena* is merely a piece of jungle, which every ten years is cleared of trees and undergrowth and sown with grain broadcast and with vegetables. The villagers owned no jungle themselves; it belonged to the Crown, and no one might fell a tree or clear a *chena* in it without a permit from the Government. It was through these permits that the headman had his hold upon the villagers. Application for one had to be made through him; it was he who reported if a clearing had been made without one, or if a man, having been given one, cleared more jungle than it allowed him to clear. Everyone in the village knew well that Babehami's friends would find no difficulty in obtaining the authority to clear a *chena*, and that the agent *Hamadoru*[1] would never hear from Babehami whether they had cleared four acres or eight. But the life of the unfortunate man, who had offended the headman, would be full of dangers and difficulties. The permit applied for by him would be very slow in reaching his hands: when it did reach his hands, if he cleared half

1 The head of a district for administrative and revenue purposes is a European Civil Servant, and is called an Assistant Government agent. The Sinhalese call him agent *Hamadoru*.

an acre more than it allowed him to clear, his fine would be heavy; and woe betide him if he rashly cleared a *chena* without a permit at all.

Babehami had never liked Silindu, who was a bad debtor. Silindu was too lazy even to cultivate a *chena* properly, and even in a good year his crop was always the smallest in the village. He was always in want, and always borrowing; and Babehami found it no easy task to gather in principal and interest after the boutique-keepers from Kamburupitiya had taken their dues. And he was not an easy man to argue with: if he wanted a loan he would, unheeding of any excuse or refusal, hang about the headman's door for a whole day. But if it were a case of repayment, he would sit staring over his creditor's head, listening, without a sign or a word, to the quiet persuasive arguments of the headman.

The headman's dislike became more distinct after the birth of Punchi Menika and Hinnihami. Silindu had resented his interference between him and his wife, and when Dingihami died bitter words had passed between them. Though Silindu soon forgot them, Babehami did not. For years Silindu did not realise what was taking place, but he vaguely felt that life was becoming harder for him. A month after Dingihami's death his store of grain was exhausted, and it became necessary for him to begin his yearly borrowings. Accordingly, he took his gun and went in the evening to the nearest water-hole to wait for deer. The first night he was unsuccessful: no deer came to drink; but on the second he shot a doe. He skinned the deer, cut it up, and carried the meat to his hut. He then carefully chose the best piece of meat, and took it with him to Babehami's house. The headman was squatting in his doorway chewing betel. His little eyes twinkled when he saw Silindu with the meat.

'*Ralahami*,'[1] said Silindu, stopping just outside the door, 'yesterday I was in the jungle collecting *domba* fruit – what else is there to eat? – when I smelt a smell of something dead some fathoms away. I searched about, and soon I came upon the carcase of a doe killed by a leopard – the marks of his claws were under the neck, and the belly was eaten. The meat I have brought to my house. This piece is for you.'

1   A respectful form of address.

The headman took the meat in silence, and hung it up in the house. He fetched a chew of betel and gave it to Silindu. The two men then squatted down, one on each side of the door. For a long time neither spoke: their chewing was only interrupted every now and then by the ejection of a jet of red saliva. At last Babehami broke the silence: 'Four days ago I was in Kamburupitiya – I was called to the *Kachcheri*[1] there. They asked me two *fanams*[2] in the bazaar for a coconut.'

'*Aiyo!* I have not seen a coconut for two years.'

'Two *fanams*! And last year at this time they were but one *fanam* each. In the bazaar I met the *Korala Mahatmaya*. The *Korala Mahatmaya* is a hard man: he said to me, "*Arachchi*, there are guns in your village for which no permit has been given by the agent *Hamadoru*." I said to him, "*Ralahami*, if there be, the fault is not mine." Then he said, "The order has come from the agent *Hamadoru* to the *Dissa Mahatmaya*[3] that if one gun be found without permit in a headman's village there will be trouble both for the *Arachchi* and the *Korala*." Now the *Dissa Mahatmaya* is a good man, but the *Korala* is hard; and they say in Kamburupitiya that the agent *Hamadoru* is very hard and strict, and goes round the villages searching for guns for which no permits have been given. They say, too, that he will come this way next month.'

There was a short silence, and then Babehami continued: 'It is five months, Silindu, since I told you to take a permit for your gun, and you have not done so yet. The time to pay three shillings has gone by, and you will now have to pay four. The *Korala* is a hard man, and the agent *Hamadoru* will come next month.'

Silindu salaamed.

'*Ralahami*, I am a poor man. How can I pay four shillings or even three? There is not a *fanam* in the house. There was a permit taken two

---

1   *Kachcheri* is the Government offices.

2   A *fanam*: six cents, one penny

3   *Dissa Mahatmaya* is the title used by villagers in referring to chief headmen or *Ratemahatmayas*. *Koralas* are subordinate headmen of *korales* under the *Ratemahatmayas*. Each *Korala* again has under him several *Arachchis*, who are headmen of single villages.

years ago. You are my father and my mother. I will hide the gun in a place that only I know of, and if it be taken or question be made, is it not easy to say that the stock was broken, and it was not considered necessary to take a permit for a broken gun?'

But the argument, which before had been successful with Babehami, now seemed to have lost its strength.

'A permit is required. It is the order of Government. I have told you the *Korala* is a hard man, and he is angry with me because I brought him but two coconuts as a present, whereas other *Arachchis* bring him an *amunam* of paddy. For I, too, am a poor man.'

Silindu sat in helpless silence. The hopelessness of raising two *rupees* to pay for a gun licence for the moment drove out of his mind the object of his coming to Babehami's house. All that he felt was the misery of a new misfortune, and, as was his nature, he sat dumb under it. At last, however, the pressing need of the moment again recurred to him, and he started in the tortuous way, habitual to villagers, to approach the subject.

' *Ralahami*, is there any objection to my clearing Nugagahahena next *chena* season?'

'There are three months before the *chena* season. Why think of that now?'

'When the belly is empty, the mouth talks of rice. Last year my *chena* crop was bad. There was but little rain, and the elephants broke in and destroyed much *kurakkan*. The Lord Buddha himself would be power-less against the elephants.'

Silindu got up as if to go. He took a step towards the stile which led into the compound, and then turned back as if he had just remembered something, and began in a soft, wheedling voice: '*Ralahami*, there is nothing to eat in the house. There is Karlinahami to feed too. If you could but lend me ten *kurunies*! I would repay it twofold at the reaping of Nugagahahena.'

Babehami chewed for some minutes, and then spat with great deliberation.

'I have no grain to lend now, Silindu.'

'*Ralahami*, it is only ten *kurunies* I am asking for only ten *kurunies* – and surely the barn behind your house is full.'

'There is very little grain in the barn now, and what there is will not last me until the reaping of the next crop. There is the old man, my father, to be fed, and my wife and her brother, and the two children.'

'Will you let me die of hunger? and my two children? Give but five *kurunies*, and I will repay it threefold.'

'If you had come last *poya*, Silindu, I could have given it. But I owed fifteen *rupees* to Nandiyas, the boutique-keeper in Kamburupitiya, for clothes, and I took *kurakkan* to pay it. The barn is all but empty.'

'*Aiyo*! We must die of hunger then. Give but one measure, and I will repay one *kuruni* at next reaping.'

'I paid away all my grain that was in the barn. The grain which remains is my father's, and he keeps it for his use. You must go to the *Mudalali* in Kamburupitiya, Silindu, and borrow from him. And when you go there remember, you must take a permit for the gun.'

Silindu felt that he had nothing more to say. He had the meat at home which he would dry and take to Kamburupitiya and sell in the bazaar. Then he would have to borrow from the *Mudalali*, who knew him too well to give anything but ruinous terms. Perhaps in that way he would manage to return to the village with a few *kurunies* of *kurakkan* and a gun licence. He walked slowly away from the headman's compound. Babehami's little eyes twinkled as he saw Silindu move away, and he smiled to himself.

Chapter 3

SILINDU made the journey to Kamburupitiya, obtained the licence for his gun and some grain, but life continued to become harder for him. The headman's ill-feeling worked against him unostentatiously, and in all sorts of little things. He never thought about the motives and intentions of those around him, and Babehami always had some excuse for refusing a loan or pressing for payment of the body tax. He did not become conscious of Babehami's enmity, or aware that many of the difficulties of his life were due to it.

The collection of the body tax was a good example of the way in which the headman worked against him. Every villager had to pay the three-shilling tax or do work on the roads, work which was the worst of hardships to them. It had always been Babehami's custom to pay himself the tax for each villager, and then recover what he had paid, with heavy interest, out of the crops at the time of reaping. But for some years after Dingihami's death, Silindu found that when the time to pay the tax came round, Babehami was always short of money. Silindu never had any money himself, and he was therefore compelled to work upon the roads.

As the years passed he became more sullen, more taciturn, and more lazy. Some evil power – one of the unseen powers which he could not understand – was, he felt, perpetually working against him. He tried to escape from it, or at any rate to forget it by leaving the village for the jungle. He would disappear for days together into the jungle, living upon roots and the fruit of jungle trees, and anything which might fall to his gun. He talked with no one except Punchi Menika and Hinni-hami. For them he never had a harsh word, and it was seldom that he returned to the hut without bringing them some wild fruit or a comb of the wild honey.

Gradually the hut of the *veddas*, as they were nicknamed, seemed to the other villagers to fall under a cloud. The headman's enmity and the strange ways of Silindu formed a bar to intercourse. And so it came about that Punchi Menika and Hinnihami grew up somewhat outside the ordinary life of the village. The strangeness and wildness of their father hung about them: as the other women said of them, they grew up in the jungle and not in the village. But with their strangeness and wildness went a simplicity of mind and of speech, which showed in many ways, but above all in their love for Silindu and each other.

Their lives were harder even than those of the other village women. As they became older the fear of hunger became more and more present with them. When Silindu was away from the village they were often compelled to live upon the fruits and leaves and roots, which they gathered themselves in the jungle. And when the *chena* season began, they worked like the men and boys in the *chenas*. They cut down the undergrowth and burnt it; they cleared the ground and sowed the grain; they lay out all night in the watch huts to scare away the deer and wild pig which came to damage the crop.

When they were fifteen, Babun Appu, the brother of Nanchohami, came to live in his brother-in-law's, the headman's, house. He had previously lived in another house with his father, an old man, toothless and brainless. When the old man whom he had supported died, he abandoned his hut and came to live with his sister and her husband. The number of houses in the village thus sank to eight.

At that time Babun Appu was twenty-one years old. He was tall for a Sinhalese, broad-shouldered, and big-boned. His skin was a dark chocolate-brown, his face oval, his nose small, his lips full and sensual. His expression was curiously virile and simple; but his brown eyes, which were large and oval-shaped, swept it at moments with something soft, languorous, and feminine. This impression of a mixture of virility and femininity was heightened by the long hair, which he tied in a knot at the back of his head after the custom of villagers. He was noted for his strength, his energy, and his good humour. The minds of most villagers are extraordinarily tortuous and suspicious, but Babun was remarkable for his simplicity. It used to be said of him in the village, 'Babun Appu could not cheat a child; but a child, who had not learnt to talk, could cheat Babun Appu.'

For two years Babun had lived in the hut adjoining Silindu's without ever speaking more than a word or two to Punchi Menika. But her presence began to move him strongly. His lips parted, and his breathing became fast and deep as he saw her move about the compound. He watched in painful excitement her swelling breasts and the fair skin, which went into soft folds at her hips when she bent down for anything.

One night in the *chena* season Punchi Menika had been watching the crop of her father's *chena*. It lay three miles away from the village, at some distance from any other *chena*. The track therefore which led from it to the village was used by no one except herself, her father, and sister. In the early morning she started back to the hut.

There had been rain during the night, and the jungle was fresh and green. That freshness, which the time of rain brings for so brief a time, was upon all things. The jungle was golden with the great hanging clusters of the *cassia* flowers. The bushes were starred with the white *karambu* flowers, and splashed with masses of white and purple *kettan*. The grey monkeys leapt, shrieking and mocking, from bough to bough; the jungle was filled with the calling of the jungle fowl and the wild cries of the peacocks. From the distance came the trumpeting and shrieking of a herd of elephants. As Punchi Menika passed a bush she heard from behind it the clashing of horns. Very quietly she peered round. Two stags were fighting, the tines of the horns interlocked; up and down, backwards and forwards, snorting, panting, and straining they struggled for the doe which stood grazing quietly beside. Punchi Menika had crept up very quietly; but the doe became uneasy, lifted her head, and looked intently at the bush behind which Punchi Menika crouched. She approached the bush slowly, stamping the ground angrily from time to time, and uttering the sharp shrill call of alarm. But the bucks fought on, up and down the open space. Punchi Menika laughed as she turned away. 'Fear nothing, sister,' she said, 'there is no leopard crouching for you. Fight on, brothers, for the prize is fair.'

Punchi Menika walked slowly on down the track. The blood in her veins moved strangely, stirred by the stirring life around her. The trumpet call of the sambur blared through the jungle, a terrific cry of desire. The girl, who had heard it unmoved thousands of times before, started at the sound of it. A sense of uneasiness came over her. Suddenly she stopped at the sight of something which moved behind a bush down the track.

She stood trembling as Babun came out of the jungle and walked towards her. His eyes were very bright; his teeth showed white between his parted lips; the long black hair upon his breast glistened with sweat. He stood in front of her.

'Punchi Menika,' he said, 'I have come to you.'

'*Aiyo!*' she answered. 'I was very frightened. I thought you were a devil of the trees crouching there for me behind the bushes. Even when we were little children our father warned us against the devils that would leap upon us from the bushes.'

'I have come to you. Come with me out of the path into the thick jungle. Last night I could not sleep for thinking of you. So I came in the early morning along the path to meet you on your way from the *chena*. I cannot sleep, Punchi Menika, for thinking of you. I have watched you in the compound and at the tank – your fair skin and the little breasts. Do not fear, I will not hurt you, Punchi Menika; but come, come quickly, out of the path.'

A strange feeling of excitement came over the girl, of joy and fear, as Babun leant towards her, and put out his hand to take her by the wrist. A great desire to fly from him, and at the same time to be caught by him came over her. She stood looking down until his fingers touched her skin; then with a cry she broke from him, and ran down the track to the village. She heard his breathing very close to her as she ran; and when she looked round over her shoulder she felt his breath on her face, saw his bright eyes and great lips, through which the teeth shone white. Another moment and she felt the great strength of his arms as he seized her. He held her close to him by the wrists.

'Why do you run, why are you frightened, Punchi Menika? I will not hurt you.'

She allowed him to take her into the thick jungle, but she struggled with him, and her whole body shook with fear and desire as she felt his hands upon her breasts. A cry broke from her, in which joy and desire mingled with the fear and the pain.

'*Aiyo! Aiyo!*'

Chapter 4

IN TOWNS and large villages there are, especially among people of the higher castes, many rigid customs and formalities regarding marriages always observed. It is true that the exclusion of women no longer exists; but young girls after puberty are supposed to be kept within the house, and only to meet men of the immediate family. A marriage is arranged formally; a formal proposal is made by the man's father or mother to the girl's father or mother. There are usually long negotiations and bargainings between the two families over the dowry. When at last the preliminaries are settled and the wedding day arrives, it is a very solemn and formal affair. All the members of each family are invited; the bridegroom goes with his friends and relations to the house of the bride, and then conducts her in procession, followed by the guests, to his own house. Much money is spent upon entertaining, and new clothes and presents.

But in villages like Beddagama, these customs and formalities are often not observed. The young girls are not kept within the house; they have to work. The young men know them, and often choose for themselves. There is no family arrangement, no formal proposal of marriage; the villagers are too poor for there to be any question of a dowry.

And yet the villager makes a clear distinction between marriage and what he calls concubinage. In the former the woman is recognised by his and her families as his wife; almost invariably she is openly taken to his house, and there is a procession and feasting on the wedding day: in the latter the woman is never publicly recognised as a wife. Marriage is considered to be more respectable than concubinage, and in a headman's immediate, family it would be more usual to find the women 'recognised' wives than 'unrecognised' wives. And though in the ordinary village life the 'unrecognised' wife is as common as, or even more common than, the 'recognised' wife, and is treated by all exactly as if she were the man's wife, yet the distinction is understood and becomes apparent upon formal occasions. For instance, a woman who is living with a man as his 'unrecognised' wife cannot be present at her sister's wedding. When a man takes a woman to live with him in this informal way, the arrangement is, however, regarded as in many ways a formal one, a slightly lower form than the recognised marriage. The man and the woman are of the same caste always: there would even be strong objection on the part of the man or woman's relations if either the one or the other did not come from a 'respectable' family.

Babun knew well his brother-in-law's dislike of Silindu, and the contempt with which the *veddas* were regarded by the other villagers. He knew that his sister and Babehami would be very angry with him if he chose a wife from such a family. But he had watched Punchi Menika, and gradually a love, which was more than mere desire, had grown up in him. The wildness and strangeness of her father and of Hinnihami were tempered in her by a wonderful gentleness. Passion and desire were strong in him: they would allow no interference with his determination to take her to live with him.

The night after his meeting with Punchi Menika on the path from the *chena*, he broke the news to Nanchohami and Babehami, as he and his brother-in-law were eating the evening meal.

'Sister,' he said, 'it is time that I took a wife.'

Nanchohami laughed. 'There is no difficulty. When you go to the *chena* the women look after you and smile and say, '*Chi! Chi!* There goes a man. O that he would take my daughter to his house.' But there are no women for you here. They are all sickly things, unfit to bear you children.'

'My father's brother married a woman of Kotegoda,' said Babehami. 'In those days wives brought dowries with them – of land. He went to live on her land at Kotegoda: it lies fifty miles away, towards Ruhuna. His sons and daughters are married now in that village, and have children. They are rich: it is a good village: rain falls there, and there are coconut lands, and paddy grows. The village spreads and prospers, and the headman is a rich man. They say that tax is paid upon sixty men every year. It would be a good thing for you to take a wife from there, for she would bring you a dowry.'

'Yes,' said Nanchohami, 'it would be a good thing for you to go to Kotegoda and take a woman from there, a daughter of my man's brother.[1] She would bring you land, and you could settle there. What use is it to live in this village? Even the *chena* crops wither for want of rain. It is an evil place this.'

' I want no woman of Kotegoda,' said Babun. 'Nor will I leave the village. There is a woman, this Punchi Menika, the daughter of Silindu. I am going to take her to live with me.'

Babehami looked at his brother-in-law, his little eyes moving restlessly in astonishment and anger. Nanchohami threw up her hands, and began in a voice which shrilled and fluted with anger: '*Ohé*! So we are to take *veddas* into the house, and I am to call a pariah sister! A fine and a rich wife! A pariah woman, a *vedda*, a daughter of a dog, *vesi, vesige duwa*! *Ohé*! The headman's brother is to marry a sweeper of jakes! Do you hear this? Will you allow these Tamils[2] in your house? Yes, 'twill be a fine thing in the village to hear that the headman has given his wife and daughters to *Rodiyas*,[3] leopards, jackals!'

Babehami broke in upon his wife's abuse; but she, now thoroughly aroused, continued throughout the conversation to pour out a stream of foul words from the background in a voice which gradually rose shriller and shriller.

'The woman is right,' Babehami said angrily to Babun. 'You cannot bring this woman to the house.'

'I will take no other woman. I have watched her there about the compound. She is fair and gentle. She is unlike the other women of this village (here he looked round at Nanchohami), in whose mouths are always foul words.'

Babehami tried to hide his anger. He knew his brother-in-law to be obstinate as well as good-humoured and simple.

1 The son of a paternal uncle is regarded as a brother.
2 A favourite form of abuse among the Sinhalese is to call someone a Tamil.
3 *Rodiyas* are the lowest Sinhalese caste.

'No doubt the woman is fair. But if you desire her, is she not free to all to take? Does she not wander, like a man, in the jungle? They say that even kings have desired *Rodiya* women. If you desire her, it is not hard to take her. But there need be no talk of marriage, or bringing her to the house.'

'This morning I took her with me into the jungle, but it is not enough; the desire is still with me. I have thought about it. It is time that I took a wife to cook my food and bear me children. I want no other than this. I can leave your compound, and build myself a new house, and take her to live with me.'

Babehami's anger began to break out again.

'Are you a fool? Will you take this beggar woman to be your wife? Is not her father always about my door crying for a handful of *kurakkan*? Fool! I tell you my brother's children in Kotegoda will bring you land, paddy land, and coconuts. There is no difference between one woman and another.'

'I tell you I want no Kotegoda woman. I will take the daughter of Silindu. I want no strange woman or strange village. I can build myself a house here, and clear *chenas*, as my father did and his father.'

'Is it for this I took you into my house? Two years you have eaten my food. How much of my *kurakkan* have you taken?'

'I have taken nothing from you. I have worked two years in the *chena*, and the crop came to you, not to me. Is not the grain now in your barn from the *chena* cleared by me?'

Babehami was too quiet and cunning often to give way to anger, but this time he was carried away by the defiance of his brother-in-law, whom he regarded as a fool. He gesticulated wildly: 'Out of my house, dog; out of my house. You shall bring no woman to my compound. Go and lie with the pariahs in their own filth!'

Babun got up and stood over Babehami.

'I am going,' he said quietly, 'and I will take Punchi Menika as my wife.'

The abuse of the headman and his wife followed him out of the compound. He walked slowly over to Silindu's hut. He found Silindu squatting under a ragged mustard tree which stood in the compound, and he squatted down by his side. He did not like Silindu; he had always an uncomfortable feeling in the presence of this wild man, who never spoke to any one unless he was spoken to; and he felt it difficult to begin now upon the subject which had brought him to the compound. Silindu paid no attention to him. Babun sat there unable to begin, listening to the sounds of the women in the hut. At last he said: 'Silindu, I have come to speak to you about your daughter Punchi Menika.'

Silindu remained quite still: he apparently had not heard. Babun touched him on the arm.

'I am talking of your daughter, Silindu, Punchi Menika.'

Silindu turned and looked at him.

'The girl is in the house. What have you to do with her?'

'I want you to listen to me, Silindu, for there is much to say. I have watched the girl from the headman's compound, and a charm has come upon me. I cannot eat or sleep for thinking of her. So I said to my sister and my sister's husband, 'It is time for me to take, a wife, and now I will bring this girl into the compound.' But they were very angry, for they want to marry me to a woman of Kotegoda, because of the land which she would bring as dowry. Tonight they abused me, and there was a quarrel. I have left their compound. Now I will make myself a house in the old compound where my father lived, and I will take the girl there as my wife.'

Silindu had become more and more attentive as he listened to Babun. The words seemed to distress him: he shifted about, fidgeted with his hands, scratched himself all over his body. When Babun stopped, he took some time before he said: 'The girl is too young to be given to a man.'

Babun laughed. 'The girl has attained her age. She is older than many a woman who has a husband.'

'The girl is too young. I cannot give her to you, or evil will come of it.'

Babun's patience began to be exhausted. His good humour had been undisturbed during the scene in the headman's compound, but this new obstacle began to rouse him. His voice rose: 'I cannot live without the girl. I have quarrelled with my sister and the headman over her; I have left the compound for her. I ask no dowry. Why should you refuse her to me?'

'They call us *veddas* in the village, while you are of the headman's house. Does the leopard of the jungle mate with the dog of the village?'

'That is nothing to me. The wild buffalo seeks the cows in the village herds. The girl is very gentle, and my mind is made up. Also the girl wishes to come to me.'

The loud voices of the two men had reached the women in the house. They had come out, and stood listening behind the men. At the last words of Babun, Silindu cried out as if he had been struck: '*Aiyo! Aiyo!* They take even my daughter from me. Is there money in the house? No. Is there rice? No. Is there *kurakkan*, or chillies, or *jaggery*,[1] or salt even? The house is empty. But there is always something for the thief to find. They creep in while I am away in the jungle; they see the little ones whom I have fed, the little ones who laughed and called me '*Appochchi*'[2] when I brought them fruits and honeycomb from the jungle. They creep in like the hooded snake, and steal them away from me. *Aiyo! Aiyo!* The little ones laugh to go.'

Punchi Menika rushed forward, threw herself at Silindu's feet, which she touched and caressed with her hands. She struck the ground several times with her forehead, crying and wailing: '*Appochchi! Appochchi!* Will you kill me with your words? I will never leave you nor my sister.'

Babun turned upon her: 'Are the words in the jungle nothing then? Did you lie to me when you said you would come to my house? They are right then when they say that women's words are lies – in the morning one thing, at night another. Did I not tell you that I cannot be without you? *Aiyo!* You told me there under the *cassia* tree that you would come to me and cook my rice. And in the evening I am homeless and without you! I shall go now into the jungle and hang myself.'

Babun moved away, but Karlinahami caught hold of his hand and pulled him back. Punchi Menika threw herself on the ground again in front of Silindu.

'*Appochchi!* It is true: I said I would go to him. Do not kill me with

1   Native sugar made from the *kitul* palm.
2   Father.

bitter words. I must go: I cannot be without him. I gave my word: what can I do?'

Punchi Menika crouched down at Silindu's feet. He sat very still for a little while, and then began in a low, moaning voice: 'Did I not often tell you of the devils of the trees that lurk for you by the way? I have stood by you against them in the day: I have held you in my arms when they howled about the house at night. I told you that the place is evil and evil comes from it. They lie in the shadows of the trees, and cast spells on you as you pass. And now one has got you, and you laugh to go from me. They sit in the trees among the grey monkeys and laugh at me as I pass in the morning: they howl at me among the jackals as I come back in the evening. They take all from me, and the house is very empty.'

'*Appochchi*! The devils are not taking me, I shall not leave you; when you come from the jungle I shall be here with my sister. But the man has called to me and I must go to him. The cub does not always remain in the cave by the father's side: her time comes, and she hears her mate call from the neighbouring rocks: she leaves her father's cave for another's. But, *Appochchi*, she will still look out for the old leopard when he returns: she will live very close to him.'

'*Aiyo*! *Aiyo*! The house will be empty.'

'The doe cannot always stay with the herd. She hears the call of the buck, and they fly together into the jungle.'

'The house is empty. There is no use for me to live now.'

Karlinahami, who had been growing more and more impatient, here broke in: 'Are you mad, brother? The child is a woman now, and it is time to give her to a man. Is she to die childless because she has a father? There is no need for her even to leave the compound. There is room for Babun to make himself a house here.'

Babun eagerly seized upon this suggestion. He assured Silindu that he had no intention of taking Punchi Menika out of the compound. Punchi Menika, still crouching at his feet, told her father that she would never leave him.

It was eventually arranged that for the present Babun should live in the house while he put up another house for himself and Punchi Menika.

Silindu took no part in the discussion. After Karlinahami intervened, he became silent: there was nothing for him to do or to say which could help him: it was only one more of the evils which inevitably came upon him. The talk died down: the others went into the house to prepare the evening meal. He sat on under the mustard tree, staring at the outline of the trees against the starlit sky. The silence of the jungle settled down upon the compound. Punchi Menika brought him his food. She tried to comfort him, to get him to come into the house, but for once she could not rouse him. He sat in the compound through the night, staring into the darkness, and muttering from time to time, '*Aiyo*, the house is empty!'

Chapter 5

BABUN put up a new hut in Silindu's compound, and three weeks after he left his brother-in-law, he and Punchi Menika began to live together in it. It was the beginning of a far greater prosperity for the family. Babun worked hard: he cleared his *chena* and watched it well: his crop was always the best in the village, and the produce went with Silindu's into a barn which served in common for the whole compound.

Silindu did not again refer to Punchi Menika's leaving him. He seemed hardly to be aware of Babun's existence in the compound: he very rarely addressed a word to him. In fact, he now scarcely ever spoke to any one except Hinnihami. When he came back to the compound from the jungle or from the *chenas*, he never went into the new hut, where Punchi Menika lived: he never called her to him as he had been used to do. If she came out in the evenings to sit with him and speak with him, he answered her questions; but he no longer poured out to her everything that was in his mind, as he still did to Hinnihami. It seemed as if he were unable to share her with another.

And Punchi Menika altered. Her blind love for her father and her sister remained, but it was swamped by a fierce attachment to Babun. She felt the barrier which had grown up and separated her from Silindu, and in a less degree from Hinnihami. And as her life became different, she lost some of the wildness which had before belonged to her. She began to lead a life more like the other village women. She no longer went to, or worked, in the *chena*; the jungle began to lose its hold on her. She had listened from the time when she first began to understand anything to the tales of her father, and imperceptibly his views of life had become hers: she and he were only two out of the countless animals which wander through the jungle, continually beset by hunger and fear. But as she became more and more separated from him and attached to Babun, this view of life – always vague and unconsciously held – became vaguer and dimmer. The simplicity of Babun reacted upon her: she became the man's woman, the cook of his food, the cleaner of his house, the bearer of his children.

There had always been considerable difference in character between Hinnihami and Punchi Menika. There was very little of her sister's gentleness in Hinnihami. There was, added to the strangeness and wildness which she derived from Silindu, a violence of feeling far greater than his. You could see this in her eyes, which gradually lost the melancholy of childhood, and glowed with a fierce, startled look through the long black hair, which hung in disorder about her pale brown face. The village women, who never tired of following Nanchohami's lead in jeering at Karlinahami and Punchi Menika, soon learned to respect the passionate anger which it was so easy to rouse in Hinnihami.

And the passion of her anger was equalled by the passion of her attachment to Silindu and Punchi Menika. The women soon learned that it was as dangerous to abuse in her presence her father or her sister, as to risk a gibe at the girl herself. It was always remembered in the village how, when Angohami once, worked up by the bitterness of her own tongue, raised her hand against Punchi Menika, Hinnihami, then a child of eight, had seized the baby which the woman was carrying on her hip and flung it into the tank water.

Hinnihami had taken no part in the discussion about her sister's marriage. But when Babun took Punchi Menika to live with him in the hut which he had built, she felt an instinctive dislike towards him, a feeling that she was being robbed of something. Her father and her sister were everything to her: for she had never felt for Karlinahami the blind affection which she felt for them. She could not understand, therefore, how Punchi Menika could turn from them to this man whom she had scarcely known the day before.

She saw and understood her father's anger and unhappiness, but she could not turn against her sister. Something had happened which she did not understand: 'an evil had come out of the jungle,' as such evils come. If any one could be blamed, it was the stranger Babun; but as her sister desired to go to him, she put on one side her own feelings of anger against him. She watched in silence the new house being put up, and she watched in silence Punchi Menika leave the old hut for the new. She felt as if she were losing something; that her sister was going away from her, and that her life had greatly altered. She turned with an increasing passion of attachment to her father; she refused to allow Karlinahami to cook his food for him; if he went out alone in the jungle, she would sit for hours in the compound watching the path by which she knew he would return; and whenever he would allow her, she followed him on his expeditions.

The marriage of Punchi Menika and Babun created a great sensation in the village. The headman and his wife did not at first hide their anger, and the thought that they had been crossed was not unpleasant to many of the villagers. Moreover, Babun was liked, and in many ways respected. The contempt in which the *veddas* had been held could no longer be shown towards a compound where he had married and where he lived. The compound was no longer avoided; the men entered it now to see Babun, and the women began to come and gossip with Punchi Menika.

It was not in Babehami's nature to remain long openly an enemy of anyone. His cunning mind was inclined to, and suited for, intrigue. He understood how much easier – and more enjoyable – it is to harm your enemy, if he thinks that you are his friend, rather than if he knows you are his enemy. He was, however, too angry with Babun for any open reconciliation. He hid his anger; and though he never went into Babun's compound, nor Babun into his, when they met in the village paths, they spoke to one another as if there was nothing between them. But he often thought over the reckoning which he was determined one day to have; and it was Silindu and his family who, he made up his mind, would feel it most heavily. He was a man who never forgot what he considered a wrong done him. He could wait long to repay a real or imaginary injury: the repayment might be made in many diverse ways, but until it was repaid with interest his mind was unsatisfied.

As time passed Silindu's family began again to enter into the ordinary village life. It was natural, therefore, that the hesitation which the villager might have felt to take a wife from the family died down before Babun's example. People who live in towns can hardly realise how persistent and violent are the desires of those who live in villages like Beddagama. In many ways, and in this beyond all others, they are very near to the animals; in fact, in this they are more brutal and uncontrolled than the brutes; that, while the animals have their seasons, man alone is perpetually dominated by his desires.

Hinnihami, both in face and form, was more desirable than any of the other women. It was about a year after Babun and Punchi Menika began to live together that proposals began to be made about her. There lived in one of the huts, with his old mother, a man called Punchirala. He was a tall, thin, dark man, badly afflicted with *parangi*. The naturally crafty look of his face had been intensified by an accident. When a young man he had been attacked by a bear, which met him crawling under the bushes in search of a hive of wild bees which he had heard in the jungle. The bear mauled him, and had left the marks of its teeth and claws upon his cheeks and forehead, and partially destroyed his right eye. The drooping lid of the injured eye gave him the appearance of perpetually and cunningly winking. He had some reputation in the village as a *vederala* or doctor, and also as a dealer in spells. The result of his quarrel with his brother had made him feared and respected. They had cultivated a *chena* in common, and a dispute had arisen over the division of the produce. Punchirala considered himself to have been swindled. He went out into the jungle and collected certain herbs, leaves, and fruit. He put them in a coconut shell together with a lime, and placed them at night in the corner of his brother's compound. The next morning his brother was found to be lying unable to speak or move. The wife and mother came and begged Punchirala to remove the spell. He denied all knowledge of the matter, and in three days his brother died. The brother's share of the *chena* produce was handed over to Punchirala, as no one else was inclined to run the risk of the curse which appeared to attach to it.

Punchirala was about thirty-eight years old. The woman who had lived with him had died about a year previously, and the marriage of Babun had directed his attention towards Hinnihami. His first proposals were made to the girl herself. He was astonished by the fury with which they were rejected, but he was not discouraged. He watched for his opportunity; and some days later, when Hinnihami was not there, he went to Silindu's compound. He found Silindu sitting in the shadow of the hut.

'I heard,' he said to him, 'that you have an ulcer in your foot. Let me see. *Aiyo!* Caused by a bad thorn! Here are some leaves. I brought them with me. They will do it good.'

Silindu had been unable to walk for some days owing to the swelling and pain. He was very glad to show the foot to the *vederala*. Punchirala sat down to examine it, and Karlinahami and Babun came out to see what was going on. This was exactly what Punchirala wanted. He heated the leaves by putting them in hot water, which he made Karlinahami fetch. He tied them on with much ceremony, and then the whole party squatted down to talk.

'This medicine I learned from my father,' he told them. 'It is of great power. It will draw the evil and the heat out of the foot into the leaves, and tomorrow you will be able to walk.'

The power of medicine and spells was a subject which never failed to appeal to Karlinahami.

'They say your father was a great man, and that in those days people came to the village from all sides for his medicine.'

'Ah, but he was a great man, and I have all my knowledge from him. Now the Government builds hospitals, and makes people go to them, and gives them Government medicine, which is useless. And so our work is taken from us, and people die of these foreign medicines. But my father was a great man. He knew of many charms: one which would bring any woman to a man. There is a tale about that charm. In those days there lived a *Korala Mahatmaya* by the sea, a big-bellied man, a great lover of women. Down the coast, beyond his village, was a village in which only Malay people live. The Malay women are before all others in beauty, very fair, with eyes shaped like pomegranate seeds. They are Mohammedan people, and no Sinhalese can approach their women; for the men are very jealous, and also strong and fearless. They are bad men. The *Korala Mahatmaya* used to go to the village on Government work, and every time he walked through the street, and saw the women peeping at him from the doorways – and he saw their eyes shaped like pomegranate seeds, shining beneath the cloths which covered their heads – he was very troubled, and longed to have a Malay woman. At last he could bear it no longer: so he lay down in his house, and sent a message to my father to say that he was very ill, and that he should come to him at once. Then my father went three days' journey to the *Korala*'s house; and, when he came there, the, *Korala Mahatmaya* sent all the women out of the house, and he made my father sit down by his side, and he said to him, '*Vederala*, I am very ill. I cannot sleep: I have a great desire day and night in me for a woman from the Malay village along the coast. I can get no pleasure from my own women. But if I be seen even talking to a Malay woman, the men of the village would rise and beat me to death. The desire is killing me. Now you, I know, have great skill in charms. You must make me one therefore which will bring a Malay woman to me to a place of which I will tell you.' Then my father said, '*Hamadoru*! I dare not do this. For I must go and make the charm in the compound of the girl's house. And I know these Malay people: they are very bad men. If they catch me there, they will kill me.' But the *Korala Mahatmaya* said, 'There is no need to fear. There is a house at the end of the village standing somewhat apart from the others. There lives in it a young girl, unmarried, the daughter of Tuwan Abdid. I will take you there on a moonless night, and you will make the charm there. And if the next night the girl comes to me, I will give you £5.'[1] Then my father thought, 'If I refuse the *Korala Mahatmaya*, he will be angry, and put me into trouble, and ruin me; and if I consent to his wish I will gain £5, which is much money, and possibly a beating from the Malay men. It is better to risk the beating.' So he agreed to make the charm on a moonless night. Then the *Korala Mahatmaya* gave out that he was very ill, and that my father was treating him. And for three days my father lived in the house, preparing the charm. On the fourth day the *Korala Mahatmaya* and my father – taking cold cooked rice with them – set out from the

1   Colloquially used for fifty *rupees*.

house, saying they were going to my father's village for the treatment of the *Korala* with medicines in my father's house. But after leaving the village they turned aside from the path, and went secretly through the jungle to a cave near the Malay village. The cave was hidden in thick jungle, and they lay there through the day. When it was night and very dark they crept out, and the *Korala* showed the house to my father. My father stood in the garden of the house, and made the charm, and buried it in the earth of the garden, and returned to the cave with the *Korala Mahatmaya*. All through the next day they lay in the cave, and ate only the cold rice, and the *Korala Mahatmaya* talked much of the Malay women, and their eyes, which were shaped like pomegranate seeds. And in the evening, at the time when the women go to draw water, the girl came to the cave, and the *Korala Mahatmaya* enjoyed her. Then he sent her away, and he called my father who was sitting outside in the jungle, and told him that the girl was cross-eyed and ugly, and not worth £5, but at the most ten *rupees*. He gave my father ten *rupees*, and told him he would give the other forty some other time – but the money was never paid. Next day they went back to the *Korala*'s house, and told a tale how the *Korala Mahatmaya* had got well on the way to my father's village, and so they had returned at once. But the girl had seen the *Korala Mahatmaya* in the village, and she recognised his black face and big belly, and she told her mother how she had been charmed to go to the cave. The mother told the Malay men, and they were very angry. Next time that the *Korala Mahatmaya* went to their village, they set upon him, and beat him with clubs and sticks until he nearly died. Then they put him in a bullock-cart, and tied his hands together above his head to the hood of the cart, and took him twelve miles into Kamburupitiya, to the agent *Hamadoru*, and said that they had caught the *Korala Mahatmaya* with a bag on his back stealing salt. And there was a great case, and the magistrate *Hamadoru* believed the story of the *Korala Mahatmaya*, who had many witnesses to show that on the very day on which the girl said she had gone to the cave they had seen him on the road to my father's village. So the Malay men all were sent to prison; but my father got a great name; for all the country, except the magistrate *Hamadoru*, knew of the charm by which he had brought the girl to the fat *Korala Mahatmaya* in the cave.'

'Did your father teach you the making of the charm?' asked Karlinahami.

'Am I not a *vederala* and the son of a *vederala*? The learning of the father is handed down to the son.'

' Yes, I remember hearing my mother speak of him: there was no one in the district, she said, so skilled in charms and medicines as your father.'

'Yes, he knew many things which other *vederalas* know nothing of. He had a charm by which devils are charmed to become the servants of the charmer. He learnt it from a man of Sinhala,[1] who lived long ago in the neighbouring village. This man was called Tikiri Banda, and he wanted to marry the daughter of the headman. The headman refused to give her, and Tikiri Banda being very angry put a charm upon a devil which lived in a *banian* tree. And the devil took a snake in his hand and touched the headman with it on the back as he passed under the tree in the dusk, and the headman's back was bent into a bow for the rest of his days.'

'Was that the village called Bogama?' asked Silindu, who had listened with interest. 'Where the *nuga* trees[2] now stand in the jungle to the south? The last house was abandoned when I was a boy, but the devil still dances beneath the *nuga* trees.'

'Yes, it was Bogama. It was a village like this in my father's time, and in your father's time. I can myself remember houses there near the *nuga* trees.'

'Of course,' said Karlinahami. Podi Sinho's wife Angohami came from there. *Aiyo!* When the jungle comes in, how things are forgotten!'

'Well, well,' said the *vederala*, 'the devils still dance under the trees, though the men have gone. The *chena* crops were bad, and every year the fever came; it is the same now in this village. The old medicines of the *vederalas* are no longer used, but people go to the towns and hospitals for

1   Kandyan district
2   The *banian* tree.

these foreign medicines. But they die very quickly, and where there was a village there are only trees and devils!'

The little group was silent for a while; nothing could be heard but the sigh of the wind among the trees for miles around them. Then the *vederala* began to speak again: 'Yes, that was a wonderful charm. The headman walked bow-backed for the rest of his life because he would not give the girl. *Aiyo!* It is always the women who bring trouble to us men, and yet what can a man do? A man without a wife, they say, is only half a man. There is no comfort in a house where there is no woman to cook the meal.'

'There is no need to use your charm, *vederala*,' said Karlinahami, 'if you want one for yourself.'

'There is only one unmarried woman in the village now,' said the *vederala*, 'and she is Silindu's daughter.'

An uncomfortable silence fell upon the listeners. Karlinahami and Babun looked at Silindu, who remained silent, his eyes fixed upon the ground. The *vederala*'s intentions were very clear, and the point of his previous stories very obvious now. Punchirala turned to Karlinahami: 'I was thinking but yesterday that it is time that the girl was given in marriage. Babun here has taken her twin sister, and it is wrong that a woman should live alone.'

'It is not for me to give the girl. She is her father's daughter.'

Silindu's face showed his distress. The *vederala* was a dangerous man to offend, but too much was being asked of him. He began in a low voice: 'The girl is too young; she has not flowered yet.'

Punchirala laughed.

'Did you bring the girl up or only filth, as the saying is? They are called twins, but the one has been married a year and the other has not flowered yet!'

'*Vederala*! I would give the girl, but she is unwilling. She told me last night that you had spoken to her. She is of the jungle, wild, not fit for your house. She was very frightened and angry.'

For a moment Punchirala was disconcerted that his rebuff was known. But anger came to his rescue.

'Am I to ask the girl then when I want a wife? Can the father not give his child? So the child is angry, and the father obeys! *Ohé*! Strange customs spring up! You are a fool, Silindu. If you tell the child to obey, there is no more to be said.'

'The girl is a wild thing, I tell you. I cannot give her against her will.'

The *vederala* got up. He smiled at Silindu, who watched him anxiously.

'You will not give the girl, Silindu?'

'I cannot, I cannot.'

'You will not give her? Remember the man of Sinhala, who taught my father.'

'*Aiyo*! How can I do this?'

'And the headman of Bogama, and the devil that still dances beneath the trees.'

Silindu's face worked with excitement.

'Ask anything else of me, *vederala*. I cannot do this, I cannot do this,'

Punchirala walked away. The others watched him in silence. When he got to the fence of the compound, he turned round and smiled at them again.

'And don't forget,' he called out, 'to tell the girl about the Malay girl who came to the *Korala Mahatmaya* in the cave. A black-faced man and big-bellied, but she came, she came. I am an ugly man, and the bear's claws have made me uglier; a poor bed-fellow for a girl! And so was he, black as a Tamil, and a great belly swaying as he walked. But she came to the cave, to the calling of my father's charm. Oh yes, she came, she came.'

Punchirala walked away chuckling. Silindu was trembling with excitement and fear. Karlinahami burst out into a wail of despair.

'*Aiyo*! What will become of us, brother? He is a bad man, a bad man; very cunning and clever. There is no protection against his charms. He will bring evil and disease upon the house: he will make devils enter us. What have you done? What have you done? *Aiyo*!'

Babun was not as excited as the other two, but he was very serious.

'It would perhaps have been better to give him the girl,' he said. 'The man is not a bad man if you do not cross him, and the girl is of age to marry. Even the bravest man does not go down the path where a devil lives.'

'Only the fool struggles against the stronger,' said Karlinahami. 'What the *vederala* says is medicine, is medicine. It is not too late, brother, to undo the evil. To whom else in the village can you give the girl?'

Silindu turned upon them in his anger and fear: 'Have you too joined to plague me? Evils come upon a man: it is fate. What can I do? The girl is unwilling: am I to throw away the *kurakkan* when the rice is already stolen? Am I to help the thief to plunder my house? I am a poor man, and the evil has come upon me; I can do nothing against it. His devils will enter me, and I shall waste away. But as for the child, what else is left to me? I will not force her to go to this son of a ——. Go into the house, woman, and cry there; and you, Babun, is it not enough that you have stolen from me one child that now you should join with this dog to steal the other from me?'

The other two were frightened by this outburst of Silindu; they saw that to argue with him would only increase his excitement. They left him. He remained squatting in the compound, and as his anger died down fear possessed him utterly. He had no doubt of the powers of Punchirala over him: he knew that he had delivered himself into his power, and the power of the devils that surrounded him. He had no thought of resistance in such a case. The terrible sense of a blank wall of fate, against which a man may hurl himself in vain, was upon him. He sat terrified and crushed by the inevitableness of the evil which must be. When Hinnihami returned, he told her what had happened, and she shared in his terror and despair.

The charms of the *vederala* did not take long to act upon Silindu. He felt that he was a doomed man, and his mind could think of nothing but the impending evil. The *banian* trees of the ruined village of Bogama obsessed his mind: he knew that ruin waited for him there, and yet a horrible desire to see them was always present with him. He could no longer remain in the hut or compound: he wandered through the jungle, fighting against the pull of the desire: his wanderings became a circle, of which the *banian* trees were the centre. He tried to go back to his hut, where he felt that there was safety for him, and found himself walking in the opposite direction. Darkness began to settle over the jungle, and the life, which awakes only in its darkness, began to stir. Voices mocked him from the canopy of leaves above him; dim forms moved among the shadows of the trees. Suddenly a blind terror came upon him, and he began to run through the dense jungle. The boughs of the trees lashed him as he ran down the narrow tracks; the thorns tore him like spurs. He lost all sense of direction; vague shapes seemed to follow him in the darkness; enormous forms broke away from the track before him, to crash away among the undergrowth and trees. The throbbing of his heart and throat became unendurable, but still his one idea was to run. As he ran the jungle suddenly became thinner; the thorny undergrowth had given way to more open spaces. Even here it was very dark. He stumbled against the knotted root of a tree; a long, straight, swinging bough struck him in the face; a wild, derisive yell came from above. The blood seemed to rise and drown his eyes: he felt about vaguely with his hands, He recognised the root-like, stringy trunks of the *banian* trees: he heard the cry ring out above his head, and he fell huddled together among the roots of the trees.

Silindu did not hear again the cry of the devil-bird from the tree-tops. He lay unconscious throughout the night. When dawn broke he came to himself stiff and cold. He dragged himself slowly to the hut. There was no necessity to tell the others what had happened. The pale yellow of his skin, his sunken glazed eyes, his shivering body told them that Punchirala's charms had already begun their work, and his devils had already entered Silindu. He lay down on a mat within the hut to wait for the slow sapping of his life by the spell.

For the next two days Silindu lay in the hut, very slowly letting go his hold of life. A kind of coma was upon him, as he felt life gradually slipping from his body. From time to time the women began a shrill wail in the compound. Babun went to expostulate with Punchirala; but the *vederala*, after listening with a malignant smile, replied that he knew nothing, and could do nothing, in the matter. Babun returned to lounge moodily about the compound.

On the second day Karlinahami determined in despair to go herself to the *vederala*. She found him sitting in his compound.

'You have come about your brother, no doubt. But I can do nothing; I'm only a poor *vederala*. There is the Government hospital in Kamburu-pitiya, and a *Mahatmaya* in trousers, a drinker of *arrack*, a clever man; he will give you Government medicines free of charge – just a *fanam* or two for the peon who stands by the door. You should take your brother there. It is only three days' journey.'

'*Vederala*! My brother lies in the hut dying. He has covered his head with his cloth, and he will neither eat nor speak. Life is slipping from him.'

'The doctor *Mahatmaya* will say it is the fever. He will give you a bottle of fever mixture – free of charge. A clever man, the doctor *Mahatmaya*. Yes, you should take him to the hospital and get the medicine – free of charge. It is a good medicine, though unpleasant to the taste, they tell me.'

'*Aiyo*! What is the good of going to the hospital? Why do you talk like that, *vederala*? You are laughing at me. We know that it is the devils that have entered my brother, and that you alone have power to save him.'

'Devils! What do I know of devils? No, they tell me the doctor *Mahatmaya* keeps no medicine in the hospital against devils. The Government says there are no devils. Surely it is fever, or fire-fever,[1] or dysentery. It is for these that they give Government medicine. No, it is no good going to the hospital for devils.'

'*Vederala*! I have brought you *kurakkan* here; it is all I have. And I will talk to the girl for you, yes, and to my brother if he gets well. But take the spell from him, *vederala*; take the spell from him, I pray you.'

'I know nothing of spells. I am a poor village *vederala* with a little knowledge of roots and leaves and fruits, which my father taught me.'

'*Vederala*, you yourself told us of the charms and spells. Your skill is known. Charm the devil to leave my brother. He meant no harm; he is a strange man – you know that, *vederala*. He never meant to injure you. The girl will come to you, I will see to that – only take the spell from my brother.'

---

1   Typhoid.

Punchirala sat and looked at Karlinahami, smiling, for a little while. Then he said, 'Is the woman mad too? What do I know of charms and spells? I can work no charm on your brother. But I have some little knowledge of devils – my father taught me. Well, well, let me think now. If a devil has entered the man, and is slowly taking his life from him, perhaps there is a way. Let me think. Do you know the village of Beragama?'

'No, *vederala*, no. I have heard of it, but I do not know it.'

'Well, it lies over there to the east, five days' journey through the jungle, beyond Maha Potana and the River of Jewels. Do you think you could take your brother there?

'Yes, *vederala*, we could go there.'

'There is a great temple there, and the great Beragama *deviyo*[1] lives in it. He is a Tamil god, so they say; but Sinhalese *kapuralas*[2] serve him in the temple. My father used to say that he is a very great god. His power is over the jungle, and the devils who live in it. The devils of the trees obey him, for his anger is terrible. If a devil has entered a man, and is harming him, and taking his life from him, the man should make a vow to the god, so my father used to say. Then he should go to the temple at Beragama at the time of the great festival, and roll in the dust round the temple three times every day, and call upon the god in a loud voice to free him from the devil. And perhaps, if he call loud enough, the god will hear him and order the devil to leave him. Then the devil will be afraid of the god's power, and will leave the man, who will be freed from the evil. Now the great festival falls on the day of the next full moon. Perhaps if your brother makes a vow to the Beragama *deviyo*, and goes to the great festival, the devil will be driven out by the god. You and the girl might take him there; and perhaps I will go too, for I have made a vow myself.'

Karlinahami fell at the *vederala*'s feet, salaaming and whimpering blessings on him. Then she hurried home. It took a long time to make Silindu understand that there was hope for him. At first he would not listen to their entreaties and exhortations. At last, when he was prevailed

1 *Deviyo* used of a god.
2 *Kapuralas* are persons who perform various services in temples.

upon to believe that it was Punchirala himself who had suggested the remedy, some spirit to fight for life seemed to creep into him. He took some food for the first time, and sat listening to the plans for the pilgrimage. It was decided that they should start on the next day, and that Babun should accompany them.

The next day the pilgrims set out on a journey which, with the enfeebled Silindu, would they knew take them at least six days. Their road the whole way led them through thick jungle; villages were few, and what there were consisted only of a few squalid huts. The only village of any size through which they were to pass was Maha Potana, an agricultural village, one day's journey from Beragama, which had sprung up around a vast tank restored by Government. They carried their food with them, and slept at night on the bare earth under bushes or trees. Every day they trudged, straggling along in single file, from seven to eleven in the morning, and from three to six in the evening. Silindu was dazed and weak, and often had to be helped along by Babun. The women carried large bundles of food and *chatties*,[1] wrapped up in cloths, upon their heads. It was the hottest time of the year, when the jungle is withered with drought, the grass has died down, the earth is caked and cracked with heat; the trees along the paths and road are white with dust. The pools had dried up, and the little streams were now mere channels of gleaming sand. Often they had to go all day without finding a pool or a well with water in it. For twelve hours every day the sun beat down upon them fiercely; the quivering heat from the white roads beat up into their faces and eyes; the wind swept them with its burning gusts and eddies of dust. Their feet were torn by the thorns, and swollen and blistered by the hot roads. As Hinnihami followed hour after hour along the white track, which forever coiled out before her into the walls of dusty trees, the old song, which Karlinahami had sung to them when they were children, continually was in her mind, and she sang as she walked:

> 'Our women's feet are weary, but the day
> Must end somewhere for the followers in the way.'

---

1   Earthenware pots.

The Village in the Jungle

Two days' journey from Beddagama they joined a larger and more frequented track. Here they continually met little bands of pilgrims bound for the same destination as themselves. The majority of them were Tamils, Hindus from India, from the tea estates, and from the north and east of the island; strange-looking men, such as Hinnihami had never seen before; very dark, with bodies naked to the waist; with lines of white and red paint on their shoulders, their foreheads smeared with ashes, and the mark of God's eye between their eyebrows. They wore clothes of fine white cotton, caught up between the legs, and they carried brass bowls and brass tongs. Their women, heavy and sullen-looking, followed, carrying bundles and children.

There were, however, also little bands of Buddhists, Sinhalese like themselves, and to one of these bands they attached themselves. Four of them were a family from a village only twenty miles north of Beddagama, and jungle people like themselves. They were taking a blind child to see whether, if they called upon the god, he would hear them and give him sight. There were a fisher and his wife from the coast; they were childless, and the woman had vowed to go to the festival and touch the heel of the *kapurala*, in order that the god might remove from her the curse of barrenness. Last, there was an old man, a trader from a large and distant village of another district; he wore immense spectacles, and all day long he walked reading or chanting from a large Sinhalese religious book, which he carried open in his hand. The rest of the party did not understand a word of what he read, but they felt that he was acquiring merit, and that they would share a little of it. He had been brought up in a Buddhist temple, and at night after the evening meal he gathered the little party round him and preached to them, or read to them, by the light of the camp-fire, how they should live in order to acquire merit in this life. And at the appropriate places they all cried out together, '*Sadhu! Sadhu!*' or he made them all repeat together aloud the *sil* or rules; and as their voices rose and fell in the stillness of the night air, Karlinahami's face shone with ecstasy, and a sense of well-being and quiet, strange to her, stole over Hinnihami. Even in Silindu there came a change; he joined in the chant:

'Búddhun sárănam gáchchāmí,'

with which they began and ended the day; he became less hopeless and sullen, and the look of fear began to leave his eyes. In the evenings, when the air grew cool and gentle after the pitiless heat and wind of the day; as they sat around the fire by the roadside; and the great trees rose black behind them into the night; and the stars blazed above them between the leaves; and up and down the road twinkled the fires of other pilgrims, and the air was sweet with the smell of the burning wood and the hum of voices; and the vast stillness of the jungle folded them round on every side; and they listened to the strange words, but half understood, of the Lord Buddha, and how he attained to Nirvana; – then the sufferings of the day were forgotten, and a feeling stole over them of peace and holiness and merit acquired.

And one evening, at Babun's suggestion, Karlinahami told them a story which had always been a favourite with the village women. At first the old man with the book and spectacles showed signs of being offended at this usurpation; but he was soothed by their saying that they did not want to tire him, and by their asking him to read to them again after the story was finished. In the end he was an absorbed listener as Karlinahami told the following story:[1]

'The Lord Buddha, in one of his previous lives, met a young girl carrying *kunji*[2] to her father, who was ploughing in the field. And when he saw her he thought, "The maiden is fair. If she is unmarried she would make me a fit wife." And she thought when she saw him, "If such a one took me to wife, I would bring fortune to my family." And he said to her, "What is your name?" Her name was Amara Devi, which means "undying", so she replied, "Sir, my name is that which never was, is, nor will be in this world." "Nothing," he said, "born in this world is undying. Is your name Amara?" She answered, "Yes, sir." Then the Buddha said, "To whom are you taking the *kunji*?" "To the first god." "You are taking it to

1 This story is taken from the *Ummaga Jataka*.
2 A sort of rice gruel.

61

your father?" "Yes, sir." "What is your father doing?" "He makes one into two." "To make one into two is to plough. Where is your father ploughing?" "He ploughs in that place from which no man returns." "No man returns from the grave. Is he ploughing near the burial ground?" "Yes, sir." Then Amara Devi offered the Buddha *kunji* to drink, and he accepted it, and he thought to himself, "If the maiden gives me the *kunji* without first washing the pot, I will leave her at once." But Amara Devi washed the pot first, and then gave the *kunji*. The Buddha drank the *kunji*, and said, "Friend, where is your house that I may go to it?" And Amara Devi answered, "Go by this path until you come to a boutique where they sell balls of rice and sugar; go on until you come to another where they sell *kunji*. From there you will see a flamboyant tree in full blossom. At that tree take the path towards the hand with which you eat rice.[1] That is the way to my father's house." And the Buddha went as Amara Devi had directed him, and found the house, and went in. Amara Devi's mother was in the house, and she welcomed the Buddha, and made him sit down. And he, seeing the poverty of the house, said, "Mother, I am a tailor. Have you anything for me to sew?" And she said, "Son, there are clothes and pillows to mend, but I have no money to pay for the mending." Then he replied, "There is no need of money; bring them for me to mend." So the Lord Buddha sat and mended the torn clothes and pillows; and in the evening Amara Devi came back from the fields carrying a bundle of firewood on her head, and a sheaf of jungle leaves in the folds of her cloth. And Buddha lived in the house some days in order to learn the behaviour of the girl. At the end of three days he gave her half a *seer*[2] of rice, and said, "Amara Devi, cook for me *kunji*, boiled rice, and cakes." She never thought to say, "How can I cook so much out of half a *seer* of rice?" but was ready to do as she was told. She cleaned the rice, boiled the whole grains, made *kunji* from the broken grains, and cakes from the dust. She offered the *kunji* to the Buddha, and he took a

1 The 'hand with which you eat rice' is a common expression for the right hand, the left hand being using for an unmentionable purpose.

2 A small measure.

mouthful and tasted the delight of its sweetness, but to try her he spat it out on the ground, and said, "Friend, since you do not know how to cook, why do you waste my rice?" Amara Devi took no offence, but offered him the cakes, saying, "Friend, if the *kunji* does not please you, will you eat of the cakes?" And the Buddha did the same with the cakes. Then Amara Devi offered him the rice, and again he spat out the rice, and pretended to be very angry, and smeared the food upon her head and body, and made her stand in the sun before the door. The girl showed no anger, but went out and stood in the sun. Then the Buddha said, "Amara Devi, friend, come here," and she came to him, and he took her as his wife, and lived with her in the city in the gatekeeper's house. And she still thought he was a tailor, and one day he sent two men to her with a thousand gold pieces to try her. The men took the gold pieces, and with them tempted her, but she said, "These thousand gold pieces are unworthy to wash my husband's feet." And three times she was tempted, and at last he told them to bring her to him by force. So they brought her to him by force, and when she came into his presence she did not know him, for he sat in state in his robes, but she smiled and wept when she looked at him. The Buddha asked her why she smiled and wept, and she said, "Lord, I smiled with joy to see your divine splendour and the merit acquired by you in innumerable births; but when I thought that in this birth you might by some evil act, such as this, by seducing another's wife, earn the pains of death, I wept for love of you." Then the Buddha sent her back to the house of the gatekeeper, and he told the king and queen that he had found a princess for his wife. And the queen gave jewels and gold ornaments to Amara Devi, and she was taken in a great chariot to the house of the Buddha, and from that day she lived happily with him as his wife.'

The other pilgrims, except the fisher, who had fallen asleep, were delighted with Karlinahami's story, and they wanted her to tell them another. But she was afraid to offend the old man again, so she refused. The old man read to them a while, and gradually, one after the other, they dropped off to sleep. And in the morning they started off again down the long white road; and at midday, when they were hot and footsore, the wall of jungle before them parted suddenly, and they came out into a great fertile plain. The green rice-fields stretched out before them, dotted over with watch-huts and clumps of coconut trees and red-roofed houses, and the immense white domes of *dagobas* gleaming in the sun. Beyond shone the pleasant sheet of water through which the jungle had yielded the smiling plain; the dead trees still stood up gaunt and black from its surface; great white birds sat upon the black branches, or flapped lazily over the water with wild, hoarse cries; its bosom was starred and dappled with pink lotus-flowers. And beyond again lay the long dark stretch of jungle, out of which, far away to the north, towered into the fiery sky the line of dim blue hills. It was the tank and village of Maha Potana; and when the weary band of pilgrims suddenly saw the monotony of the trees and of the parched jungle give place to the water, and the green fields, and the white *dagobas*, the shrines built by kings long ago to hold the relics of the Lord Buddha, they raised their hands, salaaming, and cried aloud, 'Sadhu! Sadhu!'[1]

They picked lotus-flowers, and went to the great *dagoba*, which is called after an ancient king, and laid the flowers upon the shrine as an offering, and walked three times around, crying, 'Sadhu! Sadhu!' and thus acquired merit. Then they went into the bazaar which was crowded with pilgrims, Hindus and Buddhists, and Indian *fakirs* and Moormen. Innumerable bullock-carts stood on the road and paths and open spaces, and the air rang with the bells of the bulls, which lazily fed upon the great bundles of straw tied to the carts.

And the old man, who had noted the poverty of Silindu and his family, bought them rice and curry and plantains. So they sat under the shade of a great *bo* tree, and ate a meal such as Hinnihami had never eaten before. Her eyes wandered vacantly from thing to thing; she was dazed by the crowd perpetually wandering to and fro, by the confused din of talking people, of coughing cattle, and jangling bells. In the

---

1 *Sadhu* is an exclamation of assent or approval, which people listening to the reading of Banna or Bhuddhist scriptures repeat at intervals. It is also used by pilgrims at the sight of temples or *dagobas*.

evening they went to another *dagoba*, and then returned to the *bo* tree
and lighted their fire. All about them were other little fires, around
which sat groups, like themselves, of pilgrims eating the evening meal.
They ate rice again and cakes, and Hinnihami grew heavy with sleepi-
ness. A great peace came upon her as she heard Karlinahami tell of how
she had before come on pilgrimage to the great Buddhist festival at
Maha Potana, when the crowds were tens of thousands more. And the
old man told of a pilgrimage to the sacred city of Anuradhapura on the
great *poya* day, when hundreds of thousands acquire merit by encir-
cling the shrine; and the merit to be acquired by climbing Adam's Peak,
or by visiting the ruined shrines of Situlpahuwa, which the jungle has
covered, so that the bears and leopards have made their lairs in the great
caves by the side of Buddhas, who lie carved out of rock. The air was
heavy with the smell of cooking and the pungent smell of the burning
wood; the voice of the old man seemed to come from very far away. She
covered her head with a cloth and lay down on the bare ground. For the
first time the bareness and fear and wildness of life had fallen from her;
she fell asleep in the peace of well-being, and the merit which she had
acquired.

Next morning, to the regret of all, they had to leave the pleasant
village and resting-place of Maha Potana, and face again the suffering
and weariness of the jungle. For two days their path led them through
low thorny jungle, where there was little shelter from the sun. The track
became stony and rocky; great boulders of grey lichen-covered rock
were strewn among the thick undergrowth; at intervals could be seen
enormous rocks towering above the trees. In the afternoon of the first
day they caught their first glimpse of the sacred Beragama hill, which
rises into three rounded peaks above the village and temple. Next day,
towards evening, they had reached the high forest, which, starting from
its foot, clothed the hill almost to its peaks.

Then, once again, the jungle parted suddenly, and they stood upon
the bank of a great stream. The banks were deep, and enormous trees,
kumbuk with its peeling bark and the wild fig tree, shaded them. The
season of drought had narrowed the stream of water, so that it flowed

shallow in the centre of the channel, leaving on either side a great stretch of white sand. Up and down stream were innumerable pilgrims, washing from them in the sacred waters the dust of the journey, and the impurities of life, before they entered the village. They followed the example of the other pilgrims, and performed the required ablutions; after which they put on clean white clothes, and climbed a path on the opposite bank which led them into the village.

They found themselves in a long, very broad street, on each side of which were boutiques and houses and large buildings – resting-places for the pilgrims. The street was thronged with pilgrims, idling, buying provisions, hurrying to the temple. It was near the time for the procession to start from the temple. The festival lasted fourteen days, and every night the god was taken in procession through the village: it culminated in the great procession of the fourteenth night which falls when the moon is full; and in the ceremony of the following morning, when the *kapurala* goes down, accompanied by all the pilgrims, into the bed of the river, and 'cuts the waters' with a golden knife. Silindu and his party arrived in Beragama on the ninth day of the festival, so that they would remain six days in the village, and take part in six processions.

At either end of the broad straight street stood temples. The one at the north end belonged to the Beragama *deviyo*: the temple or *dewala* itself was a small, squat, oblong building, above which at one end rose the customary dome-like erection of Hindu temples, on which are fantastically carved the images of gods. Around the temple was an enormous courtyard enclosed by red walls of roughly-baked bricks. Just outside the wall of the courtyard on the east side was another and a smaller temple belonging to the god's lawful wife. At the southern end of the street stood another temple: it was a square, dirty white building without a courtyard, but surrounded on all sides by a verandah, in which, among a litter of broken furniture and odds and ends, lounged and squatted and slept a large number of pilgrims. The only entrance to the shrine itself was through a doorway in the front, which was screened by a large curtain ornamented crudely with the figures of gods and goddesses. No one was allowed to enter behind this curtain except the *kapuralas*, for the temple belonged to the mistress of the Beragama *deviyo*.

The solemnity of the pilgrimage was intensified in the minds of Silindu and Karlinahami and the other pilgrims, who were villagers like themselves, by the mystery which surrounds the god. On the road and around the fires at night, in the streets of the village, and in the very courtyard of the temple, they listened to the tales and legends; and believing them all without hesitation or speculation they felt, through their strangeness, far more than they had ever felt with the Buddha of *dagobas* and *vihares*, that this god was very near their own lives.

Who was he, this Tamil god, living in the wilderness, whom the Tamils said was Kandeswami, the great Hindu god? These Buddhist villagers felt that they could understand him; he was so near to the devils of the trees and jungles whom they knew so well. He had once lived upon the centre of the three peaks of the great hill, ruling over the unbroken forest which stretched below him, tossing and waving north to the mountains, and south to the sea. That was why every night throughout the festival a fire blazed from the peak. But one day, as he sat among the bare rocks upon the top of the hill and looked down upon the winding river and the trees which cooled its banks, the wish came to him to go down and live in the plain beyond the river. Even in these days he was a Tamil god, so he called to a band of Tamils who were passing, and asked them to carry him down across the river. The Tamils answered, 'Lord, we are poor men, and have travelled far on our way to collect salt in the lagoons by the seashore. If we stop now, the rain may come and destroy the salt, and our journey will have been for nothing. We will go on, therefore, and on our way back we will carry you down, and place you on the other side of the river, as you desire.' The Tamils went on their way, and the god was angry at the slight put upon him. Shortly afterwards a band of Sinhalese came by: they also were on their way to collect salt in the lagoons. Then the god called to the Sinhalese, and asked them to carry him down across the river. The Sinhalese climbed the hill, and carried the god down, and bore him across the river, and placed him upon its banks under the shadow of the trees, where now stands his great temple. Then the god swore that he would no longer be served by Tamils in his temple, and that he would only have Sinhalese to perform his ceremonies; and that is why to this day, though the god is a Tamil god, and the temple a Hindu temple, the *kapuralas* are all Buddhists and Sinhalese.

The god, therefore, is of the jungle; a great devil, beneficent when approached in the right manner and season, whose power lies for miles upon the desolate jungle surrounding his temple and hill. A power to swear by, for he will punish for the oath sworn falsely by his hill; a power who will listen to the vow of the sick or of the barren woman; a power who can aid us against the devils which perpetually beset us.[1]

It was in this way that the pilgrims regarded the god, and they chose well the time of his festival to approach him. For the god loved a hind, and had made her his mistress, and had placed her in the temple which stood at the southern end of his street. On each of the fourteen nights of his festival the *kapuralas* entered his shrine, and covering the god in a great black cloth, so that no one should look upon him, carried him out, and placed him upon the back of an elephant. Then the pilgrims called upon the name of the god, and with bowls of blazing camphor upon their heads followed him in procession to his mistress's temple. There the *kapuralas*, blindfolded, took the god, hidden by the cloth, from the elephant, and carried him up the steps of the temple. Again, the pilgrims shouted the god's name, and women pressed forward to touch the *kapurala* as he passed, for in this way they escape the curse of barrenness. The *kapurala* carried the god to his mistress, and then retired. Amid the roar of tomtoms, the jangling of bells, the flaring of great lights, and the passionate shouts of the people, the pilgrims prostrated themselves. Then the *kapurala*, still blindfolded, again slipped behind the curtain into the shrine, and brought out the god and placed him upon the elephant, and the procession followed him back to his own temple.

1   There are two distinct races in Ceylon, Tamils and Sinhalese. Their language, customs, and religions are different. The Tamils are Dravidians, probably the original inhabitants of India; they are Hindus in religion. The Sinhalese are Aryans, and their religion is Buddhism. The Tamils inhabit the north and east of the island, the Sinhalese the remainder.

Silindu and the others reached the village in the evening, only a little while before the procession started. They therefore made their way at once to the great temple, and took their stand among the pilgrims who crowded the courtyard. They had eaten nothing since the midday meal; they were hungry and dizzy after the long days upon the road. Silindu seemed too dazed and weak to take much notice of what was taking place about him, and he had to be helped along by Babun. Karlinahami was awed and devout: an old pilgrim, she knew the demeanour required of her.

The effect upon Hinnihami was different. Tired and hungry though she was, even the great crowd in the courtyard excited her. As each new pilgrim arrived he called aloud upon the god; and the whole crowd took up the cry, which rose and fell around the shrine. She who had before never seen more than forty or fifty people in her life felt the weight and breath of thousands that jostled and pressed her. Her heart beat as, under the flare of the torches, hundreds of arms were raised in supplication, and to the crash of the tomtoms the name of the god thundered through the air. The tears came into her eyes and ran down her cheeks as time after time the roll of the many voices surged about her; and when at last the great moment came, and the *kapurala* appeared carrying the god under the black cloth, and over the sea of arms the elephant lifted up its trunk and trumpeted as the god was placed upon its back, she stretched out her hands and cried to the god to hear her.

They followed in the rear of the procession, where men roll over and over in the dust, and childless women touch the ground with their forehead between every step, in fulfilment of their vows.

Silindu, with drawn face and vacant eyes, dragged himself along, leaning on Babun: Karlinahami, devout and stolid, raised the ceremonial cry at the due stopping-places. But Hinnihami felt the power of the god in her and over them all: she felt how near he was to them, mysteriously hidden beneath the great cloth which lay upon the elephant's back. She felt again the awe which great trees in darkness and the shadows of the jungle at nightfall roused in her, the mystery of darkness and power, which no one can see. And again and again as the procession halted, and the cry of the multitude rolled back to them, her breath was caught by sobs, and again she lifted her hands to the god and called upon his name. She formulated no prayer to him, she spoke no words of supplication: only in excitement and exaltation of entreaty she cried out the name of the god.

They were too tired that night to go into the shrine of the big temple after the procession and see the ceremony there. They had lost sight of the old man in the crowd, so that they had to make their meal off a little food that they carried with them. Then, worn out by the journey and excitement, they lay down on the bare ground in the courtyard of the temple.

Next morning Silindu was no better. He seemed weaker and more lifeless: it was clear that the devil had not yet left him. Babun remained with him, while Karlinahami and Hinnihami went down to the river to bathe. The excitement of the previous evening had not died out of the girl, and there was much going on around her to keep it up. The village was a small one, and really consisted of little more than the one street of thirty or forty houses, which were roofed with red tiles and had brown walls of mud. Most of the houses were turned into boutiques during the pilgrimage, and the inhabitants prospered by selling provisions to the pilgrims. When Karlinahami and Hinnihami returned from the river, hundreds filled the street, lounging, strolling, gossiping, and purchasing. Every now and then the crowd would gather more thickly in one quarter, and they would see a pilgrim arrive performing some strange vow. There were some who had run a skewer through their tongue and cheeks; another had thrust through the skin of his back a long stick from which hung bowls of milk. At another time they saw a man, naked except for a dirty loin cloth, his long hair hanging about his face, and a great halo of flowers and branches upon his head; thirty or forty great iron hooks had been put through the skin of his back; to every hook was attached a long cord, and all the cords had been twisted into a rope. Another man held the rope, while the first, bearing with his full weight upon it so that the skin of his back was drawn away from his body, danced around in a circle and shouted and sang.

As Karlinahami and Hinnihami were making their way slowly through the crowd, they suddenly heard a soft voice behind them say: 'Well, mother, has not the hospital cured your brother of his fever?' They turned and saw the smiling face and winking eye of the *vederala*. Hinnihami shrank away from him behind Karlinahami.

'*Vederala*,' said Karlinahami, 'I must speak with you. Come away from all these people.'

They pushed through the crowd, and going down a narrow opening between two boutiques found themselves in the strip of quiet forest upon the bank of the river. The *vederala* squatted down under a tree and began to chew betel. Karlinahami squatted down opposite to him, and Hinnihami tried to hide herself behind her from the eye of the *vederala*, which seemed to her maliciously to wink at her.

Punchirala leaned round and peered at the girl.

'Well, daughter,' he said, ironically emphasising the word 'daughter,' 'what have you come to the god for? Have you touched the *kapurala*'s foot and prayed for a child? Truly they say he is the god of the barren wife. *Chi, chi*, she covers her face with her hands. Is the man dead then? What has the widow to do in Beragama? *Ohé*! Now, see. She has come to the god for clothing and food,[1] as they say. May the god give her a man, young and fair and strong, a prince with cattle and land. For the girl is fair, even I, the one-eyed old man, can see that – and the god is a great god.'

'Don't talk this nonsense, *vederala*,' broke in Karlinahami impatiently. 'You shame the girl and frighten her. The god is a great god, we know that, and as you told me we brought my brother here. *Aiyo*! The long road and the hot sun. We are burnt as black as Tamils, and look at our feet. On the road the strong and healthy fall sick, and the sick man grows weaker. Have you sent my brother here to kill him? He lies now in the temple with no strength in him. Last night we took him in the *perahera*,[2] and called upon the god to hear us. I pray you, *vederala* – you are a wise man, and renowned for your knowledge – tell me what wrong have we done. The devil remains; the god has not heard us, nor driven

1 An expression used frequently in stories to mean a husband.
2 Procession, usually a Sinhalese or Buddhist procession.

him out.'

'Be patient, mother. This fever is a hard thing to cure. Did I not tell you that even in the hospital there is no medicine against it? And it is hard for a man to find the lucky hour. The gecko[1] calls, and the man starts from the house: the man does not hear the sign; he is saying, "You there bring that along!" and, "You here, where is the bundle with the *kurakkan*?" So he starts on the journey in an unlucky hour.'

'We heard no gecko, nor any other bad sign. But we had to start quickly, for the time was short. We had no time to consult an astrologer to find the lucky hour.'

'Yes, perhaps that is it. And it is no easy matter, as I told you, to find a cure for these fevers.'

'But, *vederala*, what are we to do now? The man's strength goes from him. Even to take him back the long way to the village will be difficult.'

'Patience, mother, patience. You must call louder to the god nightly until the moon is full. Perhaps even now the devil – the fever – is fighting against him.'

'*Aiyo*! What help for the cultivator when the flies have sucked the strength from the paddy? He sowed in an unlucky hour, and not even the god can help him. Pity us, *vederala*. Will you not come with us and look at my brother now?'

'Why should I see your brother?' said the *vederala* angrily. 'What good can I do? Did I not tell you, woman, that I cannot cure your brother's fever? Where the god fails, can the man succeed? O the minds of these women! They say in the village' – here he looked round and smiled at Hinnihami – 'that even the little one is like an untamed buffalo cow.'

'Do not be angry with me, *vederala*. You are the only help left for us. We are weary with walking, and in grief. How can the women of the house not raise the cry when the brother and father lies dying within? If I have spoken foolishly, pardon my words.'

Punchirala sat silently looking at Hinnihami. The girl was crying. The

1 Lizard. The chirping cry of the gecko is universally regarded as a warning cry of ill omen.

memory of the great god, whom she had seen go riding by upon the elephant amid the flames and the shouts, the wild god who ruled over the jungle, and to whom the men crowned with flowers and leaves were now dancing in the street, the god to whom she cried so passionately on the night before, had left her: her excitement and exaltation had died out as she listened to the jeering words of Punchirala. She hated him as she had hated him when he approached her before; but as she listened to him talking to Karlinahami, fear – the fear that she felt for unknown evils – gradually crept upon her. She cried helplessly, and Punchirala smiled at her as he watched her. Karlinahami watched his face expectantly and anxiously.

At last Punchirala began again slowly: 'How the girl cries. And for her father too! I am thinking that there is yet something for you to do. I am a poor *vederala*, and my powers are small. But there is a man here, a great man, a holy man, who they say is very skilled in medicine and magic, and knows the mind of the god. He is a *sanyasi*[1] from beyond the sea, from India, and his hair is ten cubits[2] in length. Perhaps if you take Silindu to him, and inquire of him, he will tell you the god's mind. But you must take money for him.'

'*Aiyo*! What is the use of talking of money to the starving?'

Punchirala fumbled in the fold of his cloth, and drew out his betel-case. From this he took a very dirty rag, in which were a number of copper and silver coins. He made up the sum of ninety-five cents, and handed it over to Karlinahami.

'Here you are then, a *rupee*. Even the gods require payment. You can pay me three shillings in *kurakkan* when the crop is reaped. The *sanyasi* sits behind the little temple under a *banian* tree. Today, when the sun sinks behind the trees of the jungle, take your brother to him and make inquiry.'

Punchirala got up and began walking away, followed by the obeisances and profuse thanks of Karlinahami. The two women hurried back to the

1 A holy man or religious beggar Hindu.
2 Fifteen feet.

temple. They found that the old man and the fisher and his wife had joined Silindu and Babun. The whole party agreed that the only thing to do was to consult the *sanyasi*. They waited, dozing and talking through the hot afternoon, until the hour fixed by the *vederala* arrived.

As soon as the sun sank behind the jungle, and the shadow of the trees fell upon the courtyard, they went in a body to the *banian* trees. They found the *sanyasi* sitting with his back against the trunk of a tree with a brass bowl by his side. He was unlike any *sanyasi* whom they had seen before. He had a long black beard reaching below his waist, a big hooked nose, and little twinkling black eyes. He wore a long white cotton robe which was indescribably dirty, and an enormous dirty white turban. As they approached him he unwound the folds of his turban, and displayed his hair to the crowd which surrounded him. It was plaited and matted into two thin coils upon the top of his head, and its length had not been by any means exaggerated by Punchirala. The *sanyasi* spoke only a strange language, unintelligible to the Tamils and Sinhalese in the crowd, but there stood by him an old Tamil man who interpreted what he said.

Babun led Silindu up to the *sanyasi* and dropped the money in the bowl. He explained what he wanted to the old Tamil, who understood and spoke (very badly) Sinhalese. The crowd pressed forward to listen. The *sanyasi* and his interpreter muttered together. The old man then addressed the crowd, and told them that the holy man could not consult the god, or give an answer, with them pressing upon him. There was much talking and excitement, but at last a large circle was cleared, and the crowd was induced to move away out of earshot. Most of the people squatted down, and, though they could not hear a word of what followed, they watched in hope of some exciting development.

Babun and Silindu squatted down in front of the *sanyasi*. Karlina-hami, Hinnihami, and the others of their party stood behind them. Silindu, weak and dejected though he was, for the first time for several days seemed to take some interest in what was passing. It had been arranged that Babun should explain the case to the *sanyasi*.

'Will you tell the holy man,' he said to the interpreter, 'that we are poor folk and ask pardon of him? This man is my wife's father, a hunter, a very poor man. There is also a *yakka* who lives in the *banian* trees in the jungle over there' (Babun made a sweep with his arm towards the west). 'This *yakka* has entered this man, and his life is going from him. Why has the *yakka* entered the man? There is another man in the village; that man is skilled in charms and magic, and is angry with this man. Therefore, he charmed the devil to do this. Well, then, when this had happened, the woman went to him and prayed him to charm the devil away again. Then he said, "Take your brother to Beragama, and pray to the god there at the great festival." So we walked and walked to this place with the sick man, and we went in the *perahera* and called to the god. But the god does not hear us, and the man's life is going from him. Then the woman went again to the man, for he too is here, and told him. He said, "I can do nothing; take the man to the holy man who sits under the *banian* tree, and make inquiry of him." So we waited for the lucky hour, and have brought him.'

The interpreter talked in the strange tongue with the *sanyasi*, and then said to Babun: 'The holy man says that the offering is too small.'

'Father, it is all we have. We are very poor. Rain never falls upon our fields, and we have no land. We pray him to help us.'

There was another muttered conversation, and then the interpreter said: 'It is very little for so great a thing. But the holy man will help you.'

The little group became very still; everyone watched the *sanyasi* anxiously. He muttered to himself, fixed his eyes on the ground in front of him, made marks in the sand with his finger, and swayed his body from side to side.

Then looking at Silindu intently he began to speak very volubly. Silindu watched him, fascinated. At last the *sanyasi* stopped, and the interpreter addressed them: 'The holy man says thus: it is true that a devil of the jungle has entered the man. This devil is of great power. Why has this happened? The man is a foolish man. There has come into the holy man's mind another man, his face marked with scars, and one-eyed. He is a *vederala*, very skilled in charms. You have not told why the one-eyed man is angry, but the holy man knows because of his holiness and wisdom. The one-eyed man came and said, "Give me your daughter,"

75

but this man, being mad, refused and spoke evil. Then the one-eyed man was very angry, and went away and made a charm over the devil, and the devil entered the man. When the one-eyed man made the charm he said to the devil: "Unless she be given to me, do not leave him."'

A cry broke from Hinnihami; she covered her face with her hands, and crouched in fear upon the ground. The interpreter paid no attention to her.

'Now even the one-eyed man cannot loose the charm, so he has sent you to the god. The god is of great power over devils: he heard your prayer, and he said to this devil, "Leave the man." But the *yakka* answered, fighting against the power, "Something must be given." The master said, "Unless she be given, do not leave the man. Am I to die for this foolish man's sake?" Then the god said, "Yes, something must be given – either the man or the girl." The holy man knows this, and says that you must remain here, and take the man every night in the *perahera* until the night of the full moon, and on the morning of the next day you must return to the village. But on the evening of the first day's journey, the one-eyed man will meet you in an open stony place beside two *palu* trees. Then you must go to him and say, "There is the girl; take her." He will take the girl, and the devil will leave the man. Otherwise, if you do not do this the man will die, for something must be given – either the man or the girl. Remember, too, that the girl cannot be given during the festival.'

Hinnihami pressed her body against the ground, but her eyes were dry now. She was broken: tired and numb with fear and despair; she had always known that it was she who was bringing death upon her father. Instinctively, like a wild animal against a trap, she had fought against the idea of giving herself to Punchirala. At the thought of her body touching his, the skin seemed to shrink against her bones. Silindu was everything to her, and she knew that now she was everything to him. At first she had felt that she was being driven inevitably to sacrifice herself; but when Karlinahami returned from Punchirala's compound, and told them of the pilgrimage, hope came to her. The hardships and excitement of the road, her ecstasy before the god, had driven away her first feeling of despair. The god would certainly help them. But fear had crept in again at the first sight of Punchirala, and as she listened to his talk with Karlina-hami her hope grew cold. Now she knew that she must inevitably sacrifice herself. Had not the *sanyasi* known the truth which Babun had not disclosed? She knew that not even the god could help her; she had heard his words, 'Yes, something must be given – either the man or the girl.' Once more evil had come out of the jungle.

The effect upon the other listeners had also been great. The holy man had seen what Babun had hidden; they knew well that they had heard from him the reply of the god. They walked back to the temple talking about it in low voices. There was no suggestion of doubt in anyone as to what should be done. Even Silindu had given in. The god had spoken; it was fate, the inevitable. The girl would be given.

The remainder of the festival passed slowly for them. They followed the *perahera* dispirited, and called upon the god nightly. But there was no hope or even doubt now to excite them. Silindu, listless, waited for his release; Hinnihami was cowed and dulled by despair. The nights passed, and the morning following, the new moon came; and they went down dutifully to the river to take part in the cutting of the waters. They were a melancholy little group among the laughing, joking crowd, which stood knee-deep in the river. And when the supreme moment came, and the *kapurala* cut the waters, and the crowd with a shout splashed high over themselves and one another the waters which would bring them good fortune through the coming year, Hinnihami stood among them weeping.

The pilgrimage was over, and a line of returning pilgrims began at once to stream across the river westwards. The old man and the fisher and his wife said good-bye to them, for they felt that it was not right for them, being strangers, to be present at what was to take place upon the homeward journey. Then they too set out. They walked all that day slowly – for Silindu was very weak and in silence. When the shadows began to lengthen, the jungle became thinner, and the ground more stony. They knew that they must be nearing the place. The track turned and twisted through the scrub; the air was very still. They passed a bend, and there before them stood the *vederala* under some *palu* trees. They stopped for a moment and looked at one another. Karlinahami touched Silindu on the arm. He took Hinnihami by the hand and went up to Punchirala. His eyes seemed to be fixed upon something far away beyond Punchirala he spoke very slowly: 'Here is the girl take her.'

Punchirala looked at Hinnihami and smiled. 'It is well,' he said.

Silindu turned, and with Karlinahami and Babun walked on down the track. Neither of them looked back. Hinnihami was left standing by the *vederala*, her arms hanging limply by her side, her eyes looking on the ground.

Chapter 6

IT BECAME CLEAR on the morning after Hinnihami had been given
to the *vederala* that the *sanyasi* had rightly interpreted the will of the
god, and that the devil had left Silindu. His eyes no longer presented the
glazed appearance, which is the sign of possession. He ate eagerly of the
scanty morning meal; and, though still weak, walked with a vigour
unknown to him since the night when he fell beneath the *banian* trees in
the jungle. Throughout the homeward journey strength and health
continued to return to him; and by the time they reached the village, the
colour of his skin showed that he had been restored to his normal
condition.

Though they travelled very slowly, they had not again seen the *vederala*
and Hinnihami on the way home. Punchirala made no haste to return to
the village, and he only appeared there two days after Silindu arrived. He
showed no signs of pleasure in his triumph; he was more quiet and
thoughtful than usual. In the house he seemed to his mother to be uneasy,
and a little afraid of Hinnihami.

The girl had yielded herself to him in silence. In the long journey
together through the jungle he had, without success, tried many methods
of breaking or bending her spirit. But he had failed: his jeers and his
irony, his anger and his embraces, had all been received by her in sullen
silence. He would have put her down to be merely a passionless, stupid
village woman had he not seen the light and anger in her eyes, and the
shudder that passed over her body when he touched her.

On the morning after she arrived in the village, Hinnihami was alone
in Punchirala's compound; the *vederala* had gone out, and his mother
was in the house. She saw Silindu coming along the path, and ran out
eagerly to meet him. They sat down under a tamarind tree, just outside
the stile in the compound fence.

'The *yakka* has gone,' said Silindu. 'The god drove him out after the *vederala* took you. But now what to do? The house is empty without you, child.'

'I must come back, *Appochchi*. I cannot live in this house.'

'But, is it safe? Will not he bring evil again upon us? The god said one must be given, and now if I take you again, will he not kill you?'

'The god said that one must be given, and it was done. I was given, and the man took me. Surely the gods cannot lie. The evil has been driven out; and as for the man, I am not frightened of him.'

'*Ané!*' said the mocking voice of the *vederala* behind them. 'They are not frightened of the man. Oh no, nor of the devils either, I suppose.'

Silindu and Hinnihami got up; the old fear came upon Silindu when he saw Punchirala, but the girl turned angrily upon the *vederala*, who was astonished by her violence.

'Punchirala,'[1] she said, 'I am not frightened of you. The god did not say I was to live with you. There is no giving of food or clothing. I was given that the devil might leave my father. Was the god disobeyed? I was given to you, you dog; the devil has flown; the god heard us there at Beragama he will not allow you again to do evil.'

'Mother, mother, come out! Listen to the woman I brought to the house; she has become a *vederala*. The pilgrimage has made her a *sanyasi*, I think, knowing the god's mind, skilled in magic.'

'Keep your words for the women of the house. I am going.'

'And are there no other charms, Silindu? No other devils in the trees? You have learned wisdom surely from a wise woman.'

'Do not listen to him, *Appochchi*. He can no longer harm us. The god has aided us.' She turned upon Punchirala. 'Do you wish me to stay in the house? Yes, there are still devils in the trees. Do not I too come from the jungle? I shall be like a *yakkini* to you in the house, you dog. You can tell them, they say, by the eyes which do not blink. Rightly the village women call me *yakkini*. I will stay with you. Look at my arms. Are they not as

---

1 Hinnihami addresses Punchirala by name, and thereby shows him that she does not regard herself as living with him as his wife.

strong as a man's arms? I will stay with you, but as you lie by my side in the house I will strangle you, Punchirala.'

Punchirala instinctively stepped back, and Hinnihami laughed.

'*Ohé*! Are you frightened, Punchirala? The binder of *yakkas* is frightened of the *yakkini*. You can tell her, they say, because her eyes are red and unblinking, and because she neither fears nor loves. It is better for you that I should go to the trees from which I came, mighty *vederala*. Otherwise, I would strangle you, and eat you in the house. Come, *Appochchi*, we will go out into the jungle together again as we did long ago – *aiyo*! The long time. I was a little thing then – and the little sister too. Come, *Appochchi*; do not fear this *Rodiya* dog: he is frightened: and now I will never leave you.'

Punchirala was really frightened. He stood and watched the girl walk slowly away with Silindu along the path. Things had not happened quite as he had expected or hoped. He had enjoyed his first triumph over the girl, but he had soon grown to doubt whether her continued presence in his house would add to his comfort. He had felt, without understanding, that the giving of her body to him had only made her spirit more unyielding. Even on the way from Beragama he had felt nervous and uncomfortable with her. He was angered by his defeat and by her taunts, but he watched her disappear with a distinct feeling of relief.

The *vederala* made no further attempt to molest Silindu, and the next nine months were a period of unwonted prosperity and happiness in the *Vedda* family. Towards the end of October great clouds rolled up from the northeast, and great rains broke over the jungle. For days the rain fell steadily, ceaselessly. The tank filled and ran over; the dry sandy channels became torrents, sweeping down old rotten trunks and great trees through the jungle; a mist of moisture rose from the parched earth, and hung grey upon the face of the jungle. Suddenly the ground became green, and soon the grass stood waist-high beneath the undergrowth. The earth at last was sodden; and as the rain still fell and the streams overflowed, the water spread out in a vast sheet beneath the trees.

Not for forty years, it was said, had rain fallen so abundantly. A great *chena* crop was assured. The more energetic began to talk of rice cultivation, now that the tank was full, and to regret the want of seed paddy. Then a rumour spread that the Government was going to make advances of seed, and at last one day the *Korala Mahatmaya* appeared in the village, and the rumour was confirmed. Promissory notes were signed; buffaloes were borrowed to turn up the soil of the fields; and at last, after twelve years, the village again saw paddy standing green in the water below their tank.

Silindu's family, principally owing to Babun, had a large share in the prosperity which came to the village from the wonderful *chena* and rice-crops. Their store was full of *kurakkan* and millet and rice. They were well fed, and even Silindu became happy. After the return of Hinnihami he seemed to change greatly. They were almost always together, and the fearlessness which she had shown towards Punchirala, and which seemed to have changed her suddenly from a child into a woman, inspired him. The fear of evil overhanging him no longer oppressed him. He worked with Babun cheerfully in the *chena* and rice-fields: he began again to talk with Punchi Menika. And sometimes he would sit in the compound and tell his strange stories to her and to the child, who had been born to her eighteen months before, and he was happy as he had been happy with her and with Hinnihami years ago when they were children. His happiness and Hinnihami's was greatly increased when she gave birth to a daughter. The child, conceived during the pilgrimage, was a pledge to them from the god that, as his word had been obeyed, the evil had been finally conquered. To the physical joy which Hinnihami felt as she suckled the child, was added her exultation in the knowledge that she was holding in her arms a charm against the evil which had threatened Silindu. Her hatred for the father only increased therefore her love for his child.

But the love and care which she showed from the moment of her birth to Punchi Nona, as she called her daughter, were from the first to be shared with another. On the morning following the evening on which the child was born, Silindu came back from the jungle carrying in his arms a fawn newly dropped by its mother. He went straight to Hinnihami, who lay in the hut nursing the child, and kneeling down by her placed the fawn in her arms. Hinnihami with a little laugh took it, and nestling it against the child was soon suckling the one at one breast and the other at the other. Silindu watched in silence: he was very serious.

'It is well, it is well,' he said when he saw that the fawn was sucking quietly and nestling against Hinnihami and the child.

'The little weakling,' said Hinnihami, gently touching with her fingers the soft skin of the fawn. 'How hungry for milk the little one is! Where has it come from?'

'It has come to you from the jungle. The gods have sent it.'

She bent her head, and very softly drew her lips backwards and forwards over its back.

'It takes the milk like the child. Has the god given another gift, *Appochchi*?'

'The god sent it. Last night I went to the water-hole, but nothing came while the moon was up. Then clouds gathered and the moon was hidden, and it became very dark. I heard a doe cry near by in pain, "*Amma, amma,*"[1] but it was too dark to see, so I lay down and slept on the top of the high rock. I woke up with the first light, and, as I lay there, I heard below the moving of something among the leaves. Very slowly I looked over the rock, and there below in the undergrowth I saw the back of a doe. Her head was down, hidden by the leaves, and she murmured, licking something on the grass. Slowly, slowly I took up my gun and leaned it over the rock and fired. Everything was hidden from me by the smoke, and I lay quiet until the wind blew it from before me. When I looked again I saw the doe stand there still, the blood running down her side; and she stretched up her head toward me from the jungle, and her great eyes rolled back with fear and showed white, and she opened her mouth and cried terribly to me. I was sorry for her pain, and I said, "Hush, mother, the evil has come. What use to cry? Lie down that death may come to you easily." But again she stretched out her neck toward me, and cried loud in pain, "*Amma! Amma! Aiyo! Aiyo!* It is you who have brought the evil, *Yakka*. To the child here that I dropped last night and that lies now between my feet. Little son, I have borne you to be food for the jackal and the leopard." Then I came

---

1   Mother.

down from the rock and stood by her and said, "Mother, the daughter at home this night bore a child. I will take this one too to her, and she will give it the breast." Then she stretched out her head, and she cried out again, and fell dead upon the ground by the side of the fawn.'

Hinnihami pressed the fawn to her.

'Yes, he has come to me out of the jungle, a sign from the god, a great charm against evil. Did not the god himself take the doe as his mistress? They told it to us at Beragama. And now in the same night he has sent me a son and a daughter from the jungle.'

So Hinnihami suckled the child and the fawn together. The village looked on with astonishment and disapproval. 'The woman is as mad as the father,' was the general comment. It was commonly rumoured that she showed more love for Punchi Appu, as the fawn was called, than for her daughter. And though she did not realise it herself, it was true. 'The son from the jungle' inspired in her a passionate love and tenderness – the great eyes which watched her and the wonderful skin that she was never tired of caressing. He had come to her out of the jungle, with something of the mystery and exaltation which she had felt in Beragama towards the god who went by upon the elephant. And her love was increased by the attachment of Punchi Appu to her. Long before Punchi Nona could crawl about the compound, the fawn would trot along by her side crying to be taken up and fed; and even after it grew old enough to feed upon grass and leaves, it never left her, following her always about the house and compound, and through the village and jungle.

The year of the great rains and rice and plenty was followed by a year of scarcity and sickness. For four months, from June to October, the sun beat down from a cloudless sky. The great wind from the south-west failed at last, but even then the rain did not come, and the withering heat lay still and heavy over the jungle. The little puddle thick with mud in the tank, which supplied the village with water, dried up, and the women had to go daily four miles to fetch water from an abandoned tank in the jungle. In November the *chenas* were still standing black and unsown. At last a little rain fell and the seed was sown. The crop just showed green above the ground, and drought came again, and the young shoots died down.

Then, when it was too late to save the crops, the rains came, and with them sickness. Want had already begun to be felt by bodies weakened by the long drought, and fever and dysentery swept over the country. There was not a family in Beddagama which did not suffer, nor a house in which death did not take the old or the children. The doctor *Mahatmaya*, whom Punchirala despised, appeared in the village, bringing the medicines which he despised still more; but his efforts were no more or less successful than those of the village *vederala*. When at last the sickness passed away, it was found that the village had lost sixteen out of its forty-one inhabitants. And the jungle pressed in and claimed two of the eight houses, after dysentery and fever had taken the men, the women, and their children, who lived there.

Even Silindu's house did not escape: there death took its toll of the young. First Punchi Menika's child sickened, and then Punchi Nona. Day after day the mothers, helpless, watched the fever come and shake the children's bodies, and sap and waste their strength. The wail of the two women, each for her dead child, was raised in one night.

It was Silindu who seemed to feel the loss of the children more than any one else in the house. This time clearly the envious powers had grudged him his little happiness. He had been foolish to show his pleasure in the children crawling about the house. He had brought disaster upon them and upon himself. The misery he had felt at losing Punchi Menika came upon him again. It was his own fault: he was a fool to tempt the evil powers that stood around him eager for their opportunity.

After their first wild outburst of grief, Punchi Menika and Hinnihami felt their loss less than Silindu. The death of the child is what every mother must continually expect. They had seen it too long in the village to be surprised at their own suffering: the birth of children every year and then the coming of the fever to carry them off. Their grief was lightened by the feeling of resignation to the inevitable. And in Hinnihami's case there was a further consolation. She still had Punchi Appu, in whose attachment she could forget the child's death. All her love for the child was now merged in her love for him: he was the mysterious gift and pledge of the god; and she felt that so long as he followed by her side, so long as she felt the caress of his lips upon her hand, no real evil could come to her.

Hinnihami's extraordinary love for the deer was well known in the village, and had never been approved. At first it was regarded merely as the folly of the 'mad' woman. These views were, however, very rarely expressed to the girl herself, for most of the villagers stood in some fear of her passionate anger. But about the time when the epidemic of fever and dysentery was decreasing, a new feeling towards them made its appearance in the village. It was started by Punchirala. 'The mad woman and her child,' he would say. 'What sort of madness is that? An evil woman, an evil woman. I have some knowledge of charms and magic. I took her to my house to live with me. But did I keep her? I drove her away very soon. I did not want the evil eye and a worker of evil to bring misfortune on my house. My mother knows, for she heard her call herself a *yakkini*. Only because of my knowledge of charms was I able to keep away the evil with which she threatened me. And then comes this deer which they say is found in the jungle. Was not the woman herself in travail that very night? Do not she-devils give birth to devils? Do village women suckle deer? Surely it is a devil, born of a devil. Look at the evil that fell upon the village when it came. The crops withered, and the old and the young died. It has brought us want and disease and death.'

The village soon came to believe in Punchirala's opinions. Small children were hurried away out of sight of Hinnihami as she passed. The deer was certainly a devil, who had brought misfortune on the village. Some said that at night it went out and ate the corpses in the new graves. It had been clear for some time that the ill-feeling against them had been growing, when an event occurred which required immediate action. The son of the headman died suddenly and apparently for no cause. Then it was remembered that, three days before, the child had been carrying some leaves when he met the deer and Hinnihami. The deer had gone up to the child and tried to nibble the leaves, but the boy had snatched them away. The headman and the *vederala* were convinced that Hinnihami and the deer were the direct cause of the child's death. There was much talk between Babehami and Punchirala; other villagers were sent for;

there was much coming and going and discussion in the headman's compound, and eventually action was decided upon.

The next day Hinnihami was collecting firewood in an old *chena*. The deer was with her, feeding at a little distance from her upon the young leaves and grass. Suddenly she was aroused by noise and movements near her. A small band of men and boys from the village had crept quietly through the jungle, and now were between her and the deer. As she looked up the first stone was thrown: it missed its mark, but another followed, and struck with a thud upon the deer's side. He bounded forward. Hinnihami cried out and ran towards him: at the sound of her voice he stopped and looked round. A shower of stones fell about him; thin streams of blood began to trickle down his flanks; suddenly he plunged forward upon his head, his two forelegs broken at the knees. A cheer broke from the men. Hinnihami, as she dashed forward, was caught by two men and flung backwards upon the ground. She fell heavily and for a moment was stunned; then she heard the long, bleating cry of pain, and saw the deer vainly trying to raise itself upon its broken legs among the jeering knot of men. She felt the blood surge up to her forehead and temples as a wave of anger came over her, and she flung herself upon the two men who barred her path. Swinging their arms wildly, they gave her blow upon blow with the open hand upon her head and breast. Her jacket was torn into shreds, and at last she fell exhausted.

The sight of the bleeding deer and the woman lying on the ground, naked to the waist, seemed to send a wave of lust and cruelty through the men. They tore Hinnihami's cloth from her, and, taking her by her arms, dragged her naked up to the deer.

'Bring the *vesi* to her child,' they shouted.

'Comfort your *yakka, yakkini*. Is there no milk in your breasts for him now?'

They held her that she might see what they did. The deer was moaning in pain. One of the men cut a thick stick and struck him upon the hind legs until they were broken. Hinnihami fought and struggled, but she was powerless in their hands. At length, when they had become tired of torturing them, they threw her down by the deer's side and went away.

Hinnihami was unhurt, but she was stunned by the violence of anger and horror. The deer moaned from time to time. She tried to lift him with some vague idea of carrying him back to the house. But he screamed with pain at the slightest movement, and he had grown too big for her to carry. She felt that he was dying. She flung herself down by him, caressing his head, and calling to him not to leave her. 'Punchi Appu! Punchi Appu!' she kept repeating, 'you must not die. Surely the god who gave you to me will save you. Punchi Appu, Punchi Appu, you cannot die.'

Then gradually a sense only of dull despair settled upon her. She sat through the long day unconscious of the passing of time. She was unaware when the deer died; she knew that he was dead now, and that with him everything had died for her. There was nothing for her to live for now, and already she felt life slipping from her. She thought of the child who had died too: she had missed her, and grieved for her, but she had never loved the child as she loved the deer. He had come to her, a wild thing from the jungle, the god's mysterious gift. Now he was lying there dead, his broken limbs twisted under him, the dead white eyes bulging, the tongue hanging out from the open mouth. She shuddered as she remembered the scene, shuddered as she recalled the thud of the stones and the blows.

She was found by Silindu next morning still sitting naked by the body of the deer, her hair wet with the dew, and her limbs stiff with the chill of the jungle at night. He tried in vain to rouse her. She recognised him. 'Let me be, *Appochchi*,' she kept repeating. 'Let me die here, for he is dead. Let me die here, *Appochchi*.'

Then Silindu wrapped her cloth about her, and carried her in his arms to the house. She cried a little when she felt his tears fall upon her, but after that she showed no more signs of grief. She lay in the house, silent, and resigned to die. She had even ceased to think or feel now. Life had no more a hold upon her, and in the hour before dawn in deep sleep she allowed it to slip gently from her.

Chapter 7

SILINDU knew well now that Hinnihami had been a victim to save him. Both the devil and the god had said, 'Either the man or the girl must be given.' It was the girl who had been given; but it was he who should have died, when the devil still possessed him. He knew now, when it was too late, that in giving Hinnihami to the *vederala* he was giving her to certain death. He had gained nothing by his first refusal of the *vederala* but pain and trouble, and now the bitterest of griefs. In the end he had lost her utterly; now indeed the house was empty. He was a fool, yes, a fool; he knew that; but how can a man know how to walk surrounded by all the snares of evil and disaster? A man may wash himself clean of oil, but however much he rubs himself he will never rub off fate. And then there was Punchirala; it was he who was the real cause of the evil. Why had he ever come with his hateful face into the compound? He would go in the early morning and take his gun and shoot the *vederala* dead as he came out of his house. And yet what would be the good of that now – now that Hinnihami was dead? It would only be more evil. It would be useless. It was useless for him to do anything now.

For days Silindu sat about the compound 'thinking and thinking,' as Punchi Menika called it. She alone had any influence with him, and even she had no power to console him. In time grief lost its first bitterness, and he sank into a perpetual state of sullen despair. An air of gloom and disaster seemed to hang about the compound.

It was not long after the life of the village had been stirred by the death of Hinnihami that another event happened which caused no little excitement. It was seen that Babehami, the headman, was having a house built on the open ground adjoining his compound; and as soon as it was finished there came to live in it a man from Kamburupitiya, known as Fernando. Many of the villagers had had dealings with him: he kept a small boutique in Kamburupitiya, and lent money on the usual, and even more than the usual, interest. He was not a Sinhalese, and spoke Sinhalese very badly. Some people said he was a Tamil: his black skin and curly black hair pointed to the fact that he had Kaffir blood in his veins.

He was a typical town man, cunning, unscrupulous, with a smattering of education. He wore the ordinary native cloth, but above it a shirt and coat, and the villagers therefore called him *Mahatmaya*. It was obvious that some very peculiar circumstances had brought such a man to settle down in a village like Beddagama. The fact was that the headman and many of the villagers were deeply in his debt. The failure of the previous year's *chena* crop had made it impossible to recover anything; in fact he was pestered with requests for further loans to tide the debtors over the hot season, until the *chenas* could again be sown.

The creditor was faced with an unpleasant alternative. If he refused further loans he would lose what he had lent already through the death or emigration of his debtors, or they would borrow from others, and thus make it difficult for him to recover. On the other hand the complete failure of the *chena* crop made his own position far from easy: the debt outstanding together with the interest would be in itself a heavy charge, on the next crop, even if it were a really good one. To be safe in giving still more credit, he required additional security.

It was Babehami, the headman, who devised a scheme to meet these difficulties. Four acres of *chena* would be allowed to each debtor: the permits would be given in favour of the debtors, who were to assign their rights to Fernando for one-fifth of the crop. It was tacitly understood that if the four-fifths of the crop exceeded the amount of the loans and interest, the debts would be considered cancelled. Fernando was to come to the village, and himself supervise the working of the *chenas*. Practically, therefore, the money-lender was hiring labour for the cultivation of *chenas* for one-fifth of the crop, an exceedingly paying transaction; while his rights and power of action for the outstanding debts remained unaffected. The villagers were completely in his hands, and both sides were fully aware of it. The whole transaction, certainly, so far as the headman was concerned, was illegal. Babehami knew this, but his needs were pressing, and his own profit would be great; for, while his consent was purchased by the cancellation of his debts, by a private arrangement with Fernando, his own four acres of *chena* were not assigned to the money-lender.

To the villagers Fernando was, owing to his dress and habits, a *Mahatmaya*. He did not treat them as his equals, and they – being in his debt – treated him as a superior. He was, however, on terms of intimacy with Babehami; and although he had a small boy with him as servant, he took all his meals in the headman's house.

Punchi Menika very soon attracted Fernando's attention. Her face and form would have been remarkable even in a town: to find her among the squalid women of so squalid a village astonished him. He wanted a woman to live with him; he was always wanting a woman; and it would be far more comfortable to have his food cooked for him than to go always to the headman for his meals. He anticipated no difficulty; she was a mere village woman, and the husband was a village boor, and in his debt.

Despite his confidence Fernando decided to act cautiously. He knew very little about villages, but he knew the many proverbs about women and trouble; and he had heard many tales of violence and murder, of which women had been the cause. He was quite alone among people whom he did not really understand, far away from the boutiques and police court, the busy little town which he understood, and where alone he really felt secure. He was a timid man, and he hated the jungle; and, though he despised these people who lived in it, he was not comfortable with them.

His first move was to try to learn something about the family from the headman. He sounded Babehami cautiously. The result pleased him greatly. They were bad people according to the headman – *veddas*, gipsies, traffickers in evil, whores, and vagabonds. By evil charms they had enticed Babun to their compound, and now they boasted that he, the brother of the headman's wife, had married Punchi Menika. They were dangerous people; they had brought misfortune and death into the village. Fernando was not greatly impressed by their reputation for working harm 'by magic'; as became a townman, he was somewhat sceptical; but what was clear to him was that the headman hated the whole family; they would get in no eventuality any help or sympathy from him. This knowledge was as valuable as it was pleasing to him.

Then one evening he surprised them by coming and chatting to Babun almost as if he were an equal. It was evening, just about the time before the lamps are lit in the house, when the air grows cool, and the wind dies down, and the afterglow of the setting sun is in the sky. The work in the *chena* for the man, and in the house for the woman, was over. Babun was squatting in the compound near the house, and Punchi stood behind him, leaning against the doorpost. From time to time a word or two was spoken, but for the most part they were content to allow the silence of the evening to descend upon them, as they watched with vacant eyes the light fade out of the sky.

Punchi Menika, brought the wooden mortar in which the grain was pounded, turned it upside down, and dusted the top with a piece of cloth.

'Will you sit down, *aiya*?' said Babun. Fernando sat down upon it. Babun squatted opposite to him, while Punchi Menika, stood behind, leaning against the doorpost.

'Well, Babun' said Fernando, 'will the *chena* crop be good, do you think?'

'Who can say, *aiya*, who can say? Only a fool measures his grain before it is on the threshing-floor.'

'Then all these villagers do that, for they are all fools. *Aiyo*! What cattle! What trouble they give a man'

'We are poor men, *aiya*, and ignorant.'

'I'm not thinking of you, Babun, but of the others. There is only one man in the village; all say that, and I've seen it myself. But the others! They will ruin me. How much do they owe me! Only a very good crop will pay it, but they don't care. They don't fence the *chena* or watch it; they sit and sleep in the compound, and the deer and pig go off with my *rupees* in their bellies. Isn't that true?'

'It's true, *aiya*.'

'And what can I do, a town man, with all these *chenas*? I ought to have a *gambaraya*.'[1]

'Yes, you want a *gambaraya*.'

'So I thought, and I thought too, "This Babun is the only man in the village, why shouldn't he be my *gambaraya*?" Well, what do you say? You could look after the other *chenas*, and also cultivate your own?'

Babun was silent with astonishment; it was a piece of good fortune which he could never have dreamed of.

'I would give you one-twentieth of the crop, after the fifth had been paid to the cultivators,' Fernando went on. 'Would you do it for that?'

'Yes, *aiya*, I will do it for that, gladly.'

'Very well, that's settled. You are my *gambaraya* now.'

Fernando sighed and stretched himself. 'What a place this jungle is!' he said. 'It is not fit for a sensible man to live in. Of course these other villagers, if they went anywhere else, what could they do, the cattle? They do not know the east from the west, as the tale says. If they get into a bazaar they are frightened, and run about like a scared bull. But you, Babun, you are young and strong; you are a knowing man. Why do you starve here when you could eat rice and grow fat elsewhere?'

'So my sister and her man said, *aiya*! They wanted me to go away and marry in another village – over there; rain falls and rice grows there. But it is a great evil to live in a strange place and among strangers.'

Fernando laughed. 'An evil you call it! But how many have got wealth and fortune by going to strange places! Have you not heard of Maha Potana? Many years ago it was all trees and jungle like this, and no one lived there. Then they built the great tank in the jungle, and people went there from all the villages of the west – poor men living in villages like this. Now it is a town, and all are rich there, and eating rice.'

'Yes, *aiya*, we know that. The tank was built in my father's time. And the *Korala Mahatmaya* and the *Ratemahatmaya* came to the village and spoke as you speak now. And they said that land would be given to all that

---

1 A *gambaraya* is technically a man who oversees the cultivation of rice-fields for the owners, and is paid usually by a share of the crop.

went there, and water from the tank for the cultivation of rice. It was in a year, I remember my father telling me, when rain had not fallen – like the last crop with us – and there was want in the village, and many died of fever. They urged my father to go, for he was a good man: they knew that. And my father said to them – so he told me – "How can I go to this strange place? Can I take the woman and the child with me? I have no house there, and no money to buy in the bazaar. Among strangers and in strange places evil comes. Here my father lived, and his father before him, in this house; and they cleared the *chenas* as I do, and from time to time when rain fell sowed rice below the tank. What folly for me to leave my home and field and the *chena* to meet evil in strange places." My father said this to the headman, and all the other men of the village also refused to go, except one man – Appu they called him; he went with his wife, and was given land under Maha Potana. And nothing was heard of Appu for many months; and his brother, who still lived here, at last went to Maha Potana to inquire about him. And when he came there the people told him that Appu was dead of the fever, and that his wife had gone away, and no one knew where she had gone.'

'But people die of fever in Beddagama.'

'Yes, *aiya*, of course many people die of fever here too. But they die among their relations, and friends, and people who are known to them; in houses where their fathers lived before them. Surely it is a more bitter thing to die in a strange place. I am a poor man and ignorant, and I cannot explain it to you better. There is always trouble and evil in strange places; when a man goes even upon a journey or pilgrimage to Kamburu-pitiya or Maha Potana or Beragama, always, *aiya*, he is troubled and afraid – in the bazaars and boutiques and on the roads people unknown to him – and everywhere he is thinking of his village, and his house, and the tank, and the jungle paths which he knows there, and people living in the village, all of whom he knows. That is why a man will not leave his village, even when the crops fail and there is no food; no, not even when the headmen come – and they come now every year – and say, "There is good land to be given in such a place, there is work upon such a road, or in such a village, why starve here?" I have heard people say that far away in the west there are large towns, Colombo and Kalutara and Galle, where everyone has food and money always; but, *aiya*, not even to those towns do you see a man going who has been born and lived all his life in a village.'

'Am I not now among strangers? What evil will befall me?'

'May the gods keep it away from you, *aiya*. But how can a man tell what evil is before him? But you are not an ignorant village man like us, and besides after the *chena* is reaped you will return to your house.'

Fernando was silent for a while. When he spoke again he had a curiously seductive effect upon his listeners. His low, soft voice and broken Sinhalese, the languorousness and softness which seemed to pervade him fascinated them even more than what he said.

'What can the buffalo born in the fold know of the jungle? or does the wild buffalo know how to work in the rice-fields? I was born far away across the sea on the coast. I was only a little child when they brought me to Colombo to live there in the shop which my father kept. He had no fear to leave his village and to cross the sea, nor had he any desire to go back again there. He was a rich man. *Ohé*! What a town is Colombo. There we lived in a great building, and all around us were houses and houses, and people and people: no jungle or snakes or wild beasts; not even a paddy-field or a coconut tree. Always streets and people walking, walking backwards and forwards on the red roads (and very few even known to you by sight), and bullock-carts and carriages and rickshaws, hundreds upon hundreds. And there are houses, very high, as high as the hill at Beragama, full of white *Mahatmayas* and their women, always coming and going from the ships. How many times have I stood outside when a boy and watched them, always laughing and talking loud, like madmen, and dancing, men and women together. And how fair are the women, fair as the lotus-flower as the tale says; very fair and very shameless.'

'Is it true then that the women of the white *Mahatmayas* are shameless?' broke in Punchi Menika.

'In Colombo all say they are shameless. Very fair, very mad, and very shameless. Their eyes are like cats' eyes. The proverb says, "If the eyes of a woman are like the eyes of a cat, evil comes to the man who looks into them." The hair of the English *Mahatmayas'* women is very fair, the colour of the young coconut-flowers. Yes, they are mad. In the evening strange music is played by many men sitting high up near the roof; then every *Mahatmayas* takes a woman in his arms, and looking into her eyes goes round and round very quickly on the floor.'

'*Aiya, aiya,* is this a true tale?'

'Why should I tell you what is false? Did I not live twenty years there in Colombo? It is a great town. In the morning I went and walked on the stone road that has been built into the sea, and within is the harbour, full always of great ships bigger than villages. Always the *Mahatmayas* are coming and going in the great ships; from where they come and where they go no one can tell. You stand upon the stone road, and you see the great ship come in across the sea in the morning, filled with white *Mahatmayas*, and in the evening it carries them out again across the sea. They are all very rich, and for a thing that costs one shilling they willingly give five. Also they are never quiet, going here and there very quickly, and doing nothing. Very many are afraid of them, for suddenly they grow very angry, their faces become red, and they strike any one who is near with the closed hand.'

Fernando stopped. He had become quite excited as he recalled his life in Colombo in his youth. He had forgotten where he was. Suddenly he became aware of his surroundings, the little village so far away from everything; the ignorant, uncouth villager who listened to him; the woman behind him for whose sake he had come to the hut, and whom for the moment he had forgotten. For a while Babun did not like to disturb his silence, then he asked diffidently: 'But, *aiya,* if Colombo is your village, how is it that you now live in Kamburupitiya?

Fernando laughed. 'What talk is this of villages?' he said. 'Everywhere here the question is, "Of what village is he?" And then, "He is of Beddagama or Bogama, or Beragama, or any *gama*."[1] And the liver in villages says, as you did but now, 'How can I leave my *gama*. Did I not tell

1   *Gama* means a village.

you that I am of no village? My father's village is beyond the sea, and they say that the father's village is the son's. I have never seen that village; I have forgotten its name. I was born in Colombo, which is no village, but a town. *Aiyo!* What a town it is! How pleasant! The houses and the noise and smell of the bazaar for miles, and the dust and people everywhere! What folly to live here, like a *sanyasi* on the top of a bare rock! Perhaps one day I shall return to Colombo, and live in a great house, as my father did. My father was a rich man, but always gambling; no money stayed in the house. And I spent much money upon women. There was a nautch-girl from the coast; her eyes had made me mad, and she devoured me. It was always *rupees*, and bracelets, and anklets, and silk cloths. Then my father was very angry, for all the money had gone on the gambling and jewellery. There was no money to pay the merchants for goods for the shop, but worst of all he had no money for gambling. The girl had taunted me because I had come empty-handed, saying that she would shame me openly if I came back again with nothing. So I again asked my father for money. He drove me away, cursing me; so I went into the shop, and took goods and sold them, and taking two handfuls of silver flung them down before the girl. But when my father found what I had done, he cursed me again, and beat me, and drove me out of the house, saying, that if I returned he would give me to the police. I ran out very sad because of the girl. I was also sorry that I had given her both handfuls of silver, and had not kept one for myself. I stood at a street corner thinking that now I would die of hunger, and that it would be better to hang myself. Just then there passed a Moorman, Cassim, a man of Kalutara, a merchant, whom I had often seen in my father's shop. He laughed at me when he saw me, and said, speaking Tamil, "Now I see that the feet of the girl have danced away with the old man's wealth and the young man's life." At that the tears ran down my face, and I told him all that had happened. Then he said, "Come with me to Kalutara. You can sell there for me in my shop." So I went with him to Kalutara, and stayed there selling for him for two years. After that he sent me to sell for him in Kamburupitiya, and there I now live, and have a shop of my own.'

Fernando paused for a while; then he began again: 'You see I have no village. I live always among strangers, but no evil has come. I left Colombo without a cent, and now I have become rich. What folly to starve where one was born when there are riches to be got in the neighbouring village! Well, I am going now.'

Babun accompanied his guest to the stile of the compound, and took leave of him with the usual words, 'It is well; go and come again.'

Fernando was quite satisfied with his interview. He thought he had gauged Babun, and that he would have no difficulty with him; he seemed so simple and mild. Both the man and woman had obviously been impressed by him and by his wealth. He was, however, still cautious; he decided to make his first overture through the servant boy, whom he could trust.

The boy was instructed carefully. He was to go to Punchi Menika as if on his own initiative. His master was a rich man, and a great lover of women. He had already remarked upon her beauty. The boy was quite sure that, though his master had not actually said so, he desired her greatly. If she agreed, he would tell his master that the next night that Babun was watching in the *chena* she would come to his house or would receive him in hers. It would benefit both her and her husband, for his master was very kind and generous.

The attempt was a failure. Punchi Menika listened to what the boy had to say, and then gave him a sound smack in the face, which sent him crying back to his master. She was very angry with the 'badness of these boys from the town,' and she did not suspect that he had been sent by his master.

Fernando beat the servant boy, and himself went to Punchi Menika's compound one evening when he knew that Babun would be watching at the *chena*.

'Woman,' he said, 'you have beaten my servant boy. Why is that?'

'He came here with evil words, *aiya*.'

'Evil words? A child of eight?'

'*Chi, chi*. But he came here with evil words and lies.'

'Lies? What did he say? That your face is very fair, and that all men desire you?'

'*Aiya, aiya*, do not speak like that. He spoke shameful words. I cannot tell you what he said.'

'Nonsense. You have beaten my servant and you must tell me why, or I must go to the headman.'

'*Aiya*, why force me to tell what is shameful?'

'What nonsense. Are you a child, then? What shame is there in words?'

'The boy came here with shameful words, saying that you desired a woman. He called me to come to you secretly at night, when my man goes to the *chena*.'

Fernando looked very hard at Punchi Menika. He smiled when her eyes dropped.

'But what if the boy did not lie? What if he was sent by his master?'

'Hush, *aiya*. Do not speak like that.'

'Why? Am I so foul that the woman of the villager Babun shrinks from me?'

'It is not that.'

'What is it, then? The women of Colombo and Kamburupitiya have not found me foul. Are you afraid?'

'Yes, *aiya*, I am afraid.'

'Afraid of what? What harm can come? Who need know? And what can Babun do? He is a fool. He owes me money. What can he do?'

'I am afraid. It is difficult for me to explain to you, for I see you will grow angry. I am a village woman, ignorant: I am not a woman like that. I went to the man willingly, even against my father's will. He has been the father of my child, that is dead. He is good to me. Let me alone, *aiya*, let me alone, to keep his house and cook his meals for him as before.'

'Why not? I do not ask you to come to Kamburupitiya to be my wife. There is no talk of leaving your husband. I am rich, and can give you money and jewels. You will bring good fortune to your husband, for I will cancel his debts and give him the share of the other *chenas* which I promised him.'

'I cannot do it, *aiya*.'

'What folly! There is nothing to fear. The houses are near with the same fence. No one will know if you come to me through the fence after nightfall. If I say "Come, I want you," is it not enough? Do you wish me to lie on ground before you and pray to you?'

'Enough, enough, *aiya*. Pardon me, I cannot do it.'

'Will you bring ruin on your man, then?'

'I do not understand.'

'What? She doesn't understand. What cattle these people are! Is Babun in my debt? Is he to get a share of my *chenas*?'

'Yes, *aiya*, I heard you tell him so.'

'Well, is anything given over for nothing? Do they give you rice in the bazaar for nothing, or *kurakkan* or cloth? Do they? Fool, why do you stand there looking at me like a buffalo? You – your man, tell him that I have been here, and what I said. Will he sell you to me like a sack of *kurakkan*? If not, he is a fool too, a dog, a pig; if not, he gets no share of the crop from me, his debts stand and the interest too. I can ruin him. He – I will, too, I will ruin him. Do you hear that? Well, what do you say?'

'What is there to say, *aiya*? I cannot do it. If this thing must come to us, what can we do? Always evil is coming into this house from the jungle, my father says. At first there was no food. Then the devil entered into my father. Then more evil, upon my sister and her child, and upon my child. The children died; they killed Punchi Appu; they killed my sister. And now evil again.'

Punchi Menika had spoken in a very low voice, very slowly. Fernando stood looking at her. For a moment he was affected by the resignation and sadness of her tone. Then he thought he had been a fool to lose his temper and threaten openly. But how could one deal with cattle like these people? He began to grow angry again, but he recognised that it was useless and dangerous further to show his anger and disappointment. He returned without another word to his house.

His failure astonished him almost more than it annoyed him. His first thought was to approach Babun himself. Probably the woman was only frightened of her husband, and probably the husband would see more clearly the advantages to be gained by giving his consent. But Fernando had lost a good deal of his confidence; he felt the need of an adviser and ally. There could be no danger in consulting the headman. In any case it would be dangerous for Babehami to oppose him, and there was every reason to believe that Babehami would be only too glad of an opportunity of working against Babun and Punchi Menika.

Next day, after he had eaten the evening meal, in the headman's house, and while he was sitting in the compound with Babehami, chewing betel, he opened the subject.

'I thought to get your wife's brother to oversee my *chenas*. He is a good man, I think.'

Babehami spat. 'What will you pay him?'

'One twentieth of the crop. He is a good man to work.'

'He is a good worker. His *chena* is always the best, but he is a fool. He has brought disgrace upon us.'

'Is he married to that woman?'

'No. He went to her father's house and lives there with her.'

'It would be a good thing to take him from them. Is he not tired of her now?'

'He was mad about her. He would not listen to reason,'

'Ah, but that was at first, long ago. They say the man first finds heaven in a woman, later in a field, and last in the temple. Would you like to get him back to your house?'

'Yes.'

'Well, why not?' Fernando moved nearer to Babehami and lowered his voice. '*Ralahami*, I must live here some months. Without a woman what comfort in a house? The woman is not ill-looking and could cook my meals for me. I had thought of this for some days, so I sent my servant boy to her. She answered that she would come, but she was afraid of her man. Then I thought of speaking to the man, but it is not easy for a stranger. I thought, if he marries this woman it is a disgrace to the headman. It is better that his friends speak to him. Probably he is tired of the woman, and will marry from another village some girl who has a dowry of land.'

Babehami seemed to be considering the ground in front of him with great attention; from time to time he spat very deliberately. It was impossible to tell from his face what impression Fernando's suggestion had made upon him. His silence irritated Fernando. 'What swine these villagers are,' he thought.

'Well,' he said at last, 'what do you say?'

'Did she say she would come to you, if Babun allowed her?'

'Yes, but why do you ask that? If the man agrees, what difficulty can there be?'

'Perhaps none, perhaps none, *aiya*, but who can say? They are mad those people. It happens so sometimes to people who live as we do in the jungle. The spirits of the trees, they say, enter into a family and they are mad and a trouble to the village. Who knows what such people will do?'

'Well?'

'Is the plan good?'

'Yes.'

'But will you help me?'

'The plan is a good one certainly. But I am on bad terms with my wife's brother. We quarrelled about the girl. What can I do?'

'If you talk to him now, *Ralahami*? You quarrelled when he was hot after the girl. That was long ago; and a man soon tires of the woman that has borne him children. And there are many ways, *Ralahami*, to persuade him if you will help me. There are the debts and the *chenas*, and many other ways. What is there that a headman cannot do? It is wrong for him to sit still and watch disgrace come upon him and his family. Have you given him his permit to *chena* yet?'

'No, not yet.'

'Well, you can keep it back. How can they live without *chenas*? Then there are the courts. I can help you there, for, being of Kamburupitiya, I know the ways of the courts well. There will be cases and trouble for him, and for them.'

Babehami was not to be hurried. He considered the proposal for some minutes. It was the sort of persecution which appealed to him. He would at the same time be injuring those he disliked, helping those in whose debt he stood, and pleasing himself. He could see very little risk in it, and much to gain.

'Well, *aiya*,' he said at length, 'I will help you if I can. I will speak to Babun. Shall it be done soon?'

'Yes, quickly. Send for him now. There is no harm in doing it before me; and there is no time to lose if I am to get the woman.'

Babehami was at first averse to doing things with such precipitation; he liked to think over carefully each move in his game. But he was overpersuaded by Fernando, who could not restrain his impatience. A message was sent to Babun that the headman wanted to speak to him. Babun was very much astonished at receiving this message, and still more so at his reception. He was given a chew of betel and welcomed warmly.

'Brother,' said the headman, 'it is a bad thing for those of the same blood to quarrel. This *Mahatmaya* has been speaking of it, saying you are a good man. All that is very long ago, and it is well to forget it.'

'I have forgotten it. I have never had a bad thought of you in my mind, brother.'

'Good, good. Nor I of you, brother, really. Well, and how are things with you now?'

'The light half of the moon returns. This *Mahatmaya* is giving me his *chenas* to work for a share of the crop.'

'Good, good. Where there is food, there is happiness. Never have I known a year like this, and I am growing an old man now. On the *poya* day two months back there was not a *kuruni* of grain in all the village. I went to the *Korala Mahatmaya*; I said to him: "Can men live on air?" He is a hard man. He said (his stomach swollen with rice), "For ten years now I have told you to leave your village. There are fields and land elsewhere; there is work elsewhere; they pay for work on the roads. If you make your paddy field on rock, do you expect the rice to grow?" I said to him, "The Government must give food or the people will die." Then he said, "Go away and die quickly," and he abused me, calling me a tom-tom-beater, and drove me away. So I went to this *Mahatmaya* and arranged about the *chenas*. Had it not been for him, we should all have starved.'

'I know. The *Mahatmaya* has been very good.'

'And now again the *Mahatmaya* said to me: 'It is a foolish thing to quarrel with a brother. It is long ago and about a woman! What use is it? Send for him and be friends.'

'The *Mahatmaya* is very good to us.'

'I was wrong, brother. I say it to you myself. I used shameful words to you. But that was long ago. A young man must have a woman. It is foolish to stand in his way. Even the buck will turn upon you in the rutting season.'

'All that is forgotten now.'

'So the *Mahatmaya* says: "It is time," he said, "for him to marry. Send for him and become friends again. For the heat of youth is now past." So I sent for you.'

'I have come.'

'He said to me, "Now is the time. The boy has become a man. When he learns about the woman, he will do as you ask."'

'I do not understand that.'

'The woman has offered to go and live with the *Mahatmaya* and cook his meals for him. So the *Mahatmaya* says, 'Very well, I will take her to live with me while I am here. I will give her food and money, and also to her father. I will give work in my *chenas* to your brother. So your brother can leave the woman and marry from another village.'

'I do not understand. I do not wish to marry from another village. And what offer of the woman do you talk of?'

'The woman came to the *Mahatmaya* while you were away in the *chena*. She offered herself to him. The *Mahatmaya* said to her, "I cannot take you unless the man gives you." Then he came to me: he said to me, "This woman says this and that to me. It would be better for me to take her to live with me while I am here; and you should marry your brother to an honest woman." So I sent for you.'

'It must be lies, brother. It must be lies. Who told this to you?'

'The *Mahatmaya* himself. Would he tell lies?'

'Is this true, *aiya*?' Babun asked Fernando.

'Yes, it is true. The woman came to me.'

'The woman is a whore, brother; I told you so long ago. It is better that you should give her to the *Mahatmaya*, and marry now from another village. You can come back to my house and live here meanwhile.'

Babun was dazed. His first instinct had been to disbelieve entirely the story about Punchi Menika. He did not believe it now, but he could not disbelieve it. Why should the *Mahatmaya* lie? He could not tell him to his face that he was lying. He got up and stood hesitating. The others watched him. Fernando had difficulty in repressing his laughter. Several times Babun opened his mouth to speak, and then stopped.

'I do not understand,' he said at last. 'I do not understand this. The woman went to the *Mahatmaya*? Offered herself? *Aiya*, that cannot be so. Surely she would be afraid? Yet you yourself say it's true. *Aiyo*, I do not understand. I must go to the woman herself.'

Babehami got up and caught hold of Babun by the arm, trying to prevent his leaving the compound.

'Do not do that, brother. Let her go, let her go to the *Mahatmaya*, and do you stay here. My house is always open to you; stay now and I will tell the woman to go to the *Mahatmaya*.'

'No, no. I must see her myself.'

'What is the use? There will only be abuse and angry words. It is always lies or foul words in a woman's mouth.'

'I must go, brother. I must see her myself.'

'What folly! But you would never listen to me, and see what has come of it. She is a whore. It was known before, but you would not believe it. You would not listen. Hark, the lizard chirps. It is an evil hour, but again you do not listen. You are going, brother, to meet misfortune.'

Babun allowed himself to be brought back into the compound. His mind worked slowly, and he was dazed by the shock, and by the insinuating stream of the headman's words. But there was a curious obstinacy about him which Babehami recognised and feared. Babun came back, but he did not squat down again. He stood near Fernando; his forehead was wrinkled with perplexity. Surely the story could not be true, and yet how could it be false? Why should the *Mahatmaya* and Babehami lie to him? The simplicity of his character made him always inclined to believe at once and without question anything said to him. The headman had reckoned on this, and his plan would probably, but for Fernando, have succeeded. Suddenly, however, the latter could no longer restrain his amusement. The wrinkled forehead, the open mouth, the pain and hesitation in Babun's face as he stood before him, seemed to him extraordinarily ridiculous. He laughed. The laugh broke the spell. Babun turned again.

'I must see the woman herself,' he said as he walked away.

'That was foolish, *aiya*,' said Babehami to Fernando. 'Very foolish. He would have stayed.'

'I know. But I couldn't help it. He stood there like a bull pulled this way and that with a string in its nose. What now?'

'He will come back. Then we shall see. It is spoilt now, I think. This bull is an obstinate brute when it jibs. We may have to use the goad. It will be the only way, I think.'

They waited in silence. The headman proved right. Babun returned. He did not speak to Fernando, but addressed himself to Babehami.

'The *Mahatmaya* was right to laugh at me for a fool. Yes, I am a fool. I know that. The tale was false. It was the *Mahatmaya* who called the woman to come to him, and she refused. I knew it. Yes, brother, I knew it. But I was frightened by your words. I thought "he is my sister's man, why should he lie to me?" It was lies. The woman wept for shame when I told her.'

'It was true, brother. It is the woman who is lying now to you. She is frightened of you, frightened that you should know what she has done.'

'I am a fool, brother, but what use is there in repeating lies now? The story was false. It was the *Mahatmaya* who came to my house and called the woman to him. She refused. She would not leave me.' He turned to Fernando. '*Aiya*, why come and trouble us? We are poor and ignorant, and you have wealth, and women in the town as you told us. Leave us in peace, *aiya*, leave us in peace.'

'It is not lies,' broke in Babehami. 'Truly you are a fool. The woman is ashamed now, and lies to you, and you believe. But what has that to do with it? The *Mahatmaya* is now ready to take the woman. It is time that this folly should end. Let him take her, and come back to this house.'

'She refuses, I tell you.'

'What has that to do with it? It is time for you to marry, and leave that filth.'

'What is the good, brother, of beginning this again? It will only lead to angry words again. I told you, so many years back, that I want no other wife than this. It is the same now. I will live with no one else. All these lies and words are useless.'

'*Ohé, Ohé!* It may lead to angry words; yes, but are they useless? Last time you refused to listen to me. Well, I did nothing: I allowed you to go your own way. You brought shame on me and my family. I did nothing. I let you go. But now it is different. Suppose they were lies, the words spoken by me just now. They weren't, but suppose they were. What then? The *Mahatmaya* wants the woman now. He calls her to him: she will not come; you refuse to give her. Is it wise, wise brother? Think a little. Is there much *kurakkan* in the house after the drought? The *Mahatmaya* has made you overseer of his *chenas*. If the woman is refused, will you remain overseer? The twentieth of the crop will go, I think, to someone else. Is it wise for the bull to fight against the master, when he has the goad in his hand? Is it wise, too, always to be fighting against the headman? Even the headman has a little power still. The *chena* permit has not yet come for you. Perhaps it may never come. Who knows?'

'The *Mahatmaya* will not do that – and you – you are my brother.'

'If the woman is not given to me,' said Fernando, 'neither will the twentieth be given to you. I have not come here to be laughed at by cattle like you. First the woman is offered, and then I am refused! What does it mean? Would you try to make me out a fool?'

'Very well, *aiya*, then I will not have the twentieth. The woman cannot be given to you.'

'Fool,' said Babehami. So you refuse again to listen to me? But remember this time it will not be as it was before. You shall not always disgrace and insult me.'

'I have never spoken nor thought evil of you, brother. But I tell you, as I told you before, I will not live without this woman. It is useless to talk more, for nothing but angry words will follow. Therefore I am going.'

Babun did not wait for any answer from the two men, but went quickly from the compound. The other two sat on discussing, the matter for long. They had to take their steps quickly, for Fernando would only be a few weeks in the village, and he was very anxious, now that he was really opposed, to possess Punchi Menika. Their plans were laid that night.

Babun and Silindu very soon became aware of the web that was being spun around them. They had already begun to cultivate a *chena* together: two days after Babun's conversation with Babehami and Fernando they found another man, Baba Sinno, a near relation of Babehami, in occupation of it. Babun went to the headman to inquire what this meant. The headman was quite ready to explain it. No permit could be given to Babun and Silindu this year. It was a Government rule that permits were to be given only to fit persons. Babun and Silindu were not fit persons, therefore no permits could be given to them. That was all.

They returned to the compound amazed, overwhelmed. Babun explained to Silindu the real cause of the headman's act, the proposal of Fernando and its reception. It was clear that the two men would stop at nothing, that they had determined upon the complete ruin of Silindu's family, unless Punchi Menika were given up. For if no *chena* were given, it meant starvation; for they had at the utmost food only for a month, and besides that nothing but their debts. They saw that Baba Sinno was but a foil; they did not dare to turn him out by force, because they had no permits which would give them the right to do so. If they had felt that there was any one in the village who would openly take their part, it would have been different; but they knew that no one would dare to side with them against the headman and Fernando, who already held the whole village enmeshed in their debt.

The more they discussed it the more horrible became their fear. In a month they would be starving or forced to leave the village. There was only one thing for them to do, to put the whole case before the Assistant Government Agent. Babun set off for Kamburupitiya next morning with this object. His trouble and his fear drove him; and he did the three days' journey in two. On the morning of the third day, hours before the office opened, he was standing, haggard and frightened, on the *Kachcheri* verandah, waiting to fall at the feet of the Assistant Agent. At last a peon or two arrived, and later some clerks. At first no one took any notice of him. Then a peon came and asked him what he wanted. He told him that he had come to make a complaint to the Assistant Agent. The peon said, 'The Assistant Agent is away on circuit. You must send a petition.'

'When will he be back?'

'I don't know.'

'Where is he now, *aiya*?'

'I don't know.'

He had not the few cents necessary to buy him a fuller answer. He went from one peon to another, and from one clerk to another trying to learn more particulars. They told him nothing; they did not know, they said, when the Assistant Agent would return, or where he was; he had better have a petition written, and come again a week later. He became stupid with fear and misery. He hung about the verandah hour after hour, doing nothing, and thinking of nothing. At last, late in the afternoon, he wandered aimlessly into the bazaar. He was passing the shop of the Moorman, who had previously made many loans in Beddagama: Cassim, who was sitting within doing nothing, knew Babun and called out to him: 'What are you doing in Kamburupitiya, Babun? Like cotton down in a storm! What is the matter with you? I hear that dog Fernando is in Beddagama – may he die of the fever.'

'I have been to the *Kachcheri*[1] to lay a complaint before the agent *Hamadoru*. The agent *Hamadoru* is away on circuit. I cannot learn where he is or when he returns.'

'*Ohé*! A complaint? Those dogs of peons! Everyone knows where the agent *Hamadoru* is except the peon; and he only knows when there are *fanams* in his hand. The agent *Hamadoru* is in Galbodapattu on circuit: he will not return for another ten days. Everyone knows that.'

'*Aiyo*! Then we are ruined!'

'Why? What is it?'

'We are ruined. Only the agent *Hamadoru* could help us, and now it will be too late. Our *chena* is taken from us. *Aiyo! Aiyo*!'

'Is this one of Fernando's games? They say that the *chenas* are his now,

---

1 Kachcheri is the Government offices.

and not the Government's. The low caste fisher! *Vesige puta*! He is a *Mudalali* now: I expect he hopes to be made the agent *Hamadoru* one day.'

'It is he, *aiya*, he and the headman. They want me to give my wife to the *Mudalali*. I refused. Now they have taken my *chena* from me. They will ruin me. The agent *Hamadoru*, if he knew, would have interfered to stop this; but now it will be too late by the time I can complain to him. It will be too late, *aiya*!'

The fat Moorman rolled from side to side with laughter.

'O the dog! O the dog! O the dog! There is no one like these fishers for finding money and women everywhere. *Allah*! They call us Moormen cunning and clever. The only thing I ever found in Beddagama was bad debts. And here this swine of a fisher finds not only bags of grain, and bags of *rupees* there, but women too. But I am sorry for you, Babun. I remember you; you were a good man in that accursed village. Come in here now, and I'll see what I can do for you. I should like to stop that swine's game. But it is difficult. One wants time. We must send a petition; the agent *Hamadoru* would stop it if he knew. But there are always peons and clerks and headmen in the way before you can get to him. Cents here and cents there, and delays and inquiries! You want time, and we haven't got it. But there is nothing for it but a petition. Here now, I'll write it myself for you to spite that dog Fernando.'

The *Mudalali* made Babun give him all the particulars, and he wrote the petition, and stamped and posted it. He told Babun to come in again to Kamburupitiya in ten days' time to see him about it. He also gave him food, and made him sleep that night in his verandah. The next day Babun, somewhat comforted, set out for his village. He was very weary by the time that he reached it: he felt that he could show little gain from his journey to Silindu and Punchi Menika. Ruin seemed very near to them. They could do little, but sit gloomily talking of their fears.

But Babehami and Fernando were meanwhile not idle. The cunning headman and the townman, with his energetic fertile mind, were a strong combination. On the morning after Babun's return to the village a rumour spread through the village that the headman's house had been broken into during the night, and that Babehami had left at once to complain to the

Korala. Late in the afternoon of the same day the *Korala* and Babehami arrived in the village. They called to them three or four of the village men, and went with them straight to Silindu's compound. The *Korala*, a fat, consequential, bullying man, went in first and summoned Babun, Silindu, and Punchi Menika. They were handed over to Babehami's brother, who was instructed to keep them in the compound, and not to allow them out of his sight.

The news of the burglary had not reached Babun and Silindu. They were bewildered by what was passing. They saw the *Korala* go into the house with Babehami. They were some time in the house, while the men in the compound talked together in whispers. A little group of men and women had gathered outside the fence, and Fernando stood in the door of his house watching what was happening. At last the two headmen came out of the house. The *Korala* was carrying a bundle. He walked up to Babun and showed him the bundle: it consisted of two cloths, a pair of gold ear-rings, and some other pieces of gold jewellery. 'Where did you get these from, *yakko*?'[1] he asked.

'I know nothing about them: they are not mine.'

'Don't lie, *yakko*. They were in your house. Where did you get them from?'

'*Hamadoru*, I know nothing about them. Some one must have put them there.'

'Lies. They were stolen last night from the *Arachchi*'s house. The *Mudalali* saw you leaving the house in the night. Curse you, I shall have to take you into Kamburupitiya now to the court and the magistrate *Hamadoru*. And what about this fellow?' pointing to Silindu, 'Do you charge him as well?'

'Yes, *Mahatmaya*,' said Babehami. 'But there is the box too. Should not the jungle round the house be searched for it?'

'Yes. Hi there, you fellows! Go and search that piece of jungle there.'

Three or four men went off slowly and began a desultory search in the jungle which lay behind the compound. Suddenly there was a cry, and

---

1 A term used by superiors to inferiors meaning something like 'fellow'.

one of them lifted up a large box. He brought it to the *Korala*. The lock had been forced open. It was recognised as the headman's. The case was complete, and the onlookers recognised that the evidence against Babun was damning.

Babun and Silindu were taken off to the headman's house. They had to spend the night in the verandah with Babehami's brother, who was there to see that they did not run away. The injustice of this new catastrophe seemed to have completely broken Babun's spirit. His misfortunes were too many and sudden for him to fight against. He refused to talk, and squatted with his back against the wall silent throughout the night. The effect upon Silindu was different. He saw at last the malignity of the headman and how his life had been ruined by it. This last stroke made him aware of the long series of misfortunes, which he now felt were all due to the same cause. This knowledge roused him at last from his resignation and from the torpor habitual to his mind. He talked incessantly in a low voice, sometimes to Babun, but more often apparently to himself.

'They call me a hunter, a *vedda*? A fine hunter! To be hunted for years now and not to know it! It is the headman who is the *vedda*, a very clever hunter. I have been lying here like a fat old stag in a thicket while he was crawling, crawling nearer and nearer, round and round, looking for the shot. Where was the watching doe to cry the alarm? Always he shot me down as I lay quiet. But the old hunter should be very careful. In the end misfortune comes. Perhaps this time I am a buffalo, wounded. The wise hunter does not follow up the wounded buffalo, where the jungle is thick. Ha! ha! The wounded buffalo can be as clever as the clever hunter. He hears the man crawling and crawling through the jungle. He stands there out of the track in the shadows, the great black head down, the blood bubbling through the wound, listening to the twigs snap and the dry leaves rustle; and the man comes nearer and nearer. Fool! you cannot see him there, but he can see you now; he will let you pass him, and then out he will dash upon you, and his great horns will crash into your side, and he will fling you backwards through the air as if you were paddy straw. The old buffalo knows, the old buffalo knows; the young men laugh at him, "buffaloes' eyes," they say, "blind eyes, foolish eyes, a foolish face like a buffalo," but he is clever, *amma*! He is clever – when wounded – when he hears the hunter after him – cleverer than the cleverest hunter. And when it has gone on for years! All his life! What will he do then? Will he lie quiet then? Oh! He will lie quiet, yes, and let them take all from him, daughter and home and food. He will shake his head and sigh the great sigh, and lie quiet in the mud of the wallow, very sad. And then at last they come after his life. Shall they take that too? Then at last he knows and is angry – very angry – and he stands waiting for them. The fools! They come on, crawling still; they do not know that he is ready for them now. The fools! The fools!'

The next morning the *Korala* took with him the complainant, the accused, and the witnesses, of whom Fernando turned out to be one, and started for Kamburupitiya. Punchi Menika went with them. They travelled slowly, and reached Kamburupitiya on the fourth morning. Silindu had relapsed into his usual state of sullen silence; Babun's spirit appeared to be completely broken. He scarcely understood what the charge against him was; he knew nothing of why or on what evidence it had been made. He waited bewildered to see what new misfortune fate and his enemies would bring upon him.

The parties and witnesses in the case were taken at once to the court-house. They waited about all the morning on the verandah. The court was a very large oblong room with a roof of flat red tiles. At one end was the bench, a raised daïs, with a wooden balustrade round it. There were a table and chair upon the daïs. In the centre of the room was a large table with chairs round it for the bar and the more respectable witnesses. At the further end of the room was the dock, a sort of narrow oblong cage made of a wooden fence with a gate in it. Silindu and Babun were locked up in this cage, and a court peon stood by the gate in charge of them. There was no other furniture in the room except the witness-box, a small square wooden platform surrounded by a wooden balustrade on three of its sides.

Nothing happened all the morning: Babun and Silindu squatted down behind the bars of their cage. They were silent: they had never been in so vast or so high a room. The red tiles of the roof seemed a very long way above their heads. Outside they could hear the murmur of the sea, and the rush of the wind, and the whispered conversation of the witnesses on the verandah; but inside the empty room the silence awed them. About one o'clock there was a stir through the court: the headmen hurried in, a proctor or two came and sat down at the table. The peon nudged Babun and Silindu, and told them to stand up. Then they saw a white *Hamadoru*, an English man, appear on the daïs and sit down. The court interpreter, a Sinhalese *Mahatmaya* in coat and trousers, stood upon a small wooden step near the bench. The judge spoke to him in an angry voice. The interpreter replied in a soothing deferential tone. The conversation being in English was unintelligible to Babun and Silindu. Then the door of their cage was unlocked, and they were led out and made to stand up against the wall on the left of the bench.

The court-house stood on a bare hill which rose above the town, a small headland which ran out into the sea to form one side of the little bay. The judge, as he sat upon the bench, looked out through the great open doors opposite to him, down upon the blue waters of the bay, the red roofs of the houses, and then the interminable jungle, the grey jungle stretching out to the horizon and the faint line of the hills. And throughout the case this vast view, framed like a picture in the heavy wooden doorway, was continually before the eyes of the accused. Their eyes wandered from the bare room to the boats and the canoes, bobbing up and down in the bay, to the group of little figures on the shore hauling in the great nets under the blazing sun, to the dust storms sweeping over the jungle, miles away where they lived. The air of the court was hot, heavy, oppressive; the voices of those who spoke seemed both to themselves and to the others unreal in the stillness. The murmur of the little waves in the bay, the confused shouts of the fishermen on the shore, the sound of the wind in the trees floated up to them as if from another world.

It was like a dream. They did not understand what exactly was happening. This was 'a case' and they were 'the accused,' that was all they knew. The judge looked at them and frowned; this increased their fear and confusion. The judge said something to the interpreter, who asked them their names in an angry threatening voice. Silindu had forgotten what his *ge*[1] name was; the interpreter became still more angry at this, and Silindu still more sullen and confused. From time to time the judge said a few sharp words in English to the interpreter: Silindu and Babun were never quite certain whether he was or was not speaking to them, or whether, when the interpreter spoke to them in Sinhalese, the words were really his own, or whether he was interpreting what the judge had said.

At last the question of the names was settled. Babehami was told to go into the witness box. As he did so a proctor stood up at the table and said: 'I appear for the complainant, your honour.'

'Any one for the defence?' said the judge.

'Have you a proctor?' the interpreter asked Silindu.

'No,' said Babun, 'we are very poor.'

'No, your worship,' said the interpreter.

Babehami knew exactly what to do; it was not the first time that he had given evidence. He was quite at his ease when he made the affirmation that he would tell the truth, the whole truth, and nothing but the truth. He gave his name and his occupation. Then his proctor stood up and said to him: 'Now *Arachchi*, tell us exactly what has happened.'

Babehami cleared his throat and then told the following story in a rather sing-song voice: 'About four days ago when I woke up in the morning my wife had gone out into the compound. I heard her cry out, "*Aiyo*, some one has made a hole in the wall of the house." I ran out and saw a hole on the western side of the house. The hole was big enough for a man to crawl through. There are two rooms in the house, one on the eastern side, and one on the western side. We, my wife and I were sleeping that night in the room on the east side; in the other room was a wooden box in which were clothes and two new sarong cloths and jewellery belonging to my wife. The box was locked. When I saw the hole I ran back into the house to see if the box was safe. I found it had disappeared. At that I cried out: "*Aiyo*, my box has been stolen." Then

---

1   *Ge* is Sinhalese for house. A *ge* name answers in some respects to a surname.

the *Mudalali*, who had been staying in the hut next to mine, hearing the cries came up and asked what was the matter. I told him: he said, "Last night about four *peyas*[1] before dawn I went out into the compound for a call of nature. I heard a noise in your compound. Thinking it was a wild pig I stepped back into the doorway, and looked. Then I saw your brother-in-law come running from your compound carrying something in his hands. He ran into the jungle behind his own house. I went straight off to the village of the *Korala Mahatmaya*; it lies many miles away to the north. Then when the sun was about there (pointing about three-quarters way up the wall of the court) I met the *Korala Mahatmaya* on the road. The *Korala Mahatmaya* said, "What are you coming this way for, to trouble me? I am going to Kamburupitiya." I told him what had happened and turned with him to go back. We came to the village in the afternoon. The *Korala Mahatmaya* went to the accused's house and searched. In the roof between the thatch he found the two sarong cloths and my wife's jewellery, and the box with the lock broken was found in the jungle behind the house.'

When Babehami began his story, Babun and Silindu had not really listened to what he was saying. They were still dazed and confused, they did not quite understand what was going on. But as he proceeded, they gradually grasped what he was doing, and when he told the story about the *Mudalali*, they saw the whole plot. Their brains worked slowly; they felt they were trapped; there was no way out of it. Babehami's proctor stood up to examine him, but the judge interrupted him: 'The first accused, I understand, is the brother-in-law of the complainant. Is that correct? I propose to charge the accused now. But is there any evidence against the second accused – Silindu, isn't his name? – Mr Perera?'

The proctor called Babehami to him and had a whispered conversation with him.

'There is no evidence, sir,' he said to the judge, 'to connect him directly with the theft. But he was in the house in which the first accused

---

1 A *peya* is a Sinhalese hour, and is equal to about twenty minutes.

lived, on the night in question. He must have been an accessory. He is the owner of the house, I understand, and might be charged with receiving.'

'No, certainly not – if that's your only evidence to connect him with the theft. I should not be prepared to convict in any case, Mr Perera. I shall discharge him at once – especially as the man does not look as if he is quite right in the head.'

'Very well, sir.'

'Charge the first accused only,' said the judge to the interpreter. 'There is no evidence against the second accused. He can go.'

This conversation had been in English and therefore was again unintelligible to the two accused. Their bewilderment was increased therefore when the interpreter said to Silindu: 'You there, go away.' Silindu, not knowing where he had to go, remained where he was. 'Can't you hear, *yakko*?' shouted the interpreter. 'Clear out.' The peon came up and pushed Silindu out on to the verandah. A small group of idle spectators laughed at him as he came out.

'They'll hang you in the evening, father,' said a small boy.

'I thought the judge *Hamadoru* said ten years' rigorous imprisonment,' said a young man. Silindu turned to an old man who looked like a villager, and said: 'What does it mean, friend?' Everyone laughed.

'You are acquitted,' said the old man; 'go back to your buffaloes.'

Babun also did not understand the acquittal of Silindu. Things appeared to be happening around him as if he were in a dream. The interpreter came and stood in front of him and said the following sentence very fast in Sinhalese: 'You are charged under section 1010 of the Penal Code with housebreaking and theft of a box, clothing, and jewellery, in the house of the complainant, on the night of the 10th instant, and you are called on to show cause why you should not be convicted.'

'I don't understand, *Hamadoru*.'

'You heard what the complainant said?'

'Yes, *Hamadoru*.'

'He charges you with the theft. Have you anything to say?'

'I know nothing about this.'

'He says he knows nothing about this,' said the interpreter to the judge.

'Any witnesses?' said the judge.

'Have you any witnesses?' said the interpreter to Babun.

'How can I have witnesses? No one will give evidence against the headman.'

'Any reason for a false charge?' asked the judge.

'*Hamadoru*, the headman is on very bad terms with me; he is angry with me because of my wife. He is angry with my wife's father. He wanted me to marry from another village. Then he wanted me to give my wife to the *Mudalali* and because I refused he is angry.'

'Anything else?'

Babun was silent. There was nothing more to say. He looked out through the great doors at the jungle. He tried to think where Beddagama was; but, looking down upon it from that distance, it was impossible to detect any landmark in the unbroken stretch of trees.

'Very well, Mr Perera,' said the judge.

Mr Perera got up again and began to examine Babehami.

'How long have you been a headman?'

'Fifteen years.'

'Have you ever had a private case before?'

'No.'

'Are you on bad terms with your brother-in-law?'

'No, but he is on bad terms with me.'

'How is that?'

'There is a Government Order that *chenas* are only to be given to fit persons. The accused is not a fit person: he could do work, but he is lazy. Therefore *chenas* were refused to him. He thought that I had done this. It was a *Kachcheri* Order from the agent *Hamadoru*. Last week he was very angry and threatened me because of it. The *Mudalali* heard him.'

'Is the *Mudalali* a friend of yours?'

'How could he be, *aiya*? He is a *Mahatmaya* of Kamburupitiya. I am only a village man. How could he be a friend of mine? He comes to the village merely to collect debts due to him.'

'And when he comes, you let him stay in the unoccupied house next to yours. Otherwise you do not know him?'

'Yes, that is true, *aiya*.'

'Is the *Korala* related to you?

'No.'

'A friend of yours?'

'No; he was on bad terms with me. He said I troubled him and was a bad headman.'

Mr Perera sat down.

'Any questions?' said the judge.

'Any questions?' the interpreter asked Babun.

'I don't understand,' said Babun.

'*Yakko*,' said the interpreter angrily, 'do you want to ask complainant any questions?'

'What questions are there to ask? It is lies what he said.'

There was a pause while the judge waited for Babun to think of a question. The silence confused him, and all the eyes looking at him. He fixed his own eyes on the jungle.

At last Babun thought of a question.

'Did you not ask me to give the woman to the *Mudalali*?'

'No,' said Babehami.

'Did not the *Mudalali* call her to go to his house?'

'I know nothing of that.'

'Weren't you angry when I married the woman?'

'No.'

Babun turned desperately to the judge.

'*Hamadoru*,' he said, 'it is all lies he is saying.' The judge was looking straight at him, but Babun could read nothing in the impassive face; the light eyes, 'the cat's eyes,' of the white *Hamadoru* frightened him.

'Is that all?' said the judge.

Babun was silent.

'Who is this *Mudalali*?' said the judge sharply to Babehami.

'Fernando *Mudalali*, *Hamadoru*. He comes from Kamburupitiya; he is a trader, he lends money in the village.'

'What's he doing in the village now?'

'He has come to collect debts.'

' When did he come?'

'About a week ago.'

'When is he going?'

'I don't know.'

'Is he married?'

'I don't think so. I don't know.'

'Why do you give him a house to live in?'

'*Hamadoru*, the little hut was empty. He came to me and said: '*Arachchi*,' he said, 'I must stay here a few days. I want a house. There is that hut of yours – can I live in it? So I said, 'Why not?'

'Whose is the hut?'

'Mine.'

'Why did you build it?'

'It was built, *Hamadoru*, for this brother-in-law of mine.'

'When?'

'I don't know.'

'What do you mean?'

'*Hamadoru*, last year, I think.'

'But your brother-in-law lives with his father-in-law?'

'Yes.'

'Then why did you build him a house?'

'There was talk of his leaving the other people.'

'Has the *Mudalali* ever stayed in the village before?'

'No.'

'Do you owe anything to him?'

'No.'

'Next witness.'

Babehami stood down and the *Korala* entered the witness-box. He was examined by Mr Perera. He told his story very simply and quietly. He had met Babehami, who had told him that his house had been broken into and that a box had been stolen; he described the box and its contents; he suspected his brother-in-law, who had been seen going away from his house in the night, by the *Mudalali*. The *Korala* then described how he went into and searched the house, and how he found the cloths and jewellery which answered to Babehami's previous description. He then produced them. The proctor examined him.

'Are you on good terms with the complainant?'

'I am not on good terms or bad terms with him. I only know him as a headman.'

'Do you complain of his troubling you?'

'I complained that he was a bad headman. He has troubled me with silly question. He is an ignorant man.'

Mr Perera sat down. 'Any questions?' asked the judge.

'Any questions?' asked the interpreter of Babun.

Babun shook his head. 'What questions are there?' he said.

'Do you know this *Mudalali*?' said the judge to the *Korala*.

'I have seen him before in Kamburupitiya.'

'Have you seen him before in Beddagama?'

'No.'

'Did you know that he was there?'

'No.'

'Do you know of any ill-feeling between complainant and accused?'

'No, I did not know the accused at all. I live many miles from Beddagama.'

'Next witness.'

Fernando was the next witness. He wore for the occasion a black European coat, a pink starched shirt, and a white cloth. He was cool and unabashed. He told how he had gone out in the night for a call of nature, how he had heard a noise in the compound of the headman and had then seen Babun come out carrying something and go with it into the jungle behind his own house.

'Could you see what it was?' asked the proctor.

'Not distinctly. He walked as if it were heavy. It was rather large.'

'How did you recognise him? Can you swear it was he?'

'I can swear that it was the accused. I recognised him first by his walk. But I also saw his face in the moonlight.'

'Are you on bad terms with accused? Does he owe you money?'

'I am not on bad terms with him. I scarcely know him. He owes me for *kurakkan* lent to him. I had arranged to make him my *gambaraya*. All the villagers there owe me money.'

'How long have you been in the village?'

'About ten days. I am making arrangements for the recovery of my loans. Last crop failed and therefore much is owed to me.'

The proctor sat down.

'Any questions?' said the judge.

'Any questions?' said the interpreter to Babun. Babun shook his head. 'It is lies they are telling,' he murmured.

'Are you married?' the judge asked Fernando.

'No.'

'You live with a woman in Kamburupitiya?'

'Yes.'

'How did you come to settle in the hut in Beddagama?'

'I was getting into difficulties with my loans because the crop failed last year. I thought I must go to the village during the *chena* season and arrange for the repayment. I saw the hut empty there, and went to the headman and asked whether I might live there. He said "Yes."'

'Do you know the accused's wife?'

'I have seen her. Their compound adjoins that of the hut. Otherwise I do not know her.'

'Next witness.'

The man who had found the box gave evidence of how and where he had found it. Various villagers were then called, who identified the things found in Silindu's hut and the box as having belonged to Babehami. They all denied any knowledge of ill-feeling between Babun and the headman or of any intimacy between the headman and Fernando. This closed the case for the prosecution.

The judge then addressed Babun in a speech which was interpreted to him. Babun should now call any witnesses whom he might have. It was for him to decide whether he would himself go into the witness-box and give evidence. If he gave evidence he would be liable to cross-examination by Babehami's proctor; if he did not, he (the judge) might draw any conclusion from his refusal.

Babun did not really understand what this meant. He did not reply.

'Well?' said the interpreter.

'I don't understand.'

'Are you going to give evidence yourself?'

'As the judge *Hamadoru* likes.'

'Explain it to him properly,' said the judge. 'Now, look here. There is the evidence of the *Korala* that he found the things in your house. There is no evidence of his being a prejudiced witness. There is the evidence of Fernando that he saw you leaving the complainant's hut at night. You say that Fernando wants your wife, and that the headman is in league with him against you. At present there is no evidence of that at all. According to your story the things must have been deliberately put into your house by complainant, or Fernando – or both. Listen to what I am saying. Have you any witnesses or evidence of all this?'

'*Hamadoru*, how could I get witnesses of this? No one will give evidence against the headman.'

'I will adjourn the case if you want to call witnesses from the village.'

'What is the good? No one will speak the truth.'

'Well, then, you had better, in any case, give evidence yourself.'

'Get up here,' said the interpreter.

Babun got into the witness-box. He told his story. The judge asked him many questions. Then the proctor began cross examining.

'Are you on bad terms with the *Korala*? Do you know him well?'

'I am not on bad terms. I scarcely know him.'

'Do you know that Fernando came to the village to recover money, that he has arranged to get the *chena* crops from many of the villagers in repayment of his loans?'

'Yes.'

'Did he ask you to act as overseer of those *chenas*, and promise you a share of the crop if you did?'

'Yes.'

'Because he thought you the best worker in the village?'

'Yes, I think so.'

'When did this happen?'

'About a week ago.'

The proctor sat down. Babun called no witnesses. There was a curious look of pain and distress in his face. The judge watched him in silence for some minutes, then he told the interpreter to call Silindu. Silindu was pushed into the box, the interpreter recited the words of the affirmation to him. He said, 'I do not understand, *Hamadoru*.' It took some time to make him understand that he had only to repeat the words after the interpreter. He sighed and looked quickly from side to side like a hunted animal. The eyes of the judge frightened him. He was uncertain whether he was being charged again with the theft. He had not listened to what was going on after he had been sent out of the court. It occurred vaguely to him that the best thing would be to pretend to be completely ignorant of everything. He still thought of the wounded buffalo listening to the hunter crawling after him through the scrub: 'He doesn't move,' he muttered to himself, 'until he is sure: he stands quite stupid and still, listening always; but when he sees clear, then out he rushes charging.'

'Stop that muttering,' said the judge, 'and listen carefully to what I ask you. You've got to speak the truth. There's no charge against you; you've got nothing to fear if you speak the truth. Do you understand?'

'I understand, *Hamadoru*,' said Silindu.

But he thought, 'They are cunning hunters. They lie still in the undergrowth, waiting for the old bull to move. But he knows: he stands quite still.'

'Is there any reason why the headman should bring a false case against you and the accused?'

'I don't know, *Hamadoru*.'

'You are not on bad terms with him personally.'

'I have nothing against him. He does not like me, they say.'

'Why doesn't he like you?'

'*Hamadoru*, how should I know that?'

'You have never had any quarrel with him?'

'No, *Hamadoru*.'

'Are you related to him?'

'I married a cousin of his wife.'

'The accused lives in your house? He is married to your daughter?'

'Yes, *Hamadoru*.'

'Do you know of any quarrel between him and the headman?'

'How should I know that?'

'There was no quarrel at the time of the marriage?'

'They say this and that, but how should I know, *Hamadoru*?'

'You know nothing about it yourself, then?'

'No, *Hamadoru*.'

'Do you know the *Mudalali* Fernando?

'No, *Hamadoru*.'

'You don't know him? Doesn't he stay in the hut adjoining your compound?'

'I have seen him there. I have never spoken with him.'

'Did you hear of anything between him and your daughter?'

'They talk, *Hamadoru*.'

'What did they say?'

'They said he wanted my daughter.'

'Who said? When?'

'This man' (pointing to Babun).

'When?'

'Three or four days ago.'

'You know nothing more, yourself, about this?'

'No, *Hamadoru*.'

Neither Babun nor Babehami's proctor asked Silindu any questions; he was told to go away, and was pushed out of court by the peon. The case was over, only the judgment had to be delivered now. The judge leant back in his chair, gazing over the jungle at the distant hills. There was not a sound in the court. Outside, down on the shore, the net had been hauled in, and the fish sold. Not a living being could be seen now, except an old fisherman sitting by a broken canoe, and looking out over the waters of the bay. The wind had died away, and sea and jungle lay still and silent under the afternoon sun. The court seemed very small now, suspended over this vast and soundless world of water and trees. Babun became very afraid in the silence. The judge began to write; no one else moved, and the only sound in the world seemed to be the scratching of the pen upon the paper. At last the judge stopped writing. He looked at Babun, and began to read out his judgment in a casual, indifferent voice, as if in some way it had nothing to do with him. The interpreter translated it sentence by sentence to Babun.

'There is almost certainly something behind this case which has not come out. There is, I feel, some ill-feeling between complainant and accused. The complainant impressed me most unfavourably. But the facts have to be considered. There can be no doubt that complainant's things were found hidden in the house in which accused lives, and that the box was found in the jungle behind the house. The evidence of the *Korala* is obviously trustworthy on these points. There is clear evidence, too, that a hole had been made in complainant's house wall. Then there is the evidence of the *Mudalali*. As matters stand, it was for the accused to show that that evidence was untrustworthy. He has not really attempted to do this. His father-in-law's evidence, if anything, goes to show that there is nothing in complainant's story that Fernando wanted to get hold of his wife. Accused's defence implies that there was a deliberate conspiracy against him. I cannot accept his mere statement that such a conspiracy existed without any corroborating evidence of motive for it. He has no such evidence. Even if there were ill-feeling over the refusal of a *chena* or something else, it would cut both ways; that is, it might have been accused's motive for the theft. I convict accused, and sentence him to six months' rigorous imprisonment.'

Babun had not understood a word of the broken sentences of the judgment until the interpreter came to the last words, 'six months' rigorous imprisonment.' Even then, it was only when the peon took hold of him by the arm to put him back again into the cage, that he realised what it meant – that he was to be sent to prison.

'*Hamadoru*,' he burst out, 'I have not done this. I cannot go to prison, *Hamadoru*! It is all lies, it is lies that he has said. He is angry with me. I have not done this. I swear on the Beragama temple I have not done this. I cannot go to prison. There is the woman, *Hamadoru*, what will become of her? Oh! I have not done this. I have not.'

The proctors and idlers smiled; the peon and the interpreter told Babun to hold his tongue. The judge got up and turned to leave the court.

'I am sorry,' he said, 'but the decision has been given. I treated you very leniently as a first offender.'

Everyone stood up in silence as the judge left the court. As soon as he had left, everything became confusion. Proctors, witnesses, court officials, and spectators all began talking at once.

Babun crouched down moaning in the cage. Punchi Menika began to shriek on the verandah, until the peon came out and drove her away. Only Silindu maintained his sullenness and calmness. He followed Babun when he was taken away by the peon to the lock-up. At one point, when he saw that the peon was not looking, he laid his hand on Babun's arm and whispered: 'It is all right, son, it is all right. Don't be afraid. The old buffalo is cunning still. Very soon he will charge.' He smiled and nodded at Babun, and then left him to find Punchi Menika.

It took some time for Silindu to find Punchi Menika. She had wandered aimlessly away from the court through the bazaar. Silindu was now extraordinarily excited, he seemed to be almost happy. He ran up to her, took her by the hand, and began leading her quickly away out of the town.

'We must go away at once,' he said. 'There is much to think of and much to do. It is late, but we at least do not fear the jungle. The jungle is better than the town. We can sleep by the big trees at the second hill.'

'But, *Appochchi*, my man. What will become of him? What will they do to him? Will they kill him?'

'Babun is all right. I have told him. The Government do not kill. There is no killing here. But in the jungle, always killing – the leopard and jackal, and the hunter. Yes, and the hunter, always killing, the blood of deer and pig and buffalo. And at last, the hunting of the hunter, very slow, very quiet, very cunning; and at the end, after a long time, the blood of the hunter.'

'But, *Appochchi*, stop, do. What does it mean? They are taking him to prison. What will they do with him? Shall we never see him again?'

'The hunter? Yes, yes we shall see him again. Very soon, but he will not see us.'

127

'What is this about the hunter? It is my man I am talking about.'

'Oh, Babun. He is all right. The white *Hamadoru* said, "Six months' rigorous imprisonment." I heard that quite clear at the end. 'Six months' rigorous imprisonment.' It was all that I heard clearly. He is all right. There is no need for you to cry. They will take him away over there – (Silindu pointed to the east) – there is a great house – I remember I saw it a long time ago when I went on a pilgrimage with my mother. They will put him in the great house, and give him rice to eat, so I hear. Then he will come back to the village – but it will be after the hunting.'

'O *Appochchi*, are you sure?'

'Yes, child, all will be well after the hunting. But now I must think.'

Punchi Menika saw that it would be impossible to get anything more out of Silindu in his present state. They walked on in silence. As they walked his excitement began to die down. He seemed to be thinking deeply. From time to time he muttered to himself. Late in the evening they came to the big trees. Silindu collected some sticks and made a fire. Then he squatted down while Punchi Menika cooked some food which they had carried with them.

Once or twice as they sat round the fire, after having eaten the food, Punchi Menika began to question Silindu about Babun, but he did not reply; he did not seem to hear her. Her mind was numbed by the fear and uncertainty. She lay down on the ground, and an uneasy sleep came to her. Suddenly she was aroused by Silindu shaking her. She saw in the light of the fire how his face was working with excitement.

'Child, there are two of them, two of them the whole time, and I never saw it.'

'What do you mean? Where?'

'Hunting me, child, hunting us all – me, you, and Babun, and Hinni-hami. They killed Hinnihami, your sister. I found her lying there in the jungle, dying. They did that. But they shall not get you. There are two of them. Listen! I hear them crawling round us in the jungle, do you hear? Now – there! I thought there was only one, fool that I was – the little headman. But now I hear them both. The little headman first and then the other; the man with the smooth black face and the smile. It was he, wasn't it? Didn't Babun say so? He came to you and called you to come to his house. Babun said so, I heard him. Fernando – the *Mudalali* – he wanted to take you away, but he couldn't. Then he went to the headman and together they went to hunt us. Isn't that true? Isn't that true?'

'Yes, *Appochchi*, yes. It was because they wanted me for the *Mudalali*. Then they took the *chena* away and then they brought the case. They have taken my man from me, what shall I do?'

'Hush, I am here. They shall do no more. Listen, child. It is true that they have taken Babun from you. For six months he will be over there. "Very well," they think. They thought to send me there too, but the judge *Hamadoru* was wise. 'Get out,' he said to me. I did not understand then, and they laughed at me, but I understand now. Well, those two will come back to the village. "The man," they think, "is away over there for six months, only the woman and the mad father are here. What can they do? The *Mudalali* can now take the woman." Is this true?'

'*Appochchi*! It is what I fear. It is true.'

'It is true. But do not be afraid. The old father is there, but he is not altogether mad. The *Mudalali* will come back tomorrow, perhaps, or the next day, with the headman. Then they will begin again.'

'Yes, yes. That is what I fear, *Appochchi*. What can we do? we must go away.'

'Hush, child. Do not cry out. There is no need to be afraid. We cannot go away. How can we live away from the village and the jungle which we know. That is foolish talk. There in the town I do not understand even what they say to me; and the noise and the talking in the bazaar, and people always laughing, and the long hard roads and so many houses all together! How could we live there? But in the village I am not altogether mad. It is folly to talk of leaving it and the jungle. Very soon I shall feel the gun in my hand again. Then I shall be a man again, slipping between the trees – very quietly. Ha, ha! We know the tracks, little *Arachchi*. I remember child, when I was but a boy, I went out once with my father for skins and horns. He was a good hunter and knew the jungle well. We went on and on – many days – round and round too – he leading, and I following. And at last we came to very thick jungle which not even he knew. And a sort of madness came on us to go on and on always, and we had forgotten the village and the wife and mother. The jungle was tall, dense, and dark, and the sky was covered with cloud – day after day so that one could not tell the west from the east. And at last, when we had many skins and horns, my father stopped, and stood still in the track and laughed. "Child," he said, "we are mad, we have become like the bear and the elephant; it is time to return to the village." Then he turned round and began to walk. Soon he stopped again, frowning. It was very dark. He stood there for a little, thinking; and then climbed a very big tree and looked around for a long time. Then he came down and I saw from his face that he was very afraid. We said nothing, but started off again. For many *peyas* we walked and always through very thick jungle. Again he stopped and climbed a tree and again, when he came down, there was great fear in his face. *Aiyo*! That was the first time that I saw the fear, the real fear of the jungle; but then I did not understand. "*Appochchi*," I said, "what is the matter?" "Boy," he said, and his voice trembled; "we are lost. I do not know where we are, nor where the village lies, nor how we came, nor which is east and which is west. From the trees I can see nothing which I know, not even the hill at Beragama, only the tops of the trees everywhere. Therefore we must be very far from the village. I have heard of such things happening to very good hunters; but always before I have known the way. Punchi Appu must have died like that. Wandering on and on until no powder is left and no food. *Aiyo*! The jungle will take us, as they say." Then I said, "*Appochchi*, do not be afraid. I do not know which way we came, and I cannot tell just now which is west and which is east because of the clouds; but I know where the village lies. It is over there." "Can you lead the way?" he asked, and I said, "Yes." Then he said, "Perhaps you know, perhaps you do not; but now one way is as good as another for me. You go first." At that I was pleased, and led on straight to where I knew the village must lie. For two days I led the way and my father said nothing, but I saw that he became more and more afraid. And on the third day, suddenly he cried out, "I know this: this track leads to the village. You are going right." It was a track I had never been on, but I still led the way; and on the fourth day we entered the village – well, what was I saying? Yes, I know the tracks, even in those days when I was a boy I knew the jungle. But this time it requires clever hunting.'

'Yes, *Appochchi*, but what to do now, when they come back to the village?'

'Those two! Ah! Now you listen, child. I have thought over it all this time and there is only one way. I shall kill them both.'

'Kill them! O *Appochchi*, no, no. You are mad!'

'Am I mad? And what if I am? Haven't they always called me mad, the mad *vedda*. Well, now let them see if I am mad or not. Have they not hunted me for all these years and am I always to go running like a stupid deer through the jungle? No, no, little *Arachchi*; no, no. This time it is the old wounded buffalo. Three times, four times that night in the hut when I saw it first I got up to get my gun and end it. And again, after the court, I would have done it, had I had a gun. But I thought – no, not yet, for once we must act cunningly, not in anger only. The buffalo's eye is red with anger, but he stands quiet until the hunter has passed. Then he charges.'

'But, *Appochchi*, you must not say that. You cannot do it. You must come away. They will take you and hang you.'

'What can I do? I cannot leave the village; I will not; I have told you that. There is no other way.'

'But what are you going to do?'

'Ah! I must think. It needs cunning and skill first. I must think.'

'No, no, *Appochchi*; no, no. It would be better to give me to the *Mudalali*.'

'I would rather kill you than that. Do you hear? I shall kill you if you go to the *Mudalali*.'

'Oh! oh! isn't it enough that they should have taken my man from me? And now more evil comes.'

'I tell you that I will end this now. Now I shall sleep and tomorrow think of the way.'

Silindu refused to listen any further to Punchi Menika's expostulations. He lay down by the fire and soon slept. Next day, and throughout their journey to the village, he was very silent, and refused to discuss the subject at all with her. The lethargy habitual to him had left him completely. He was in an extraordinary state of excitement, goaded on perpetually by great gusts of anger against Babehami and Fernando. When he got back to his house he sat down in the compound in a place from which he could see the headman's house, and waited. He watched the house all day, and, when in the evening he saw the headman return, he smiled. Then he got up and went into the hut. He took his gun which stood in the corner of the room, unloaded it, and reloaded it again with fresh powder and several big slugs. He examined the caps carefully, chose two, and put them in the fold of his cloth. Then he lay down and slept.

Next morning he was very quiet and thoughtful; but if any one had watched him closely he would have seen that he was really in a state of intense excitement. After eating the morning meal he took his gun and went over to the headman's house. To the astonishment of Babehami and his wife he walked into the house, put his gun in the corner of the room, and squatted down. Babehami watched him closely for a minute or two; he felt uneasy; he noted that the curious wild look in Silindu's eyes was greater than ever.

'Well, Silindu, what is it?' he said.

'*Arachchi*, I have come to you about this *chena*. I cannot live without *chena*. You must give it back to me.'

'You heard in the court that the *chena* cannot be given to you. It has been given to Appu. Let us have an end of all this trouble.'

'Yes, *Arachchi*, that is why I have come to you. I want an end of all this trouble. Do you hear that? An end now – today – of trouble. Trouble, trouble, for years. We must end it today. Do you hear?'

'What do you mean?'

'Yes. What did I say? This, this. Now, *Arachchi*, that was nothing; do not mind what I said then. I was thinking, thinking. You know they call me mad in the village. Well, I was thinking, you know, now that Babun is over there for six months, I heard the judge *Hamadoru* say that clearly, but to me he said merely, "Clear out" – I was never a friend of that Babun – all the trouble has come from him – he took Punchi Menika from me, and then Hinnihami. I saw her lying in the jungle by the deer – what did we call him? Kalu Appu? Punchi Appu? Yes, yes, Punchi Appu, that was long ago. They beat her. They threw stones at her. That was long ago – in the jungle. But now Babun is away for six months. When he comes back, I shall say to him, "Clear out," as the judge *Hamadoru* said. They laughed at me then. A foolish old man, a mad old man, eh? Ha, ha! little *Arachchi*, little *Arachchi*, you have laughed at me too-for years, haven't you, haven't you?'

'What is all this, Silindu? What do you mean? I don't understand.'

'Ah, *Arachchi*, it is nothing. Do not mind what I say. I do not know what I was saying. I am a poor man, *Arachchi*, very ignorant, a little mad. But I am a quiet man; I have given no trouble in the village. You know that well, *Arachchi*, don't you? I cannot speak well – like you, *Arachchi* – in the court. But this is what I want to say. I do not like this Babun; all the trouble has come from him. I am a quiet man in the village, you know that. I said to my daughter on the way here by the big *palu* trees at the second hill – I said to her, "The man is now sent away; he will be over there for six months. He is a foolish man. It is he who has brought the trouble. The *Mudalali* is a good man. The *Arachchi*, too, is a good man. Why should we quarrel with those two? There is no shame in your going to the *Mudalali*." Then my daughter said, "I will do as you think best, *Appochchi*." Do you understand now, *Arachchi*?'

Silindu stopped. The *Arachchi* had been watching him narrowly. He began to understand the drift of Silindu's incoherent words. But he still felt uneasy. As Silindu spoke, his suppressed excitement became more and more apparent in his voice and words. But Babehami knew well that he was mad, and that he was also wonderfully stupid. It was just like him to do things in this wild way. The more Babehami thought of it, the more he became convinced that the conviction of Babun had done its work. Silindu and Punchi Menika had given in.

'Yes, I think I understand,' he said. ' It is true that the *Mudalali* will take your daughter. He is a good man; and the trouble came from Babun, as you say.'

'That is it, *Arachchi*, that is it. Let the *Mudalali* take Punchi Menika. My daughter cannot live with thieves now. She will go to the *Mudalali*. Do you understand?'

'Yes, Silindu. But it must be done quietly. She cannot go openly to his house, or there will be silly talk, after what was said in the court.'

'No, no. It must be done quietly, very quietly.'

'I will tell the *Mudalali*, and she can come at night to him. Afterwards, perhaps, she can live at the house; but at first she must go secretly at night.'

'Ha, ha, *Arachchi*. You are clever! How clever you are! You think of all things. Yes, it must be all done quietly, quietly.'

'Very well, Silindu, I will tell the *Mudalali*. It is a good thing to end all this trouble, like this.'

'Yes, it is a very good thing to end it – like this. Yes – like this, like this. But now the *chena*, *Arachchi*. I cannot live without the *chena*. Without a *chena* I must starve. You cannot see me starve. Even now there is no grain in my house. You must give me the *chena*.'

Babehami thought for a while, then he said: 'Well, I will see what can be done; perhaps I can arrange with Appu about the *chena*. We will see.'

'Yes, *Arachchi*, but let us have done with it once for all. The thing is settled. Appu cannot be left there. Come.'

'Why, what do you want? Don't you trust me?'

'Yes, I trust you – why not, *Arachchi*? But I am afraid of Appu. If he is left there to do work, he will refuse to go. He is in the *chena* now. It would be better to go and tell him at once.'

'I cannot go now. Tomorrow, perhaps.'

'*Arachchi*, it is but two miles. You said it is a good thing to end the trouble, Let us settle it now, today, and the *Mudalali* can have Punchi Menika tonight.'

Babehami was silent. He disliked being hurried. On the other hand he would be very glad to see the whole matter settled. His action with regard to the *chena* troubled him because it was dangerous. He knew that the petition had been presented, and he was not at all sure that he would come off as well in an inquiry as he had in the court. It would also be wise to bind Silindu to him by giving him back the *chena*, and not to risk his changing his mind about the *Mudalali* and Punchi Menika. He argued a little more, and stood out half-heartedly against Silindu's urgings to start at once. At last he gave in, and they started for the *chena*.

They followed a narrow jungle track which had been lately cleared. The tangle of shrubs and undergrowth and trees was like a wall on each side of the track. The headman walked first, and Silindu, carrying his gun, followed. For the first three-quarters of a mile they walked in silence, except for a word or two which the headman shouted back to Silindu without turning his head. Silindu had fallen somewhat behind; he quickened his pace, and came up close to the headman; he was muttering to himself.

'What do you say?' asked Babehami.

'What? Was I talking? I do not know, *Arachchi*. They say the hunter talks to himself in the jungle. It is a custom. Have you ever been a hunter, *Arachchi*?'

'No. You know that well enough.'

'Oh yes. You are no hunter. Who should know that better than I? But do they call me a good hunter, *Arachchi*? skilful, cunning? Do I know the tracks, *Arachchi*?'

'Of course, everyone knows you to be the best hunter in the district.'

'*Aiyo*, the best hunter in the district. And do you know, *Arachchi*, that I am afraid of the jungle?'

'So they say. What are you afraid of?'

Silindu began to speak with great excitement. As he went on his voice began to get shriller and shriller; it trembled with anger and fear and passion.

'I am afraid of everything, *Arachchi*; the jungle, the devils, the darkness. But, above all, of being hunted. Have you ever been hunted, *Arachchi*? No, of course you are not a hunter, and therefore have never been hunted. But I know. It happens sometimes to the cleverest of us. The elephant, they say; but that I have never seen. But the buffalo: I have seen that – here – on this very track – before it was cleared – many years ago. The buffalo is stupid, isn't he, little *Arachchi*? Very stupid; he does not see – he does not hear – he goes on wallowing in his mud. And they hunt him year after year – year after year – he does not know – he does not see them – he does not hear them. Do you know that? I know it – I am a hunter. Then – then having crept close, they shoot him. It was near here. At first, crash – he tears away through the jungle, the blood flowing down his side. He is afraid, very afraid – and in pain. But the pain brings anger, and with anger, anger, *Arachchi*, comes cunning. And now, *Arachchi*, now comes the game, the dangerous game. The young men laugh at it, but the wise hunter would be afraid. There he stood, do you see? – There – under that *maiyilittan* tree, head down, very still. And the hunter – fool, fool – crept after him through the undergrowth: there was no track then. Ah, it was thick then: he could not see anything but the shrubs and thorns; he did not see the red eyes behind him nor the great head down. For the other was cunning now, cunning, and very angry. And when the hunter had gone on a little – just where you are now, *Arachchi* – then – do you hear, little *Arachchi*? Then, out and crash, he charged, charged, like this – '

Babehami had at first hardly listened, but the fury and excitement of Silindu had at last forced his attention. As Silindu said the last words, Babehami half stopped and turned his head: he just saw Silindu's blazing eyes and foam on the corner of his lips; at the same moment he felt the cold muzzle of the gun pressed against his back. Silindu pulled the trigger and Babehami fell forward on his face. A great hole was blown in the back, and the skin round it was blackened and burnt; the chest was shattered by the slugs which tore their way through. The body writhed and twisted on the ground for a minute, and then was still. Silindu kicked it with his foot to see whether it was dead. There was no movement. He reloaded his gun and turned back towards the village. His excitement had died down: the old lethargy was coming upon him again. He felt this himself and walked faster, muttering, 'Even now it is not safe. There were two of them. There is still the other.'

When Silindu got back to the village, Fernando was in the headman's compound. When he saw Silindu he came down towards the fence and called out to him, 'Where is the *Arachchi*? They say he went out with you.' Silindu walked up towards the stile, and stopping levelled his gun at the *Mudalali*. Fernando stepped back, his mouth wide open, his eyes staring, his whole face contorted with fear. He cowered down behind the stile, stretching his hands vaguely out between the wooden bars, and shouted: 'Don't shoot! Don't shoot!'

The stile was little or no protection: between the two bottom bars

Silindu could see the *Mudalali*'s fat stomach and legs. He took careful aim between the bars and fired. Fernando fell backwards, writhing and screaming with pain. Silindu went and looked over the stile: at the same moment Babehami's wife rushed out of the house. But he saw that his work had been accomplished; blood was pouring from the *Mudalali*'s stomach; his two legs and one of his hands were shattered. 'The trouble is ended,' he muttered.

He walked very slowly to his house. He put the gun in the corner of the room, thought for a minute, and then immediately left the hut. He saw that already there was a crowd of people in the headman's compound: the women were screaming. Silindu turned into the jungle at the back of his house, and walking quickly cut across to the track which led to Kamburupitiya.

Chapter 8

BEFORE SILINDU reached the Kamburupitiya track, he stopped and squatted down with his back against a tree. He wanted to think. After the wild excitement which had possessed him now for three days, a feeling of immense lassitude came upon him. His mind worked slowly, confusedly; he had no clear idea of where he was going, or of what he ought to do. He was very tired, very unhappy now; but he felt no regret for what he had done – no remorse for the blood of the *Arachchi* and of Fernando could trouble him. So far as they were concerned, he only felt a great relief.

He wanted to lie down and sleep. He leant back against the tree and began to doze, but he started up again immediately, listening for footsteps of pursuers. His first idea had been simply to run away into the jungle, to get away at any rate from the village. The hunt would begin; he would be hunted once again, he knew that. Then he thought of going east where the thick jungle stretched unbroken for miles. He could live there in some cave among the rocks; he could live there safe from his hunters for months. He had heard stories of other men doing this: strange men from other districts, whom the Government and the police, were hunting down for some crime. They came down from the north, so it was said, flying to the sanctuary of the uninhabited jungle where they lay hidden for years; they lived alone in caves and in trees, eating leaves and wild fruit and honey, and the birds and animals which they managed to snare or kill. They were never caught; there were no villages in that wilderness from which information could come to the police. Sometimes one of the few bold hunters, who were the only people to penetrate these solitudes, would catch a glimpse of a wild, naked man in a cave or among the shadows of the trees. Some of them perhaps eventually, trusting to the lapse of time and to the short memory of the Government, went back to their villages and their homes. But most of them died of fever in the jungle to which they had fled.

If such a life were possible for men from distant villages, who did not know the jungle, it would be easy for Silindu. But as he squatted under the trees thinking of what he should do, a feeling of horror for such a life crept over him, and his repugnance to flying became stronger and stronger. He was very tired. What he desired – and the desire was sharp – was to rest, to be left alone untroubled in the village – in his hut, in his compound – to sleep quietly there at night, to sit hour after hour through the hot day under the mustard tree in the compound. But in the jungle there would be no rest. It was just in order to escape that terror – the feeling of the hunted animal, the feeling that some one was always after him meaning evil – that he had killed the *Arachchi* and the *Mudalali*. And if he fled into the jungle now, he would have gained nothing by the killing. He would live with that feeling for months, for years, perhaps for ever. The hunt would begin again, and again it was he who would be the hunted.

Then he thought of returning to the village, but that too would be useless; he would get no peace there. He knew well what would happen. The *Korala* would be sent for; he would be seized, worried, bullied, ill-treated probably. That would be worse than the jungle. Suddenly the conviction came to him that it would be best to end it all at once, to go into Kamburupitiya and give himself up to the *Ratemahatmaya* and the white *Hamadoru*, to confess what he had done. He got up and started for the town immediately, keeping to the game tracks in the thick jungle, and avoiding the main tracks, for he did not wish to meet any one.

He walked slowly, following instinctively the tangled winding tracks. His lassitude and fatigue increased. He reached Kamburupitiya in the evening of the third day, and asked his way to the *Ratemahatmaya's* house.

When Silindu reached the *Ratemahatmaya's* house, no news of the murder had yet come to Kamburupitiya. He had walked slowly, but what was a slow pace for him was faster than that of the other villagers. He went into the compound, and walked cautiously round the house: in the verandah through the lattice' work he saw the *Ratemahatmaya* lying in a long chair. There was a table with a lamp upon it beside him. Silindu coughed. The *Ratemahatmaya* looked up and said sharply: 'Who is there?'

'*Hamadoru*, it is I. May I come into the verandah?'

'What do you want at this time? Come tomorrow. I can't attend to anything at night.'

'*Hamadoru*, I come from Beddagama. There has been a murder there.'

'Come in, then.'

Silindu came into the verandah and salaamed. He stood in front of the *Ratemahatmaya*.

'*Hamadoru*,' he said, 'I have killed the *Arachchi* and the *Mudalali*.'

The *Ratemahatmaya* sat up. 'You? What? What do you mean? Who are you?'

'I am Silindu of Beddagama. The *Arachchi* brought a false case against me and my son-in-law. May I sit down, *Hamadoru*? I am very tired. Babun was sent to prison by the judge *Hamadoru*, but to me he said, "Clear out." The case was false. They were trying to bring evil upon me and my daughter. The *Mudalali* wanted the girl. They were still trying to bring evil on me, so I said, "Enough." I took the gun and I went out with the *Arachchi* over there to the *chena*, and I shot him through the back. He is dead, lying there on the track. Then I went back to the village and shot the *Mudalali* in the belly through the stile. He was not dead then, but I looked over and saw the blood coming fast from the belly low down. He must be dead now.'

The *Ratemahatmaya* was not a brave man. As he listened to Silindu's short expressionless sentences, the bald description of the shedding of blood, given in the tired voice of the villager, he became afraid. He sat up in his chair looking at Silindu, who crouched in front of him, motionless, watching him. The light of the lamp fell upon the dark, livid face. It was the face of the grey monkeys which leap above the jungle among the tree-tops, and peer down at you through the branches; a face scarred and pinched by suffering and weariness and fear. It was as if something, evil from the darkness, which he did not understand, had suddenly appeared in his quiet verandah. He looked out nervously over Silindu's head into the night: the light of the lamp in the verandah made it seem very dark outside. The *Ratemahatmaya* became still more afraid in the silence which followed Silindu's speech. He suddenly got up and shouted for his servant. There was the sound of movements in the back of the house, and a dirty servant boy, in a dirty vest and cloth, came blinking and yawning into the verandah. The *Ratemahatmaya* told him to stand by Silindu.

The *Ratemahatmaya* drew in a deep breath of relief. The beating of his heart became, quieter.

'Now, *yakko!*' he said in a sharp angry tone, 'stand up.'

Silindu did not move; he looked up at the *Ratemahatmaya* with weary eyes and said, '*Hamadoru!* I am very tired. For days now there has been no rest for me. *Aiyo!* I cannot remember how long it is now since I sat quiet in my compound. Let me sleep now. I have come straight to you and told you all. I thought at first I would run away. I could have lived out there for months, and you would not have caught me. But I was tired of all this: I am very tired. I thought: No. What is the good? Out there away from the village, and the hut, and the compound, and the daughter? It is the evil all over again. *Aiyo!* How tired I am of it. It is better to end it now. So I came here. I have told you no lies. What harm can I do now? Let me sleep here, and tomorrow you can do what you like to me.'

'Do you hear what I say? Stand up, *yakko*, stand up. Make him stand up.'

The servant boy kicked Silindu in the ribs, and told him to stand up. Silindu rose slowly.

'Now, then. You say you have killed the *Arachchi* and the *Mudalali*. Is that Fernando, the boutique-keeper ?'

'Yes, *Hamadoru*, yes. Fernando, the boutique-keeper.'

'Fetch me ink and paper and a pen.'

The servant boy fetched the paper, ink, and pen. Meanwhile Silindu again squatted down. The *Ratemahatmaya* prepared to write.

'Didn't you hear me tell you to get up?

'Get up, *yakko*' (the servant boy kicked Silindu again). 'Now, then. When did you kill them, and how?'

'Three or four days ago. It was in the morning. I went with the *Arachchi* to the *chena*. I shot him through the back.'

'Where did you get the gun?'

'It was my gun. I had it in my house.'

'Was it licensed?'

'Yes, *Hamadoru*. I am very tired. What is the good of all these questions? I tell you I killed them both. Let me be. I cannot think of these things now. Tomorrow, perhaps, tomorrow. Surely you have me here safe, and can do with me what you like tomorrow.'

The *Ratemahatmaya* was a self-important, fussy little man; he was also timid, and not fond of taking responsibilities. The sudden appearance of Silindu with this strange story out of the darkness had upset him. He was very annoyed when Silindu again sank down into a squatting position. 'Stand up, fellow,' he said. 'Stand up. Didn't you hear me, pariah? Stand up. You've got to answer my questions. Now, then. What did I ask last? Now, then' – He paused and thought for a moment. 'It is not, perhaps, too late. Perhaps I had better take him at once to the magistrate. Yes, that's better. You there get the bull put into the hackery. No, no, stop there; you must look after the man. Keep him there. Kalu Appu! Kalu Appu! Call Kalu Appu! Kalu Appu! Hoi! D'you hear? Wake up! Put the bull in the hackery and hurry up.'

At last another servant boy was woken up, the bull was put into the hackery. The *Ratemahatmaya* put on a dark coat, and, with many curses and complaints, got into the cart. Silindu followed slowly with the servant boy. They trailed wearily along the dark roads for three-quarters of a mile: then the cart stopped in the compound of the magistrate's bungalow. The *Ratemahatmaya* got out and went round to the back of the house to announce his arrival through the servants. Silindu squatted down near the hackery; he was no longer quite conscious of what was going on around him; after a while the *Ratemahatmaya* called to him to come round into the house, and the boy who had driven the bullock poked him up with the goad.

He was taken along a broad dark verandah, and suddenly found himself in a large well-lit room. Had it not been for the stupor of his fatigue he would have been very frightened, for he had never seen anything like this room before. It seemed to him to be full of furniture, and all the furniture to be covered with strange objects.

In reality there was only a little travel-battered furniture in the barn-like white-washed room. There was matting on the floor, and rugs on the matting. An immense writing-table littered with letters and papers stood in front of the window. There were three or four tables on which were some ugly ornaments, mostly chipped or broken, and a great many spotted and faded photographs. A gun, a rifle, and several sentimental pictures broke the monotony of the white walls. The rest of the furniture consisted of a great many chairs, two or three lamps, and a book-case with thirty or forty books in it.

When Silindu entered the room with the *Ratemahatmaya*, the magistrate was lying in a long chair reading a book. He got up and went over to sit down at the writing-table. He was the white *Hamadoru*, whom Silindu had seen before in the court. He was dressed now in black, in evening-dress. He sat back in his chair and stared at Silindu in silence for a minute or two with his 'cat's eyes'; he looked cross and tired. Silindu had instinctively squatted down again. The *Ratemahatmaya* angrily told him to stand up. The magistrate seemed to be lost in thought: he continued to stare at Silindu, and as he did so the look of irritation faded from his face. He noted the hopelessness and suffering in Silindu's face, the slow weariness of effort with which he moved his limbs. 'He need not stand,' he said to the *Ratemahatmaya*. 'He looks damned tired, poor devil. You can take a chair yourself, *Ratemahatmaya*. God! This is a nice time to bring me work, and you seem to've brought me a miserable-looking wretch. You say it's a murder case?'

'Yes, sir. Or rather it appears so. I do not know much about it. In fact, sir, only what this man has told me. He appeared at my place just now – not half an hour ago – and says that he has killed the *Arachchi* of his village and another man. I brought him straight to you, sir.'

'Oh, damn it! That means I'll have to go out there tomorrow. How far is it? Beddagama? I don't know the place.'

'It's up the north track, in the jungle, sir. It must be between fifty or sixty miles away, sir.'

'Oh, damn! And there are any number of cases fixed for tomorrow. Well – poor devil – he looks pretty done himself! By Jove! I believe he is the man who was before me as an accused in that theft case the other day. I would not charge him, I remember – no evidence against him. It might have been better for him, perhaps, if I had, and convicted him, too.' He turned to Silindu, and said in Sinhalese, 'You were accused of theft before me a few days ago, weren't you?'

'Yes, *Hamadoru.*'

'Ah, I thought so. Well, *Ratemahatmaya*, I suppose I had better record your statement first in form. Come on, now.'

The *Ratemahatmaya* made a short statement of how Silindu had come to him, and what he had said. The magistrate wrote it down, and then turned to Silindu, and explained to him that the offence with which he was charged was murder, and that he was prepared to take down anything he wished to say, and that anything which he did say would be read out at his trial.

Silindu did not quite understand, but he felt vaguely encouraged by the white *Hamadoru.* He had spoken Sinhalese to him; he had not spoken in an angry voice, and he was the same *Hamadoru* who had told him to clear out of the court when he was charged before.

'It is as the *Dissa Mahatmaya*[1] said. I have killed the *Arachchi* and the *Mudalali.* If the *Hamadoru* sends to the village, he will find that what I say is true. The *Hamadoru* remembers the previous case; he knew that they brought a false case against me. He told me to clear out. But the whole case was false – against Babun, too. Am I to tell everything? I am very tired, *Hamadoru.* For three days now I have been walking, and no food but the jungle fruit and leaves. If I might rest now a little, and sleep until tomorrow ... What can I do? I have told all. I am almost an old man, very poor. What can I do?'

---

1   A term commonly used by villagers, referring to the *Ratemahatmaya.*

'I think I had better take down what you have to say now. But you need not stand. You had better begin from the case. What happened after that?'

'*Aiyo, Hamadoru, aiyo*! I am very tired. After the case – It was a false case. The *Arachchi* for long had been trying to do me harm. How long I cannot remember, but for many years it seems to me. At that time it was because of my daughter; he wanted to take her from Babun and give her to the *Mudalali*. Well, after the case I set out for the village with the daughter. And all the way I was thinking – thinking how to end this evil. For I knew well that when they came back to the village it would begin again, all over again. They had put Babun in jail – it was a false case, but how should the *Hamadoru* know that? – with all the lies they told. And they would get Punchi Menika for the *Mudalali*. Then, as I went, I thought of the old buffalo who is wounded and charges upon –' Silindu caught sight of the gun and rifle, and stopped. 'Ah! The *Hamadoru* is a hunter, too? He knows the jungle?' he asked eagerly.

'Yes, I know the jungle.'

'Good; then the *Hamadoru* will understand. The evil and the killing there – "Yes, it is time," I thought, "to end the evil. I must kill them both." I was a quiet man in the village, all know that. I harmed no one; I wanted to live quietly. I went back to my compound, and sat down and waited. In the evening came the Punchi *Arachchi* to his house; I saw him go in. Then I took my gun, and went to him, and said: '*Ralahami*, you may give the woman to the *Mudalali*, and in return give me back my *chena*.' The *Arachchi* thought to himself: 'Here is a fool.' But he said: 'Very well, I will give the *chena* back to you.' Then we started for the *chena*, and as we went on the track I shot him from behind. He is lying dead there now – on the track which leads from the village to the *chena*. If the *Hamadoru* sends some one, he can find the body.'

'Yes, and then?'

'Then, *Hamadoru*, I loaded the gun again, and went back to the village. There was still the *Mudalali*. I saw him in the *Arachchi's* garden. He called to me. 'Where is the *Arachchi*?' I went close up to him – he was standing by the stile, and through it I saw his big belly. I shot him too. He must be dead now.'

'Yes, and then?'

'Then? I went to my house, for the women ran out screaming. I put the gun in my house, and went out into the jungle. I was tired. I am a poor man, and I have harmed no one in the village. I am getting old: I wanted to live quietly in my hut. I wanted to rest, *Hamadoru*. What good, I thought, to fly into the jungle? Only more evil. So I came straight to the *Dissa Mahatmaya*. I told him what I had done. That is all.'

The magistrate wrote down what Silindu said, and when he had finished, sat thinking, the pen in his hand, and looking at Silindu. It was very quiet in the room; outside was heard only the drowsy murmur of the sea. Suddenly the quiet was broken by the heavy breathing and snoring of Silindu, who had fallen asleep where he squatted.

'Leave him alone for a bit,' the magistrate said to the *Ratemahatmaya*. 'There's nothing more to be got from him tonight. We shall have to push on to Beddagama early tomorrow. I suppose it's true what he says.'

'I think so, sir.'

'Damned curious. I thought he wasn't right in the head when I saw him in court before. Well, I'm glad *I* shan't have to hang him.'

'You think he will be hanged, sir?'

'He'll be sentenced at any rate. Premeditation, on his own showing – clearly. And a good enough motive for murder. A very simple case – so they'll think it. You think so, too?'

'It seems to be a simple case, sir.'

'I see you would make a very good judge, *Ratemahatmaya*. I don't mind telling you unofficially of course – that I'm a very bad one. It does not seem at all a simple case to me. *I* shouldn't like to hang Silindu of Beddagama for killing your rascally headman. Now then, *Ratemahatmaya*, here you are; a Sinhalese gentleman; lived your whole life here, among these people. Let's have your opinion of that chap there. He's a human being, isn't he? What sort of a man is he? And how did he come suddenly to murder two people?'

'It's difficult, Sir, for me to understand them; about as difficult as for you, sir. They are very different from us. They are very ignorant. They become angry suddenly, and then, they kill like – like – animals, like the leopard, sir.'

'Savages, you mean? Well, I don't know. I rather doubt it. You don't help the psychologist much, *Ratemahatmaya*. This man, now: I expect he's a quiet sort of man. All he wanted was to be left alone, poor devil. You don't shoot, I believe, *Ratemahatmaya*, so you don't know the jungle properly. But it's really the same with the other jungle animals, even your leopard, you know. They just want to be left alone, to sleep quietly in the day, and to get their food quietly at night. They won't touch you if you leave them alone. But if you worry 'em enough; follow I 'em up and pen 'em up in a corner or a cave, and shoot four-hundred and fifty bullets at them out of an express rifle; well, if a bullet doesn't find the lungs or heart or brain, they get angry as you call it, and go out to kill. I don't blame them either. Isn't that true?'

'I believe it is, sir.'

'And it's the same with these jungle people. They want to be left alone, to reap their miserable *chenas* and eat their miserable *kurakkan*, to live quietly, as he said, in their miserable huts. I don't think that you know, any more than I do, *Ratemahatmaya*, what goes on up there in the jungle. He was a quiet man in the village, I believe that. He only wanted to be left alone. It must take a lot of cornering and torturing and shooting to rouse a man like that. I expect, as he said, they went on at him for years. This not letting one another alone, it's at the bottom of nine-tenths of the crime and trouble; and in nine-tenths of that nine-tenths there's one of your headmen concerned – whom you are supposed to look after.'

'It's very difficult, sir. They live far away in these little villages. Many of them are good men and help the villagers. But they are ignorant, too.'

'Oh, I'm not blaming you, *Ratemahatmaya*. I'm not blaming any one. And it's late if we are to start early tomorrow. You had better take your friend away with you and put him in the lock-up. Tell them to give him some food if he wants it. Good night.'

The *Ratemahatmaya* shook Silindu until he woke up. It was some little while before he realised where he was, and then that he had to set out again with the *Ratemahatmaya*. He turned to the magistrate.

'Where are they taking me to, *Hamadoru?*'

'You will be taken to the prison. You will have to stay there until you are tried.'

'But I have told the truth to the *Hamadoru*. Let him give his decision. It is to end it all that I came here.'

'I can't try you. You will have to be tried by the great judge.'

'*Aiyo*, it is you I wish to judge me. You are a hunter, and know the jungle. If they take me away now, how do I know what will happen? What will they do to me? Let it end now, *Hamadoru.*'

'I am sorry, but I can't do anything. You will be charged with murder. I can't try you for that. The great judge tries those cases. But no harm will come to you. You will be able to rest in the jail until the trial.'

'And what will they do to me? Will they hang me?'

'I'm afraid I can't tell you even that. You must go with the *Dissa Mahatmaya* now.'

Silindu, passive again, followed the *Ratemahatmaya* out of the room. The latter, grumbling at the late hour and the foolish talk of the magistrate, got into his hackery, and the procession trailed off again into the darkness towards the lock-up. Here a long delay occurred. A sleepy sergeant of police had to be woken up, and the whole story had to be explained to him. Eventually Silindu was led away by him and locked up in a narrow bare cell, which, with its immense door made of massive iron bars, was exactly like a cage for some wild animal. In it at last he found himself allowed to lie down and sleep undisturbed.

The rest, which the magistrate had promised him, seemed however to be still far off; for early next morning he was taken out of his cell and made to start off with the police sergeant for Beddagama. The magistrate, riding on a horse, and the *Ratemahatmaya*, in his hackery,[1] passed them when they were two or three miles from the town. A little while afterwards a messenger from Beddagama met the party, bringing the news of the murder to the *Ratemahatmaya*.

Silindu was being taken to Beddagama to be present at the magis-

---

1   A hackery is a single bullock cart.

trate's inquiry, but he did not understand this. He was weak and tired after the excitement of the trial and the murder, the long days upon the road, and the little food. He began to think that he had been a fool to give himself up; as he walked behind the police sergeant through the jungle, of which he knew every tree and track, a great desire for it and for freedom came upon him again. He thought of the great bars of the cell door through which he had seen the daylight for the first time that morning. Babun was even now lying behind such bars, and would lie there for six months. And he himself? He might never see the daylight except through such bars now for the rest of his life – unless they hanged him. He thought of the great river that cut through the jungle many miles away: it was pleasant there, to bathe in the cool clear water, and to lie on the bank under the great wild fig trees in the heat of the day. If he had not given himself up, he might have been there by now, watching the elephant sluicing water over its grey sides or the herd of deer coming down the opposite bank to drink. The thought came to him even now to slip into the jungle and disappear; the fool of a police sergeant would never catch him, would go on for a mile or two probably without knowing that his prisoner had escaped. But he still followed the police sergeant and had not the will or the energy for so decisive a step, for breaking away from the circumstances to which he had always yielded, for taking his life in his hands and moulding it for himself. He had tried once to fight against life when he killed the *Arachchi* and the *Mudalali*; he was now caught again in the stream; evil might come, but he could struggle no more.

He had forgotten Punchi Menika until he was a mile or two from the village, and he saw her waiting for him by the side of the track. The rumour had reached the village that Silindu was being brought back by the police in chains. Some said that he was going to be hanged there and then in the village. Punchi Menika had started off to meet him. Her first terror when she had been told of what her father had done had given place to bewilderment, but when she saw him in charge of the police sergeant she ran to him with a cry: 'Is it true, *Appochchi*; is it true, what they say?'

'What do they say? That I killed those two? It is true I killed them.

Then I went to Kamburupitiya and told it all to the *Dissa Mahatmaya* and the magistrate *Hamadoru*.'

'*Aiyo*, and will they hang you now?'

'What? Do they say that?'

'They say that in the village. It isn't true, is it, *Appochchi*?'

'I don't know; perhaps it is true, perhaps it isn't. But the magistrate *Hamadoru* said I would be tried by the great judge.'

'*Aiyo*! You were mad, *Appochchi*. It would have been better to have given me to the *Mudalali*.'

'Hold your tongue, hold your tongue!' burst out Silindu angrily, but his anger died down as rapidly as it had sprung up. 'Don't say that, child, don't say that. No, that is not true, is it, daughter? It is not true. It was for you I did it; and now – after all that – surely in a little while all will be well for you.'

'Well? What is to become of me? What am I to do? They will take you away again and hang you, or keep you in the great house over there. And my man, *aiyo*, is there too. I shall be alone here. What am I to do, *Appochchi*?'

'Hush! All will be well with you, I tell you. There is no one here to trouble you now. There will be quiet for you again – and for me, perhaps, why not? The killing was for that. Surely, surely, it must be, child. And Babun? Why, in a little while Babun will come back – in a month or two; you will wait in the village, you will sit in the house, in the compound, under the little mustard tree – so quietly, and the quiet of the great trees, child, round about – nothing to trouble you now. And in a month or two he will come back; he is a good man, Babun, and there will be no evil then – now that the *Arachchi* is dead and the *Mudalali*. There will be quiet for you then, and rest.'

'How can I live here alone? There is no food in the house even now.'

'Are not there others in the village? They will help you for a month or two, and they know Babun. He will work hard in the *chena* and repay them.'

'And you? What will they do to you? *Aiyo, aiyo*!'

'What does it matter? What have I ever done for you? It was true when they said that I was a useless man in the village. To creep through the leaves like a jackal; yes, I can do that; but what else? Isn't the bad crop in the *chena* rightly called Silindu's crop. There was never food in my house. The horoscope was true – nothing but trouble and evil and wandering in the jungle. It is a good thing for you that I leave the compound; when I go, good fortune may come.'

'Do not say that, *Appochchi*; do not say that! To whom did we run in the compound, Hinnihami and I? What father was like you in the village? Must I forget all that now, and sit alone in another's compound begging a little *kunji* and a handful of *kurakkan*? No, no! I cannot stay here. Won't they take me away with you to the jail? I cannot live here alone – without you!'

The sergeant looked back and angrily told Punchi Menika to stop making such a noise. They were nearing the village.

'Hush, child,' said Silindu. 'You must stay here. They will not take you, and what could you do in the big town there? You must wait here for Babun.'

The inquiry began as soon as they reached the village. Silindu went with the magistrate, the *Ratemahatmaya*, the *Korala* (who had been sent for), and most of the men of the village to the place where the *Arachchi* had been shot. The body lay where it had fallen; a rough canopy of boughs and leaves had been raised over it to shade it from the sun. A watcher sat near to keep off the pigs and jackals. When the canopy was removed for the magistrate to inspect the body, a swarm of flies rose and hung buzzing in the air above the corpse. The body had not been moved; it lay on its face, the legs half drawn up under the stomach. The blood had dried in great black clots over the wounds on the back. The magistrate looked at it, and then the *Korala* turned it over. A glaze of grey film was over the eyes. The hot air in the jungle track was heavy with the smell of putrefaction. The crowd of villagers, interested but unmoved, stood watching in the background, while the magistrate, sitting on the stump of a tree, began to write, noting down the position and condition in which he had found the body. Then the doctor arrived and began to cut up the body, where it lay, for post-mortem examination.

The Village in the Jungle

The magistrate walked back slowly to the village, followed by Silindu and the headman and such of the spectators as were more interested in the inquiry than in the post-mortem. The same procedure of inspection was gone through with Fernando's body, which lay under another little canopy, where he had died by the stile of the *Arachchi's* compound. After the inspection came the inquiry: a table and chair had been placed under a large tamarind tree for the magistrate to write at. The witnesses were brought up, examined, and their statements written down. After each had made his statement, Silindu was told that he could ask them any questions which he wanted them to answer. He had none. The afternoon dragged on; there was no wind, but the heat seemed to come in waves across the village, bringing with it the faint smell of decaying human flesh. The dreary procession of witnesses, listless and perspiring, continued to pass before the tired irritable magistrate. One told how he had seen Silindu and the *Arachchi* leave the village, Silindu walking behind and carrying a gun; another had heard a shot from the direction of the *chena*; another had seen Silindu return by himself to the village carrying a gun. The *Arachchi's* wife told of Silindu's early visit to the hut, of how he left with the *Arachchi*, of how later, hearing the report of a gun followed by screams, she ran out of the house to see Silindu standing with a smoking gun in his hand and Fernando writhing on the ground near the stile.

Late in the afternoon the inquiry was over. As the *Ratemahatmaya* had said, it was a simple case. Silindu was remanded, and would certainly be tried for murder before a Supreme Court judge. For the present he was handed over to the police sergeant, with whom he slept that night in a hut in the village. Next day he was taken back to Kamburupitiya, where he again spent the night in the lock-up. Then he was handed over to a fiscal's peon, who put handcuffs on him and started with him along the dusty main road which ran towards the west. They walked slowly along the road for two days. The peon was a talkative man, and he tried to make Silindu talk with him, but he soon gave up the attempt. He had to fall back for conversation on any chance traveller going the same way towards Tangalla where the prison was.

'This fellow,' he would explain to them, pointing to Silindu, 'has killed two men. He will be hanged, certainly he will be hanged. But he's mad. Not a word can you get out of him. He walks along like that mile after mile, looking from side to side – never a word. He thinks there are elephants on the main road I suppose. He comes from up there – in the jungle. They are all cattle like that there of course. I would rather drive a bull along the road than him.'

They passed through several villages, where Silindu was an object of great interest. People came, out of the houses and boutiques, and discussed him and his crimes with the peon. The first night they slept in a boutique in one of these villages. The boutique was full of people; they gathered round to watch Silindu eat his curry and rice with his hand-cuffed hands. They too discussed him in loud tones with the peon. There were two traders on their way to Kamburupitiya; the rest, with the exception of one old man, belonged to the village. This old man was one of those wanderers whom one meets from time to time in villages, upon the roads, or even sometimes in the jungle. Very old, very dirty, with long matted hair and wild eyes, he sat mumbling to himself in a corner. A beggar and mad, he had two claims to the charity of the boutique-keeper, who had taken him in for the night and given him a good meal of curry and rice.

The peon had for the twentieth time that day told Silindu's story with many embellishments, and complained bitterly of his silence and stupidity. The others sat round in the reeking atmosphere watching Silindu eat his rice by the dim light of two oil wicks.

'Will they hang him, *aiya*?' asked the boutique-keeper.

'Yes, he'll be hanged, sure enough,' said the peon. ' He confessed it himself, you see.'

'But they never really hang people, I am told. They send them away to a prison a long way off. They say they hang them just to frighten people.'

The other villagers murmured approval. The peon laughed.

'Of course they hang them. I've known people who were hanged. Why Balappu, who lived next door to me in Kamburupitiya, was hanged. He quarrelled with his brother in the street outside my house – it was about a share in their land – and he stabbed him dead. They hanged him. I took him along this same road to the prison three years ago. A good man he was: wanted to gamble all along the road.'

'But you don't know that he was hanged, *aiya*. No one saw it, no one ever sees it.'

'Nonsense,' said one of the traders. 'In Maha Nuwara they hang them. I knew a man there whose nephew was hanged, and afterwards they gave him the body to bury. The head hung over like this, and the mark of the rope was round the neck.'

The old beggar had listened to what was going on, squatting in his corner. He did not get up, but shuffled slowly forward into the circle, still in a squatting position. Silindu, who had before shown little interest in the conversation, looked up when the beggar intervened.

'*Aiyo*! What's that you say?' the old man asked. 'They are going to hang this man? Why's that?'

'He shot two men dead up there in the jungle.'

'*Chi*! *Chi*! Why did he do that?'

'He's mad, father, as mad as you.'

The old man turned and looked hard at Silindu, while Silindu stared at him. The spectators laughed at the curious sight. The old man smiled.

'He's not mad,' he said. 'Not as mad as I am. So he killed twice, did he? Dear, dear. The Lord Buddha said: kill not at all, kill nothing. It is a sin to kill. If he saw a caterpillar in the path, he put his foot on one side. Man, man, why have you killed twice? Were you mad?'

'I'm not mad,' said Silindu. 'They were hunting me: they would have killed me. Therefore I killed them.'

'The man is not mad, no more mad than you, or you – but I – I am mad. So at least they say. Why do they say that I'm mad? My son, do you see this paper?' (He showed a very dirty English newspaper to Silindu.) 'Well, if you are quite quiet and no gecko[1] cries and the jackals don't howl, I will look at it like this afterwards, for some short time staring

---

1 The gecko's 'chirp' is always considered by the Sinhalese to be a warning or sign of ill omen.

hard – then I shall see things on the paper, not the writing – I have wandered all my life – a wanderer on the path, seeking merit by the Three Gems – I cannot read writing or letters – but I shall see things themselves, a little hut up there in the jungle, if you desire it – your hut, my son – and I'll tell you what is doing there, that the woman is lying in the hut, crying perhaps. This paper was given to me by a white *Mahatmaya* whom I met out there once, also in the jungle. It is of great power: before I could only see what was doing in this country; but now, by its help, I can see over the sea, to the white *Mahatmaya's* country. Then they say: this is a mad old man. Well, well, who knows? I am always on the path – tomorrow I shall leave this village – from village to village, from town to town, and from jungle to jungle. I see many different men on the path. Strange men, and they do strange things. Thieving, stabbing, killing, cultivating paddy. I do not cultivate paddy, nor do I thieve or kill. I am mad perhaps. But very often it is they who seem to me to want but a little to be mad. All this doing and doing – running round and round like the red ants – thieving, stabbing, killing, cultivating this and that. Is there much good or wisdom in such a life? It seems to me full of evil – nothing but evil and trouble. Do they ever sit down and rest, do they ever meditate? Desire and desire again, and no fulfilment ever. Is such a life sane or mad? Did they call you mad in the village even before this, my son?'

'Yes, the mad hunter,' said Silindu, and the others laughed again.

'Ah, you are a hunter too. That also I have not done. But I know the jungle, for I travel through it often on my path. Do the beasts in it speak to you, son hunter?'

'Yes. They used to speak to me.'

'So they called you mad. All the beasts in the jungle speak to me too, except the elephant. The elephant is too sad even to talk. Usually when I see him he is eating; for he is always hungry because of his sins in the previous birth. But sometimes I find him standing alone away among the rocks, swaying from side to side. He is very sad, thinking of his sins in the previous birth. Then I say to him, "Brother, your feet too are upon the path. It is good to think of the sins of the previous birth, but there is no need of such sadness." Then he sways more and more, and his trunk moves from side to side, and he lifts one foot up after the other very slowly, but he never says a word, watching me with his little eye. Once, indeed, I remember, he lifted up his trunk and screamed. I too lifted up my hands and cried out with him, for we were both on the path.'

'You do not know the jungle, father,' said Silindu. 'It is of food and killing and hunting that the beasts talk to me. They know nothing of your path, nor do I.'

'*Aiyo*, it is not only in the jungle that they say that. They say the same in the small villages and the great towns. What do you say, sir?' he said, turning to one of the traders.

'I do not go into the jungle or talk to elephants, old man,' said the trader. ' I know the bazaar, and there they think of *fanams*[1] first and the path last.'

'A man must live,' said the other trader. It is only priests and beggars who have full bellies and idle hands.'

'The Lord Buddha was a beggar and a priest too,' said the old man, and began to mumble to himself. The laugh was against the trader.

'*Aiya*,' said the old man to the peon, 'who is going to hang this hunter?'

'The Government of course. He will be tried by the judge, and then they will hang him.'

'This is another thing which I do not understand. To the madman this seems foolish to kill a man because he has killed. If it is a sin, will he not be punished in the next birth?'

The old beggar had a strange influence on Silindu, who watched him the whole time, fascinated. The mumbled words seemed to excite him greatly.

'What do you mean, father?' he said, his voice rising. 'How punished in the next birth? They will punish me here – the judge – they do that – they will hang me – you hear what these have said.'

'I do not know about that. I only know of the path. On my way through the villages I hear them say this or that, but I do not understand.

1 Pence

Tomorrow I shall be gone, to the east, and you to the west. Do you know, my son, where you will sleep tomorrow night? No, no. Nor I either. But we go on the path each of us, because of the sins in our previous births. As the Lord Buddha said to the she-devil, "O fool! Fool! Because of your sins in the former birth, you have been born a she-devil: and yet you go on committing sins even now. What folly!" Is not that clear? Of these punishments of the Government I know nothing. If they are punishments they are because of sins committed in your previous birth; but be sure that for the sins which you commit in this birth – for the killing – for that is a sin, a great sin – you will be punished in the next birth. How many will hell await there! Surely, son, it is better to wander on and on from village to village, always, begging a little rice and avoiding sin.'

'But surely I have committed no sin. All these years they plagued me, and did evil to me. Was I to be starved by them, and my daughter starved? Was I to allow them to take her from me and from Babun?'

'The Lord Buddha said, "It is a sin to kill, even the louse in the hair must not be cracked between the nails." The other things I do not understand. I have no daughter and no wife and no hut. It is better to be without. They stand in one's way on the path. And to starve? What need to starve, my son? In every village is a handful of rice for the wanderer. As for the hanging, that is very foolish; the judge must be a foolish man, but I do not think it will hurt you. Remember it is not for the killing of the two men, but for the previous birth. Then there comes hell. You must have killed many deer and pig.'

'Yes, yes, I am a hunter, but what of that, father, what of that?'

'Each is a sin, for I told you, didn't I, that the Lord Buddha said, "It is a sin to kill." My son, you are a hunter, you know the jungle; surely you have seen the evil there, and the pain – always desire and killing. No peace or rest there either for the deer or the pig, or the little grey mongoose. They have sinned, and are far from Nirvana and happiness; and, like the she-devil, they sin again only to bring more evil on themselves by their blindness. What happiness is there in it, my son? The deer and the pig, they too are upon the path. It was greater sin to kill them than the other two. For those two, you say, were bringing evil upon you; but what did the deer and pig do to you? eh, hunter? tell me that.'

'Do? Nothing, of course. But there is no food up there. One must have food to live.'

'No food up there? There is always food upon the path, a handful of rice in every village, for the beggar. I have been forty years now on the path. Have I starved?'

'What was your village, father?'

'The name – I have forgotten – but it lay up there in the hills – a pleasant place – rain in plenty, and the little streams always running into the rice-fields, and coconut and *areca* nut trees all around.'

'*Ohé!*' murmured one of the villagers, 'it is easy to avoid killing in a place like that.'

'Have you ever worked, old man?' said the peon. 'Have you ever earned a *fanam* by work? In this part of the country *rupees* don't grow on *wara*[1] bushes.'

'No,' said the old man; 'I have never done anything like that. I am mad, you know. I remember once they took me to the field to watch – I was a boy – I had to scare the birds away. I was there alone, sitting under a small tree beside the field. The little birds came in crowds to feed on the young paddy. They were very hungry. What harm, I thought, if they eat a little? Plenty will remain for the house. So I sat there thinking of other things, and I forgot about the paddy and the birds until my father came and beat me. After that they took me no more to the fields; and I sat in the compound all day, thinking foolish things, until at last an old priest came by, and he told me of the path, and how to meditate, and I followed him. He died many years ago, many years. I have been no more to my village, it is forgotten; but I think it was up there in the hills; it is very long ago, and I have seen many villages since then. They are all the same; even the names I never know; always some huts, and men and women and children, suffering punishment for their sins and sinning again.'

'This is fool's talk,' said the peon impatiently. 'We cannot all beg upon

---

1   A shrub which grows in waste places.

the road. I have heard the priests themselves say that everyone cannot reach Nirvana. Nor are we all mad. There are the women and the children. Are they too to become holy men? It is hard enough to live on the eleven *rupees* which the Government gives us. I don't kill deer, but I eat it when I can get it. Is that too a sin, old man?'

But before the old beggar could answer, Silindu threw himself down on the ground in front of him, and touching his feet with his hands burst out: 'It is true, father, it is true what you say. I did not understand before, though I knew; yes, I knew it well. I have seen it all so long in the jungle. But I did not understand. How many times have I told the little ones – not understanding – about it all. Always the killing, killing, killing; everything afraid: the deer and the pig and the jackal after them, and the leopard himself. Always evil there. No peace, no rest – it was rest I wanted. It is true, father, I have seen it, it is the punishment for their sins. And always evil for me too, there; hunger always and trouble always. You should have shown me this path of yours before, father; even now I do not understand that, and it would be useless now. Through all the evil I have but sinned more, killing, the deer and the pig, and now these two men. It is too late. They will hang me, they will hang me, and what then, old man, what then?'

The old man began to shake with laughter. He mumbled incoherently, pulling at his beard and long hair with his hands. The scene caused great pleasure and amusement to all the others, except the peon, who was annoyed at finding that he was no longer playing the most important part. After a while the old man's laughter began to subside, and he regained sufficient control to make himself intelligible.

'Well, well,' he said, 'well, well, I'm not the Lord Buddha, my son. Well, well. D' you see that? He touches my feet as though I were the Lord Buddha himself. I have never seen that before, and I have seen many strange things. I am become a holy man; well, well.' Here again he was overcome with silent laughter.

'Do not laugh, father,' said Silindu. 'Why do you laugh? Is it lies that you told me just now?'

The other became serious again at once.

'Lies? No, no. I do not tell lies. *Aiyo*, it is all true. But what was it you

159

were saying just then? Ah, yes. You were afraid, afraid of the hanging and the punishment, and of the next birth. Too late, you said, too late for the path. My son, it is never too late to acquire merit. Perhaps they will hang you, perhaps not. Who can say? It matters little, for it will be as it will be. I do not think it will hurt very much. And before that, it is possible for you to acquire much merit. It will help you much in the next birth. You must meditate: you must think of holy things. Here are holy words for you to learn.' He repeated a *Pali* stanza, and tried to make Silindu learn it. It was a difficult task, and it was only after innumerable repetitions that Silindu at last got it by heart. When he had at last done so, he sat mumbling it over to himself again and again, so as not to forget it.

'That is good,' went on the old man. 'Along the road as you go wherever you are going – to the prison or to the hanging – repeat the holy words many times. In that way you will acquire merit. Also meditate on your sins, the sin of killing the deer and pig which you have killed. So you will acquire merit too. And avoid killing. Remember, if there were a caterpillar in the path, he put his foot on one side. So too you will acquire merit. It will help you in the next birth. I think you are already on the path, my son. And perhaps if my path too leads me to the west, who knows? I shall see you there again, and we shall talk together. Now, however, I grow tired.'

So saying the old man shuffled back into a corner, and covering his head and face with a dirty cloth, soon fell asleep. Silindu continued to mumble the *Pali* stanza, which he did not understand. The villagers, seeing that no more amusement was to be obtained from the strangers, left the boutique; and the boutique-keeper and the other travellers soon after spread out their mats on the ground, and lay down to sleep.

The next day the peon and Silindu started off very early in the morning. All along the road Silindu repeated the holy words to the great annoyance of the peon. They reached the prison at Tangalla late in the evening. It was dark when they arrived, and Silindu was at once locked up in a cell. He fell asleep, still repeating the *Pali* stanza.

Silindu remained three weeks in the prison. It seemed to him an immense building. It was a large and ancient Dutch fort, with high battlemented grey walls of great thickness. The inside formed a square paved courtyard in which the prisoners worked at breaking stones and preparing *coir*[1] by hammering coconut husks with wooden mallets. Round the courtyard were built the cells, oblong bare rooms with immense windows and gates, iron barred, which looked out upon the yard. Silindu, not being a convicted person, was not made to do any work. He squatted in his cell, watching the prisoners working in the yard, and thinking of what the old beggar had told him. He tried to meditate upon his sins, but soon found that to be impossible. He began, however, to forget the village and Punchi Menika, and all the trouble that had gone before. He repeated the *Pali* stanza many times during the day. He was very happy; he grew fat upon the good prison food.

Only once was the monotony of the days broken for him. He was watching a group of prisoners, in their blue and white striped prison clothes; they all looked almost exactly alike. They were quite near the gate of his cell, filling the bathing-trough with water. Suddenly in one of them he recognised Babun. He jumped up and ran to the bars of the gate, crying out: '*Ohé*! Babun! Babun!'

Babun looked round. There was no surprise or interest in his face, when he saw that it was Silindu. A great change had come over him in the short time during which he had been in prison. His skin, a sickly yellow colour, seemed to have shrunk with the flesh and muscle, which had wasted; he was bent and stooping; his eyes were sunken; a look of dullness and hopelessness was in his face. He looked at Silindu frowning. Silindu danced about with excitement behind the bars.

'You know me, Babun?' he shouted. 'You know me? Why do you look like that? All is well, all is well. I shot the *Arachchi* and Fernando: they are dead. But all is well. They'll hang me. That's why I'm here. But I have my feet on the path. I've acquired merit. The old man was right,'

A jail guard shouted across the courtyard to Silindu to 'shut his mouth.'

'And the woman,' said Babun, in a low, dull voice. 'Where is the woman?'

---

1 *Coir,* fibre of the coconut husk.

'She is there in the village waiting for you. All is well, I tell you. They are dead: I killed them. It was the only way, though a sin, a great sin, the old man said. They will hang me, everyone says so; but all is well, I've found the path. And you – you'll go back to the village. Punchi Menika is there, waiting. The evil is over.'

Babun stared at him, frowning. His face had lost completely the open cheerful look which it had once had. At last he said slowly: 'You are mad. I don't understand you. If you have killed those two, you are a fool, madman. What's the good? I shall never go back there. I shall die here. And you? Yes, they'll hang you, as you say. What's the good? You are mad, mad – you always were.'

He turned away, and slowly lifting the pail of water emptied it into the trough.

Silindu often saw Babun again in the yard, but never spoke to him. Babun seemed purposely to avoid passing near his cell, and if he had to do so, he kept his eyes fixed on the ground. The day of Silindu's trial arrived. In the morning he was taken out of his cell, and handed over with four other prisoners to an escort of police. They put handcuffs on his hands, and led him through the streets to the court.

Silindu's case was the first case for trial. He did not pay much attention to the proceedings – he continued to mumble the *Pali* stanza but he felt the greater pomp and solemnity of this court compared with the police court. The judge was a grey-haired man in a dull scarlet gown. There was a jury, among which were several white *Mahatmayas*; there were a great many lawyers sitting round the table in the centre of the court; and there was a crowd of officials and policemen standing about.

Silindu had an advocate assigned to him by the court to defend him. The lawyer soon found it useless to discuss the case with the prisoner: the line of defence was clear, however; he would admit the killing, and plead insanity and provocation. The indictment for murder was read, and the witnesses for the prosecution then gave, their evidence. They were cross-examined by Silindu's advocate, only with a view to showing that it had been well known in the village that Silindu was mad: they admitted that he had always been '*tikak pissu*.' They none of them knew anything about a quarrel with the *Arachchi* before the theft and the conviction of Babun.

Silindu's advocate then put him in the witness-box. He repeated the statement which he had made to the magistrate. He was asked very few questions in cross-examination, but the judge examined him at some length. The judge's object was to make it clear, when the idea of killing the two men first came to Silindu, and what was in Silindu's mind during his walk to the *chena* with the *Arachchi*. Silindu understood nothing of what was going on; he did not know, and could not have been made to understand the law; he understood the point and reason for no single question asked him. He knew he would be hanged; he was tired of this continual slow torture of questions which he had to answer; he wanted only to be left in peace to repeat the holy words again and again: he had told them of the killing so many times; why should they continue to bother him with these perpetual questions? He answered the questions indifferently, baldly. Most of those in the court listening to his bare passionless sentences describing how he determined to kill the two men, how he watched for their return to the village, sitting all day long in his compound, and how he finally killed them on the next day, were left with the conviction that they had before them a brutal and cold murderer.

The summing up of the judge, however, showed that he was not one of those who regarded it as a simple case. He laid stress on the fact that the prisoner had never been considered in the village to be completely sane, and he directed the notice of the jury to the 'queer' ideas which the prisoner seemed to have had in his mind about the hunting and his own identification with the buffalo. It was right for them also to consider the demeanour of the prisoner while in court, his apparent listlessness and lack of interest in what was going on. They must, however, remember that if the defence of insanity was to succeed, they must be satisfied that the prisoner was actually incapable, owing to unsoundness of mind, of knowing the nature of his act, or of knowing that he was doing what was wrong or contrary to law.

After the judge had summed up, the jury were told they could retire to consider their verdict, but after consulting with them, the foreman stated they were all agreed that the prisoner was guilty of murder. Silindu was still muttering his stanza; he had not tried to understand what was going on around him.

The court interpreter went close up to the dock and told him that the jury had found him guilty of murder. Was there anything which he had to say why sentence of death should not be passed on him? A curious stillness had fallen on the place. Silindu suddenly became conscious of where he was: he looked round and saw that everyone was looking at him; he saw the faces of the crowd outside staring through the windows and craning round the pillars on the verandah; all the eyes were staring at him as if something was expected from him. For a moment the new sense of comfort and peace left him; he felt afraid again, hunted; he looked up and down the court as if in search of some path of escape.

'*Aiyo!*' he said to the interpreter, 'does that mean I am to be hanged?'

'Have you anything to say why you should not be sentenced to be hanged?'

'What is there to say? I have known that a long time. They told me that I should be hanged – all the people – along the road. What is there to say now, *aiya?*'

Silindu's words were interpreted to the judge, who took up a black cloth and placed it on his head. Silindu was sentenced to be hanged by the neck until he should be dead. The words were translated to him in Sinhalese by the interpreter. He began again to repeat the stanza. He was taken out of the court, handcuffed, and escorted back to his cell in the prison by five policemen armed with rifles.

He was to be hanged in two weeks' time, and the days passed for him peacefully as the days had passed before the trial. He had no fear of the hanging now. If he had any feeling towards it, it was one of expectancy, even hope. Vaguely he looked forward to the day as the end of some long period of evil, as the beginning of something happier and better. He scarcely thought of the actual hanging, but when he did, he thought of it in the words of the old beggar, 'I do not think it will hurt much.'

Four days before the day fixed for the execution, the jailer came to Silindu's cell accompanied by a Sinhalese gentleman dressed very beautifully in European clothes and a light grey sun-helmet. Silindu was told to get up and come forward to the window of the cell. The Sinhalese gentleman then took a document out of his pocket and began reading it aloud in a high pompous voice. It informed Silindu that the sentence of death passed on him had been commuted to one of twenty years' rigorous imprisonment. When the reading stopped, Silindu continued to stare vacantly at the gentleman.

'Do you understand, fellow?' said the latter.

'I don't understand, *Hamadoru*.'

'Explain to him, jailer.'

'You are not going to be hanged, d'you understand that? You'll be kept in prison instead – twenty years.'

'Twenty years?'

'Yes, twenty years. D'you understand that?'

Silindu did not understand it. He could understand a week or two weeks, or a month, or even six months, but twenty years meant nothing to him. It was just a long time. At any rate he was not, after all, to be hanged. For the moment a slight sense of uneasiness and disappointment came over him. In the last four days he had grown to look forward to the end, and now the end was put off for twenty years, for ever, it seemed to him. He squatted down by the gate of his cell, holding the great iron bars in his hands and staring out into the courtyard. He thought of the past three weeks which he had spent in the cell; after all, they had been very peaceful and happy. He had been acquiring merit, as the old man told him to do. Now he would have more time still for acquiring it. He would be left in peace here for twenty years – for a lifetime – to acquire merit, and at the end he might make his way back to the village and find Babun and Punchi Menika there, and sit in their compound again watching the shadows of the jungle. It was very peaceful in the cell.

A jail guard came and unlocked the cell gate. Silindu was taken out and made to squat down in the long shed which ran clown the centre of the courtyard. A wooden mallet was put into his hand and a pile of coconut husks thrown down in front of him. For the remainder of that day, and daily for the remainder of twenty years, he had to make *coir* by beating coconut husks with the wooden mallet.

Chapter 9

PUNCHI MENIKA had been present at the inquiry of the magistrate in the village, but she had not spoken to Silindu after her meeting with him when he was being brought to Beddagama by the police sergeant. The magistrate and the headman and the prisoner had left for Kamburupitiya very early in the morning following the day of the inquiry. She and the other villagers woke up to find that the village had already been left to its usual sleepy life. There was nothing for her to do but to obey Silindu's instructions, to wait for Babun's release, living as best she might in the hut with Karlinahami. Her present misfortunes, the imprisonment of Babun, the loss of her father, and the fate (and the uncertainty of it) which hung over him, weighed numbly upon her. And the future filled her with vague fears; she did not, could not plan about it, or calculate about it, or visualise it, or anything in it. She did not even think definitely of how she was going to live for six months, until Babun should return. There was scarcely food in the house for her and Karlinahami to exist in semi-starvation through those six months. Yet the future loomed somehow upon her, filling her with a horrible sense of uneasiness, uncertainty. It was a new feeling. She sat in the hut silent and frightened the greater part of the day. She thought of Silindu's stories of hunters who had lost their way in the jungle. Their terror must have been very like hers; she was alone, terribly alone and deserted; she too had lost her way, and like them one path was as good or as bad to her as another.

Karlinahami was nearly fifty years old now, and in a jungle village a woman – and especially a woman without a husband – is very old, very near the grave at fifty. The sun and the wind, the toil, the hunger, and the disease sap the strength of body and mind, bring folds and lines into the skin, and dry up the breasts. A woman is old at forty or even thirty. No one, man or woman, in the jungle, lives to the term of years allotted to man. It would have been difficult to say whether Karlinahami looked nearer eighty than ninety, nearer ninety than a hundred. The jungle had left its mark on her. Her body was bent and twisted, like the stunted trees, which the south-west wind had tortured into grotesque shapes. The skin, too, on her face and thin limbs reminded one of the bark of the jungle trees; it was shrunken against the bones, and wrinkled, and here and there flaking off into whitish brown scales, as the bark flakes off the *kumbuk* trees. The flesh of the cheeks had dried and shrunk; the lips seemed to have sunk into the toothless mouth, leaving a long line damp with saliva under the nose. And under the lined forehead were the eyes, lifeless and filmy, peering out of innumerable wrinkles. The eyes were not blind, but they seemed to be sightless – the pupil, the iris, and even the white had merged – because the mind was dying. It is what usually happens in the jungle – to women especially – the mind dies before the body. Imperceptibly the power of initiative, of thought, of feeling, dies out before the monotony of life, the monotony of the tearing hot wind, the monotony of endless trees, the monotony of perpetual hardship. It will happen at an age when in other climates a man is in his prime, and a woman still bears children. The man will still help at the work in the *chena*, cutting down the undergrowth and sowing the crop; but he will do so unthinking, without feeling, like a machine or an animal; and when it is done he will sit hour after hour in his compound staring with his filmy eyes into nothing, motionless, except when he winds one long thin arm round himself, like a grey monkey, and scratches himself on the back. And the woman still carries the waterpot to the muddy pool to fetch water; still cooks the meal in the house. While they still stand upright, they must do their work; they eat and they sleep; they mutter frequently to themselves; but they do not speak to others, and no one speaks to them. They live in a twilight, where even pain is scarcely felt.

Karlinahami was sinking rapidly into this twilight. In the jungle decay and growth are equally swift. The trial of Silindu and Babun, the murder of the *Arachchi* and Fernando, and now the loss of Silindu had meant very little to her. She had felt vaguely that many evils were happening, but facts no longer had meaning for her clouded mind. She fetched the water as usual for the cooking, muttering to herself; but she did not speak to Punchi Menika, and Punchi Menika knew that to talk to her or consult with her would be useless.

A month after the conviction of Silindu the life of the village would at first sight have appeared to have regained its ordinary course. But in reality a great change had come over it. It had been a small village, a dwindling village before; one of those villages doomed to slow decay, to fade out at last into the surrounding jungle. Now at a blow, in a day, it lost one out of its six houses, and seven out of its twenty-five inhabitants. For after the death of the *Arachchi*, Nanchohami, his wife, decided to leave the village. Her children were too young to do *chena* work; so that it was not possible any longer to support herself in Beddagama. In Kotegoda, where the *Arachchi's* relations lived, there was paddy land and coconuts, and rain fell in plenty every year. They would give her a hut, and a little land; she would marry her children there; she had always said that Beddagama was an unholy place, full of evil and evil omens. She packed up her few possessions in a bullock hackery, which she borrowed from the *Korala*, and set out for Kotegoda. The *Arachchi's* house was abandoned to the jungle. There was no one to inhabit it; and indeed no one would have been foolhardy enough to go and live in it. It was ill-omened, accursed, and very soon came to be known as the haunt of devils. It seemed to make a long fight against the jungle. The fence itself merged into the low scrub which surrounded it, growing into a thick line of small trees. The wara bushes, with their pale grey thick leaves and purple flowers the rank grass, the great spined slabs of prickly pear, crawled out from under the shadow of the fence over the compound up to the walls and the very door. But the walls were thicker and better made than those of most huts: the roof was of tiles; there was no cadjan thatch to be torn and scattered by the south-west wind. The rains of the north-east monsoon beat against the mud walls for two years in vain; they washed out great holes in them, through which you could see the jungle sticks upon which the mud had been plastered. The sticks exposed to the damp air took root and burst into leaf. Great weeds, and even bushes, began to grow up between the tiles, from seeds dropped by birds or scattered by the wind. An immense twisted cactus towered over the roof. The tiles were dislodged and pushed aside by the roots. The jungle was bursting through the walls, overwhelming the house from above. The jungle moved within the walls: at last they crumbled; the tiled roof fell in. The grass and the weeds grew up over the little mound of broken red pottery; the jungle sticks of the walls spread out into thick bushes. Tall saplings of larger trees began to show themselves. By the end of the third rains the compound and the house had been blotted out.

It was as if the jungle had broken into the village. Other huts had been abandoned, overwhelmed, blotted out before, but they had always lain on the outside of the village. The jungle had only drawn its ring closer round the remaining huts; it had not broken into the village – the village had remained a whole, intact. But now the jungle cut across the village, separating Silindu's and Bastian Appu's hut from the rest. The villagers themselves noted it: they felt that they were living in a doomed place. 'The village is dying,' Nanchohami had said before she left. 'An evil place, devil-haunted. It is dying, as its young die with the old. No children are born in it now. An evil place. In ten years it will have gone, trampled by the elephants.'

It was, however, only very gradually that this feeling of doom came to be felt by the village and the villagers. At first, after the excitement of the trials and the murder, they seemed to have settled down to the old monotonous life, as it had been before. The *vederala* was appointed *Arachchi*. Punchi Menika waited for Babun. She did not and could not count the passing of time: a week was only some days to her, and six months only many months; but she waited, watching the passage of time, vaguely but continuously, for the day when Babun should return. She heard the rumour which eventually reached the village that after all Silindu was not to be hanged; he was to be kept in prison, they said, for ever, for the remainder of his life. It brought no comfort to her; he had been taken out of her life, she would never see him again; did it matter whether he was dead or in prison?

She waited month after month. Her first feelings of fear were lost in the perpetual sense of expectancy as the time slipped away. And she had to work, to labour hard in order to keep herself and Karlinahami alive. The little store of *kurakkan* in the house dwindled rapidly. She had to search the jungle for edible leaves and wild fruit and roots, like the wild onions which the pig feed upon. When the *chena* season came she worked in the others' *chenas*, Balappu's and Bastian Appu's, and even Punchirala's. She worked hard like a man for a few handfuls of *kurakkan*, given to her as a charity. The others liked her, and were in their way kind to her; they liked her quietness, her gentleness and submission. Even Punchirala said of her: 'She goes about like a doe. They used to call the mad *vedda* a leopard. The leopard's cub has turned into a deer.'

As the months passed, she gradually began to feel as if each day might be the one on which Babun would return. And as each day passed without bringing him, she tried to reckon whether the six months had really gone. She talked it over with the other villagers. Some said it was five months, others seven months since the conviction. They discussed it for hours, wrangling, quarrelling, shouting at one another. He had been convicted two months – about two months – before the Sinhalese New Year. No, it was one month before the New Year.' 'It couldn't be one month before, because the *chena* crop was not reaped yet.' 'Reaped? Why it had only just been sown.' It must have been three months before.' 'Three months, you fool? Is a *chena* crop like ninety days' rice?' 'Fool? Who is a fool?' 'Hold your tongue! Hold your tongue! At any rate, it was before the New Year, and it's already six months since the New Year.' '*Aiyo!* Six months since the New Year. It is only a month since I sowed my *chena*. Who ever heard of sowing a *chena* five months after the New Year? It is not three months since the New Year.'

Punchi Menika would stand listening to them going over it again and again, hour after hour. She listened in silence, and would then slip quietly away to wander in the evening down the track towards Kamburupitiya. It was on the track that she hoped, that she was certain that she would meet him. Then all would be well; the evil would end, as Silindu had said. But as the days went by, the certainty left her; even hope began to tremble, to give place to forebodings, fears. The time came when all were agreed that the six months had passed; something must have happened to him; he was ill, perhaps, or he had just been forgotten there; one can never tell, anything may happen when a man gets into prison; 'they' simply have forgotten to let him out.

Punchirala, the new headman, was consulted. 'The man,' he said, 'is probably dead.' Punchi Menika shuddered. Her great eyes, in which the look of suffering had already grown profound and steady, did not leave the *vederala's* face. 'Yes, I expect the man's dead. They die quickly over there in prison. Especially strong men like Babun. They lie down in a corner and die. There is medicine for diseases, but is there any medicine for fate? So they say, and lie down in the corner and die. There is nothing for you to do. No. I can give you no medicine for fate either. You must sit down here in the village and marry a young man – if you can find one, and if not, perhaps, an old one. Eh? Why not? Though the jackals are picking the bones of the elephant on the river bank, there are other elephants bathing in the river. Nor are they all cows. Well, well.'

'*Ralahami*, do you really know anything? Have you heard that he is dead?'

'I have heard nothing. From whom could I hear? If you want to hear anything you must go to the prison. It will take you many days – first to Kamburupitiya, and then west along the great road, three days to Tangalla, where the prison is. You must ask at the prison. They can tell you.'

Punchi Menika left the *vederala* in silence. She walked away very slowly to the hut; the conviction had come to her at once that she must go to the prison. The thought of the journey alone into an unknown world frightened her; but she felt that she must go, that she could not bear any longer this waiting in doubt in the village. She made some cakes of *kurakkan*, tied them up in a handkerchief, together with some uncooked grain which the villagers gave her when they heard of her intended journey, and started next day for Kamburupitiya.

The first part of her journey, the track to Kamburupitiya, she knew well. She had, too, no fear, as other women have, of being alone in the jungle. It was when she turned west along the main road to Tangalla that her real troubles began. She felt lost and terribly alone on the straight, white, dusty road. The great clumsy bullock carts, laden with salt or paddy, perpetually rumbled by her; the carters she knew were bad men, terrible tales were told about them in the villages. The life of the road frightened her far more than the silence and solitude of the jungle. That she understood: she belonged to it. But the stream of passers-by upon the road, the unknown faces and the eyes that always stared strangely, inquiringly at her for a moment, and had then passed on for ever, made her feel vaguely how utterly alone she was in the world. And nowhere was this feeling so strong for her as in the villages which she slunk through like a frightened jackal. Everywhere it was the same; the crowd of villagers and travellers staring at her from in front of the village boutique, the group of women gossiping and laughing round the well in the paddy field – not a known face among them all. She had not the courage even to ask to be allowed to sleep at night in a boutique or hut. She preferred to creep into some small piece of jungle by the roadside, when darkness found her tired and hungry.

She was very tired and very hungry before she reached Tangalla. Her bewilderment was increased by the network of narrow streets. She wandered about until she suddenly found herself in the market. It was market-day, and a crowd of four or five hundred people were packed together into the narrow space, which was littered with the goods and produce which they were buying and selling: fruit and vegetables and grain and salt and clothes and pots. Everyone was talking, shouting, gesticulating at the same time. The noise terrified her, and she fled away. She hurried down another narrow street, and found herself at the foot of a hill which rose from the middle of the town. There were no houses upon its sides, but there was an immense building on the top of it. There was no crowd there, only an old man sitting on the bare hillside watching five lean cows which were trying to find some stray blades of parched brown grass on the stony soil.

She squatted down, happy in the silence and solitude of the place after the noise of the streets and market. Nothing was to be heard except the cough of one of the cows from time to time, and from far off the faint, confused murmur from the market-place. She looked up at the great white building; it was very glaring and dazzling in the blaze of the sun. She

wondered whether it was the prison in which Babun lay. She looked at
the old man sitting among the five starved cows. He reminded her a little
of Silindu; he sat so motionless, staring at a group of coconut trees that lay
around the bottom of the hill. He was as thin as the cattle which he
watched: as their flanks heaved in the heat you saw the ribs sticking out
under their mangy coats, and you could see, too, every bone of his chest
and sides panting up and down under his dry, wrinkled skin. The
insolent noisy townspeople had terrified her; this withered old man
seemed familiar to her, like a friend. He might very easily have come out
of the jungle.

She went over to where he sat, and stood in front of him. For a
moment he turned on her his eyes, which were covered with a film the
colour of the film which forms on stagnant water; then he began again to
stare at the palms in silence.

'Father,' she said, 'is that the prison?'

The old man looked up slowly at the great glaring building as if he had
seen it for the first time, and then looked from it to Punchi Menika.

'Yes,' he said in a dry husky voice. 'Why?'

'My man must be there,' said Punchi Menika gazing at the white
walls. 'He was sent there many months ago. They sent him there for six
months. It was a false case. The six months have passed now, but he has
not returned to the village. I have come to ask about him here – a long
way. I am tired, father, tired of all this. But he must be there.'

The old man's eyes remained fixed upon the coconut palms; he did
not move.

'What is your village, woman?' he asked.

'I come from Beddagama.'

'Beddagama, I know it. I knew it long ago. I, too, come from over
there, from Mahawelagama, beyond Beddagama. You should go back to
your village, woman.'

'But my man, father, what about my man?'

The old man turned his head very slowly and looked up at the prison.
The sun beat down upon his face, which seemed to have been battered
and pinched and folded and lined by age and misery. His eyes wandered

from the prison to one of the cows. She stood still, stretching out her head in front of her, her great eyes bulging; she coughed in great spasms which strained her flanks. He waited until the coughing had stopped, and she began again to search the earth for something to eat. Then he said, speaking as if to himself: 'They never come out from there – not if they are from the jungle. How can they live in there, always shut in between walls? These town people – they do not mind, but we – surely I should know – I am from Mahawelagama, a village in the jungle over there. I would go back now, but I am too old. When one is old, it is useless; but you go back to your village, woman. It is folly to leave the village. There is hunger there, I know, I remember that; but there is the hut and the compound all by themselves, and the jungle beyond. Here there is nothing but noise and trouble, and one house upon the other.'

'But I must ask at the prison first for my man. Why are they keeping him there?'

'They never come out. Surely I should know. My son was sent there. He never came out. The case was in this town, and I came here and spent all I had for him. Then I thought I will wait here until they let him out; but he never came. It will be the same with your man. Go back to the village.'

Punchi Menika wept quietly from weariness and hunger and misery at the old man's words: 'It is no good crying,' he said; 'I am old, and who should know better than I? They never come out. It is better to go back to the village.'

Punchi Menika got up and walked slowly up the hill, and then round the prison. There was only one entrance to it, an immense solid wooden gate studded with iron nails. She knocked timidly, so timidly that the sound was not heard within. Then she sat down against the wall and waited. Hours passed, and nothing happened; the gate remained closed; no sound could be heard from within the prison; the hill was deserted except for the five cows whose coughing she could hear from time to time below her. But she waited patiently for something to happen, only moving now and again into the shadow of the wall, when the sun in its course beat down upon her.

At last the door opened, and a man in a khaki uniform and helmet, carrying a club in his hand, came out. He looked at Punchi Menika, and said sharply: 'What do you want here?'

'I have come about my man, *aiya*. A long time ago he was sent here for six months. The time has passed, but he has not returned to the village. They say he is dead. Is it true, *aiya*?'

'What was his name and village?'

'He was from Beddagama.'

'His name?'

'*Aiya*, how can I tell his name?'

'What was his name, fool?'

'They called him Babun.'

'What was he convicted for?'

'It was a false case. They said he had robbed the *Arachchi*.'

'Oh, that man, yes. The *Arachchi* was killed afterwards, wasn't he?'

'Yes, yes, my father did that.'

'Well, he was here, too. Have you any money, woman?'

'No, *aiya*, none; we are very poor.'

'Ah! Well. We can't tell you anything here. You must go to Kamburu-pitiya, and send a petition to the agent *Hamadoru*.'

'But you know my man, *aiya*; you said you did. What harm to tell me? Is he here now? What has happened to him? I have come many days' journey to ask about him, and now you send me away to more trouble.'

The jail guard looked at Punchi Menika for a minute or two.

'Well,' he said, 'charity they say is like rain to a parched crop. You are asking for drought in a parched field. I knew the man; he was here, but he is dead. He died two months back.'

The jail guard expected to hear the shrill cry and the beating of the breast, the signs of a woman's mourning. Punchi Menika astonished him by walking slowly away to the shade, and sitting down again by the prison wall. The blow was too heavy for the conventional signs of grief. She sat dry-eyed; she felt little, but the intense desire to get away to the village, to get away out of this world, where she was lost and alone, to the compound, where she could sit and watch the sun set behind the jungle. She did not wait long; she set out at once down the hill. The old man still sat among his cows looking at the coconut trees.

'Ah,' he said, as she passed him, 'they never come out. I told you so.'

'He is dead, father.'

'Yes, they never come out. Go back to the village, child.'

'I am going, father.'

Chapter 10

TWO YEARS LATER, Punchi Menika was still living in the hut which had belonged to Silindu, but she lived alone. Karlinahami had died slowly and almost painlessly, like the trees around her. Her death had brought no difference into Punchi Menika's life, except that now she had to find food for herself alone.

The years had brought more evil, death, and decay upon the village. Of the five houses which stood when Punchi Menika returned from her journey to the prison, only two remained, her own, and that of the headman *vederala* Punchirala. Disease and hunger visited it year after year. It seemed, as the headman said, to have been forgotten by gods and men. Year after year, the rains from the north-east passed it by; only the sun beat down more pitilessly, and the wind roared over it across the jungle; the little patches of *chena* crop which the villagers tried to cultivate withered as soon as the young shoots showed above the ground. No man, traveller or headman or trader, ever came to the village now. No one troubled any longer to clear the track which led to it; the jungle covered it and cut the village off.

Disease and death took the old first, Podi Sinho, and his wife Angohami, and the jungle crept forward over their compound. And three years later two other huts were abandoned. In one had lived Balappu with his wife and sister, and his two children; in the other Bastian Appu with his two sons, a daughter, a daughter-in-law, and a grandchild. They had tried to help Punchi Menika by letting her work in their *chenas*, and by giving her a share in the meagre crop. They struggled hard against the fate that hung over them, clinging to the place where they had been born and lived, the compound they knew, and the sterile *chenas* which they had sown. No children were born to them now in their hut, their women were as sterile as the earth; the children that had been born to them died of want and fever. At last they yielded to the jungle. They packed up their few possessions and left the village for ever, to try and find work and food in the rice-fields of Maha Potana.

They tried to induce Punchi Menika to go with them, but she refused. She remembered her misery and loneliness upon the road to Tangalla, and the words of the old man from Mahawelagama, who sat among the cows upon the hill there. She remembered Babun's words to the *Mudalali*, 'Surely it is a more bitter thing to die in a strange place.' It might be a still bitterer thing to live in a strange place. She was alone in the world; the only thing left to her was the compound and the jungle which she knew. She clung to it passionately, blindly. The love which she had felt for Silindu and Babun – who were lost to her for ever, whose very memories began to fade from her in the struggle to keep alive – was transferred to the miserable hut, the bare compound, and the parched jungle.

So she was left alone with Punchirala. He was an old man now, weak and diseased. After a while he became too feeble even to get enough food to keep himself alive. She took him into her hut. She had to find food now for him, as well as for herself, by searching the jungle for roots and fruit, and by sowing a few handfuls of grain at the time of the rains in the ground about the hut. He gave her no thanks; as his strength decayed, his malignancy and the bitterness of his tongue increased; but he did not live long after he came to her hut; hunger and age and *parangi* at last freed her from his sneers and his gibes.

The jungle surged forward over and blotted out the village up to the very walls of her hut. She no longer cleared the compound or mended the fence, the jungle closed over them as it had closed over the other huts and compounds, over the paths and tracks. Its breath was hot and heavy in the hut itself which it imprisoned in its wall, stretching away unbroken for miles. Everything except the little hut with its rotting walls and broken tattered roof had gone down before it. It closed with its shrubs and bushes and trees, with the impenetrable disorder of its thorns and its creepers, over the rice-fields and the tanks. Only a little hollowing of the ground where the trees stood in water when rain fell, and a long little mound which the rains washed out and the elephants trampled down, marked the place where before had lain the tank and its land.

The village was forgotten, it disappeared into the jungle from which it had sprung, and with it she was cut off, forgotten. It was as if she was the last person left in the world, a world of unending trees above which the wind roared always and the sun blazed. She became one of the beasts of the jungle, struggling perpetually for life against hunger and thirst; the ruined hut, through which the sun beat and the rains washed, was only the lair to which she returned at night for shelter. Her memories of the evils which had happened to her, even of Babun and her life with him, became dim and faded. And as they faded, her childhood and Silindu and his tales returned to her. She had returned to the jungle; it had taken her back; she lived as he had done, understanding it, loving it, fearing it. As he had said, one has to live many years before one understands what the beasts say in the jungle. She understood them now, she was one of them. And they understood her, and were not afraid of her. They became accustomed to the little tattered hut, and to the woman who lived in it. The herd of wild pigs would go grunting and rooting up to the very door, and the old sows would look up unafraid and untroubled at the woman sitting within. Even the does became accustomed to her soft step as she came and went through the jungle, muttering greetings to them; they would look up for a moment, and their great eyes would follow her for a moment as she glided by, and then the heads would go down again to graze without alarm.

But life is very short in the jungle. Punchi Menika was a very old woman before she was forty. She no longer sowed grain, she lived only on the roots and leaves that she gathered. The perpetual hunger wasted her slowly, and when the rains came she lay shivering with fever in the hut. At last the time came when her strength failed her; she lay in the hut unable to drag herself out to search for food. The fire in the corner that had smouldered so long between the three great stones was out. In the day the hot air eddied through the hut, hot with the breath of the wind blowing over the vast parched jungle; at night she shivered in the chill dew. She was dying, and the jungle knew it; it is always waiting; can scarcely wait for death. When the end was close upon her a great black shadow glided into the doorway. Two little eyes twinkled at her steadily, two immense white tusks curled up gleaming against the darkness. She sat up, fear came upon her, the fear of the jungle, blind agonising fear.

'*Appochchi, Appochchi!*' she screamed. 'He has come, the devil from the bush. He has come for me as you said. *Aiyo*! Save me, save me! *Appochchi!*'

As she fell back, the great boar grunted softly, and glided like a shadow towards her into the hut.

Pearls and
Swine

A short story by

LEONARD WOOLF

Pearls and Swine

I HAD FINISHED my hundred up – or rather he had – with the Colonel and we strolled into the smoking room for a smoke and a drink round the fire before turning in. There were three other men already round the fire and they widened their circle to take us in. I didn't know them, hadn't spoken to them or indeed anyone except the Colonel in the large gaudy uncomfortably comfortable hotel. I was run down, out of sorts generally, and – like a fool, I thought now – had taken a week off to eat, or rather to read the menus of interminable *table d'hote* dinners, to play golf and to walk on the 'front' at Torquay.

I had only arrived the day before, but the Colonel (retired) a jolly tubby little man – with white moustaches like two Ss lying side by side on the top of his stupid red lips and his kind choleric eyes bulging out on a life which he was quite content never for a moment to understand – made it a point, my dear Sir, to know every new arrival within one hour after he arrived.

We got our drinks and as, rather forgetting that I was in England, I murmured the Eastern formula, I noticed vaguely one of the other three glance at me over his shoulder for a moment. The Colonel stuck out his fat little legs in front of him, turning up his neatly shoed toes before the blaze. Two of the others were talking, talking as men so often do in the comfortable chairs or smoking rooms between ten and eleven at night, earnestly, seriously, of what they call affairs, or politics or questions. I listened to their fat, full-fed assured voices in that heavy room which smelt of solidity, safety, horsehair furniture, tobacco smoke, and the faint civilised aroma of whisky and soda. It came as a shock to me in that atmosphere that they were discussing India and the East: it does you know every now and again. Sentimental? Well, I expect one is sentimental about it, having lived there. It doesn't seem to go with solidity and horsehair furniture: the fifteen years come back to one in a moment all in a heap. How one hated it and how one loved it!

I suppose they had started on the Durbar and the King's visit. They had got on to Indian unrest, to our position in India, its duties, responsibilities, to the problem of East and West. They hadn't been there of course, they hadn't even seen the brothel and *café chantant* at Port Said suddenly open out into that pink and blue desert that leads you through Africa and Asia into the heart of the East. But they knew all about it, they had solved, with their fat voices and in their fat heads, riddles, older than the Sphinx, of peoples remote and ancient and mysterious whom they had never seen and could never understand. One was, I imagine, a stock-jobber, plump and comfortable with a greasy forehead and a high colour in his cheeks, smooth shiny brown hair and a carefully grown small moustache: a good dealer in the market: sharp and confident, with a loud voice and shifty eyes. The other was a clergyman: need I say more? Except that he was more of a clergyman even than most clergymen, I mean that he wore tight things – leggings don't they call them? or breeches? – round his calves. I never know what it means: whether they are bishops or rural deans or archdeacons or archimandrites. In any case I mistrust them even more than the black trousers: they seem to close the last door for anything human to get in through the black clothes. The dog collar closes up the armour above, and below, as long as they *were* trousers, at any rate some whiff of humanity might have eddied up the legs of them and touched bare flesh. But the gaiters button them up finally, irremediably, for ever.

I expect he was an archdeacon; he was saying: 'You can't impose Western civilisation upon an Eastern people – I believe I'm right in saying that there are over two hundred millions in our Indian Empire – without a little disturbance. I'm a Liberal you know. I've been a Liberal my whole life – family tradition – though I grieve to say I could not follow Mr Gladstone on the Home Rule question. It seems to me a good sign, this movement, an awakening among the people. But don't misunderstand me, my dear Sir, I am not making any excuses for the methods of the extremists. Apart from my calling – I have a natural horror of violence.

Nothing can condone violence, the taking of human life, it's savagery, terrible, terrible.'

'They don't put it down with a strong enough hand', the stock-jobber was saying almost fiercely. 'There's too much Liberalism in the East, too much namby-pambyism. It is all right here, of course, but it's not suited to the East. They want a strong hand. After all they owe us something: we aren't going to take all the kicks and leave them all the halfpence. Rule 'em, I say, rule 'em, if you're going to rule 'em. Look after 'em, of course: give 'em schools, if they want education – schools, hospitals, roads, and railways. Stamp out the plague, fever, famine. But let 'em know you are top dog. That's the way to run an eastern country. I am a white man, you're black; I'll treat you well, give you courts and justice; but I'm the superior race, I'm master here.'

The man who had looked around at me when I said 'Here's luck!' was fidgeting about in his chair uneasily. I examined him more carefully. There was no mistaking the cause of his irritation. It was written on his face, the small close-cut white moustache, the smooth firm cheeks with the red-and-brown glow on them, the innumerable wrinkles round the eyes, and above all the eyes themselves, that had grown slow and steady and unastonished, watching that inexplicable, meaningless march of life under blazing suns. He had seen it, he knew. 'Ah,' I thought, 'he is beginning to feel his liver. If he would only begin to speak, we might have some fun.'

'H'm, h'm.' said the archdeacon. 'Of course there's something in what you say. Slow and sure. Things may be going too fast, and, as I say, I'm entirely for putting down violence and illegality with a strong hand. And after all, my dear Sir, when you say we're the superior race you imply a duty. Even in secular matters we must spread the light. I believe – devoutly – I am not ashamed to say so – that we are. We're reaching the people there, it's the cause of the unrest, we set them an example. They desire to follow. Surely, surely we should help to guide their feet. I don't speak without a certain knowledge. I take a great interest, I may even say that I play my small part, in the work of one of our great missionary societies. I see our young men, many of them risen from the people, educated often, and highly educated (I venture to think), in Board Schools. I see them go out full of high ideals to live among those poor people. And I see them when they come back and tell me their tales honestly, unostentatiously. It is always the same, a message of hope and comfort. We are getting at the people, by example, by our lives, by our conduct. They respect us.'

I heard a sort of groan, and then quite loud, these strange words: 'Kasimutal Rameswaramvaraiyil terintavan.'

'I beg your pardon,' said the archdeacon, turning to the interrupter.

'I beg yours. Tamil, Tamil, proverb. Came into my mind. Spoke without thinking. Beg yours.'

'Not at all. Very interesting. You've lived in India? Would you mind my asking for a translation?'

'It means "He knows everything between Benares and Rameswaram". Last time I heard it, an old Tamil, seventy or eighty years old, perhaps – he looked a hundred – used it of one of your young men. The young man, by the bye, had been a year and a half in India. D'you understand?'

'Well, I'm not sure I do: I've heard, of course, of Benares, but Rameswaram, I don't seem to remember the name.'

I laughed; I could not help it; the little Anglo-Indian looked so fierce.

'Ah!' he said, 'you don't recollect the name. Well, it's pretty famous out there. Great temple – Hindu – right at the southern tip of India. Benares, you know, is up north. The old Tamil meant that your friend knew everything in India after a year and a half: *he* didn't you know, after seventy, after seven thousand years. Perhaps you also don't recollect that the Tamils are Dravidians? They've been there since the beginning of time, before we came, or the Dutch or Portuguese or the Muhammadans, or our cousins, the other Aryans. Uncivilised, black? Perhaps, but, if they're black, after all it's *their* suns, through thousands of years, that have blackened them. They ought to know, if anyone does: but they don't, they don't pretend to. But you two gentlemen, you seem to know everything between Kasimutal – that's Benares – and Rameswaram, without having seen the sun at all.'

'My dear sir,' began the archdeacon pompously, but the jobber interrupted him. He had had a number of whiskies and sodas, and was quite heated. 'It's very easy to sneer: it doesn't mean because you've lived a few years in a place . . . '

'I? Thirty. But they – seven thousand at least.'

'I say, it doesn't mean because you've lived thirty years in a place that you know all about it. Ramisram, or whatever the damned placed is called, I've never heard of it and don't want to. You do, that's part of your job, I expect. But I read the papers, I've read books too, mind you, about India. I know what goes on. One knows enough – enough – data: East and West and the difference: I can form an opinion – I've a right to it even if I've never heard of Ramis what d'you call it. You've lived there and you can't see the wood for the trees. We see it because we're out of it – see it at a distance.'

'Perhaps', said the archdeacon 'there's a little misunderstanding. The discussion – if I may say so – is getting a little heated – unnecessarily, I think. We hold our views. This gentleman has lived in the country. He holds others. But I confess I didn't quite gather them from what he said.'

The little man was silent: he sat back, his eyes fixed on the ceiling. Then he smiled.

'I won't give you views', he said. 'But if you like I'll give you what you call details, things seen, facts. Then you can give me *your* views on 'em.'

They murmured approval.

'Let's see, it's fifteen, seventeen years ago. I had a district then about as big as England. There may have been twenty Europeans in it, counting the missionaries, and twenty million Tamils and Telegus. I expect nineteen million of the Tamils and Telegus never saw a white man from one year's end to the other, or if they did, they caught a glimpse of me under a sun helmet riding through their village on a flea-bitten grey Indian mare. Well, Providence had so designed it that there was a stretch of coast in that district which was barren wilderness of sand and scrubby thorn jungle – and nothing else – for three hundred miles; no towns, no villages, no water, just sand and trees for three hundred miles. Oh, and sun, I forget that, blazing sun. And in the water off the shore at one place there were oysters, millions of them lying and breeding at the bottom, four or five fathoms down. And in the oysters, or some of them, were pearls.

'Well, we rule India and the sea, so the sea belongs to us, and the oysters are in the sea and the pearls are in the oysters. Therefore of course the pearls belong to us. But they lie in five fathoms. How to get 'em up, that's the question. You'd think being progressive we'd dredge for them or send down divers in diving dresses. But we don't, not in India. They've been fishing up the oysters and the pearls there ever since the beginning of time, naked brown men diving feet first out off long wooden boats into the blue sea and sweeping the oysters off the bottom of the sea into baskets slung at their sides. They were doing it centuries and centuries before we came, when – as someone said – our ancestors were herding swine on the plains of Norway. The Arabs of the Persian Gulf came down in dhows and fished up pearls which found their way to Solomon and the Queen of Sheba. They still come, and the Tamils and Moormen of the district come, and they fish 'em up in the same way, driving out of long wooden boats shaped and rigged as in Solomon's time, as they were centuries before him and the Queen of Sheba. No difference, you see, except that we – Government I mean – take two thirds of all the oysters fished up: the other third we give to the driver, Arab or Tamil or Moorman, for his trouble in fishing 'em up.

'We used to have a Pearl Fishery about once in three years. It lasted six weeks or two months just before the two monsoons, the only time the sea is calm there. And I had, of course, to go and superintend it, to take the Government's share of oysters, to see them, to keep order, to keep out KDs – that means Known Depredators – and smallpox and cholera. We had what we called a camp, in the wilderness remember, on the hot sand down there by the sea: it sprang up in a night, a town, a big town of thirty or forty thousand people, a little India, Asia almost, even a bit of Africa. They came from all districts: Tamils, Telegus, fat Chetties, Parsees, Bombay merchants, Sinhalese from Ceylon, the Arabs and their negroes, Somalis probably, who used to be their slaves. It was an immense gamble: everyone brought oysters for the chance of the prizes in them: it would have taken fifty white men to superintend that camp properly: they gave me one, a little boy of twenty-four fresh cheeked from England, just joined the service. He had views, he had been educated at Board School, won prizes, scholarships, passed the Civil Service 'Exam'. Yes, he had views; he used to explain them to me when he first arrived. He got some new ones I think before he got out of that camp. You'd say he only saw details, things happen, facts, data. Well, he did that too. He saw men die – he hadn't seen that in his Board School – die of plague or cholera, like flies, all over the place, under the trees, in the boats, outside the little door of his own little hut. And he saw flies, too, millions, billions of them all day long buzzing, crawling over everything, his hands, his little fresh face, his food. And he smelt the smell of millions of decaying oysters all day long and all night long for six weeks. He was sick four or five times a day for six weeks; the smell did that. Insanitary? Yes, very. Why is it allowed? The pearls, you see, the pearls: you must get them out of the oysters as you must get the oysters out of the sea. And the pearls are very often small and embedded in the oyster's body. So you put all the oysters, millions of them, in dug out canoes in the sun to rot. They rot very well in that sun, and the flies come and lay eggs in them, and maggots come out of the eggs and more flies come out of the maggots; and between them all, the maggots and the sun, the oysters' bodies disappear, leaving the pearls and a little sand at the bottom of the canoe. Unscientific? Yes, perhaps; but after all it's our camp, our fishery – just as it was in Solomon's time? At any rate, you see, it's the East. But whatever it is, and whatever the reason, the result involves flies, millions of them and a smell, a stench – Lord! I can smell it now.

'There was one other white man there. He was a planter, so he said, and he had come to 'deal' in pearls. He dropped in on us out of a native boat at sunset on the second day. He had a red face and a red nose, he was unhealthily fat for the East: the whites of his eyes were rather blue and rather red: they were also watery. I noticed that his hand shook, and that at first he refused and then took a whisky and soda – a bad sign in the East. He wore very dirty white clothes and a vest instead of a shirt: he apparently had no baggage of any sort. But he was a white man, and so he ate with us that night and a good many nights afterwards.

'In the second week he had his first attack of DT. We pulled him through, Robson and I, in the intervals of watching over the oysters.

When he hadn't got DT, he talked: he was a great talker, he also had views. I used to sit in the evenings – they were rare – when the fleet of boats had got in early and the oysters had been divided, in front of my hut and listen to him and Robson settling India and Asia, Africa too probably. We sat there in our long chairs on the sand looking out over the purple sea, towards a sunset like blood shot with gold. Nothing moved or stirred except the flies which were going to sleep in a mustard tree close by; they hung in buzzing clusters, billions of them on the smooth leaves and little twigs: literally it was black with them. It looked as if the whole tree had suddenly broken out all over in some disease of living black currants. Even the sea seemed to move with an effort in the hot, still air; only now and again a little wave would lift itself up very slowly, very wearily, poise itself for a moment and then fall with a weary little thud on the sand.

'I used to watch them, I say, in the hot still air and the smell of dead oysters – it pushed up against your face like something solid talking, talking in their long chairs, while the sweat stood out in little drops on their foreheads and trickled from time to time down their noses. There wasn't, I suppose, anything wrong with Robson, he was all right at bottom, but he annoyed me, irritated me in that smell. He was too cocksure altogether, of himself, of his Board School education, of life, of his 'views'. He was going to run India on new lines, laid down in some damned *Manual of Political Science* out of which they learn life in Board Schools and extension lectures. He would run his own life, I dare say, on the same lines, laid down in some other text or primer. He hadn't seen anything, but he knew exactly what it was all like. There was nothing curious, astonishing, unexpected, in life, he was ready for any emergency. And we were all wrong, all on the wrong tack of dealing with natives! He annoyed me a little, you know, when the thermometer stood at ninety-nine, at six pm, but what annoyed me still more was that they – the natives – were all wrong too. They too had been taught how to live – and die, too, I gathered.

'But his views were interesting, very interesting – especially in the long chairs there under the immense Indian sky, with the camp at our hands –

just as it had been in the time of Moses and Abraham – and behind us the jungle for miles, and behind that India, three hundred millions of them listening to the piping voice of a Board School boy, are the inferior race, these three hundred millions – mark race, though there are more races in India than people in Peckham – and we, of course, are superior. They've stopped somehow on the bottom rung of the ladder of which we've very nearly, if not quite, reached the top. They've stopped there hundreds, thousands of years: but it won't take any time to lead 'em up by the hand to our rung. It's to be done like this: by showing them that they're our brothers, inferior brothers; by reason, arguing them out of their superstitions, false beliefs; by education by science, by example, yes, even he did not forget example, and White, sitting by his side with his red nose and watery eyes, nodded approval. And all this must be done scientifically, logically, systematically: if it were, a Commissioner could revolutionise a province in five years, turn it into a Japanese India, with all the ryots as well as all the vakils and students running up the ladder of European civilisation to become, I suppose, glorified Board School angels at the top. "But you've none of you got clear plans out here", he piped, "you never work on any system; you've got no point of view. The result is" – here, I think, he was inspired, by the dead oysters, perhaps – "instead of getting hold of the East, it's the East which gets hold of you."

'And White agreed with him, solemnly, at any rate when he was sane and sober. And I couldn't complain of his inexperience. He was rather reticent at first, but afterwards we heard much – too much – of his experiences – one does, when a man gets DT. He said he was a gentleman, and I believe it was true; he had been to public school; Cheltenham or Repton. He hadn't, I gathered, succeeded as a gentleman at home, so they sent him to travel in the East. He liked it, it suited him. So he became a planter in Assam. That was fifteen years ago, but he didn't like Assam: the luck was against him – it always was – and he began to roll; and when a man starts rolling in India, well – he had been a clerk in merchants' offices; he had served in a draper's shop in Calcutta; but the luck was always against him. Then he tramped up and down India, through Ceylon, Burma; he had got at one time or another to the Malay States, and when he was very bad one day, he talked of cultivating camphor in Java. He had been a sailor on a coasting tramp; he had sold horses (which didn't belong to him) in the Deccan somewhere; he had tramped day after day begging his way for months in native bazaars; he had lived for six months with, and on, a Tamil woman in some little village down in the south. Now he was "dealing in" pearls. "India's got hold of me", he'd say, "India's got hold of me and the East".

'He had views too, very much like Robson's, with additions. "The strong hand" came in, and "rule". We ought to govern India more; we didn't now. Why, he had been in hundreds of places where he was the first Englishman that the people had ever seen. (Lord! Think of that!). He talked a great deal about the hidden wealth of India and exploitation. He knew places where there was gold – workable too – only one wanted a little capital – coal probably and iron – and then there was this new stuff, radium. But we weren't go-ahead, progressive, the Government always put difficulties in his way. They made 'the native' their stalking-horse against European enterprise. He would work for the good of the native, he'd treat him firmly but kindly – especially, I thought, the native women, for his teeth were sharp and pointed and there were spaces between each, and there was something about his chin and jaw – *you* know the type, I expect.

'As the fishing went on we had less time to talk. We had to work. The divers go out in the fleet of three hundred or four hundred boats every night and dive until midday. Then they sail back from the pearl banks and bring all their oysters into an immense Government enclosure where the Government share is taken. If the wind is favourable all the boats go back by 6 pm and the work is over at 7. But if the wind starts blowing off shore, the fleet gets scattered and boats drop in one by one all night long. Robson and I had to be in the enclosure as long as there was a boat out, ready to see that, as soon as it did get in, the oysters were brought to the enclosure and Government got its share.

'Well, the wind never did blow favourably that year. I sat in that enclosure sometimes for forty-eight hours on end. Robson found managing it rather difficult, so he didn't like to be left there alone. If you get two thousand Arabs, Tamils, Negroes, and Moormen, each with a bag or two of oysters, into an enclosure a hundred and fifty yards by a hundred and fifty yards, and you only have thirty timid native 'subordinates' and twelve native policemen to control them – well, somehow or other he found a difficulty in applying his system of reasoning to them. The first time he tried it, we very nearly had a riot; it arose from a dispute between some Arabs and Tamils over the ownership of three oysters which fell out of a bag. The Arabs didn't understand Tamil and the Tamils didn't understand Arabic, and when I got down there, fetched by a frightened constable, there were sixty or seventy men fighting with great poles – they had pulled up the fence of the enclosure for weapons – and on the outskirts was Robson running round like a distracted hen with a white face and tears in his blue eyes. When we got the combatants separated, they had only killed one Tamil and broken nine or ten heads. Robson was very upset by that dead Tamil, he broke down utterly for a minute or two, I'm afraid.

'Then White got his second attack. He was very bad: he wanted to kill himself, but was worse than that, before killing himself, he wanted to kill other people. I hadn't been to bed for two nights and I knew I should have to sit up another night in that enclosure as the wind was all wrong again. I had given White a bed in my hut: it wasn't good to let him wander in the bazaar. Robson came down with a white face to tell me that he had "gone mad up there again". I had to knock him down with the butt end of a rifle; he was a big man and I hadn't slept for forty-eight hours, and then there were the flies and the smell of those dead oysters.

'It sounds unreal, and perhaps a nightmare, all this told here to you behind blinds and windows in this – ' he sniffed – 'in this smell of – of – horsehair furniture and paint and varnish. The curious thing is it didn't seem a nightmare out there. It was too real. Things happened, anything might happen, without shocking or astonishing. One just did one's work, hour after hour, keeping things going in that sun which stung one's bare hands, took the skin off even my face, among the flies and the smell. It wasn't a nightmare, it was just a few thousand Arabs and Indians fishing up oysters from the bottom of the sea. It wasn't even new, one felt; it was old, old as the Bible, old as Adam, so the Arabs said. One hadn't much time to think, but one felt it and watched it, watched the things happen quietly, unastonished, as men do in the East. One does one's work, – forty-eight hours at a stretch doesn't leave one much time or inclination for thinking, – waiting for things to happen. If you can prevent people from killing one another or robbing one another, or burning down the camp, or getting cholera or plague or small-pox, and if one can manage to get one night's sleep in three, one is fairly satisfied; one doesn't much worry about having to knock a mad gentleman from Repton on the head with the butt end of a rifle between-whiles.

'I expect that's just what Robson would call "not getting hold of India but letting India get hold of you". Well, I said I wouldn't give you views and I won't: I'm giving you facts: what I want, you know, too is to give you the feeling of facts out there. After all that is data for your views, isn't it? Things here feel so different; you seem so far from life, with windows and blinds and curtains always in between, and then nothing ever happens, you never wait for things to happen, never watch things happening here. You are always doing things somehow – Lord knows what they are – according I suppose to systems, views, opinions. But out there you live so near to life, every morning you smell damp earth if you splash too much in your tin bath. And things happen slowly, inexorably by fate, and you – you don't do things, you watch with the three hundred millions. You feel it there in everything, even in the sunrise and sunset, every day, the immensity, inexorableness, mystery of things happening. You feel the whole earth waking up or going to sleep in a great arch of sky; you feel small, not very powerful. But who ever felt the sun set or rise in London or Torquay either? It doesn't: you just turn on or turn off the electric light.

'White was very bad that night. When he recovered from being knocked down by the rifle, I had to tie him down to the bed. And then Robson broke down – nerves, you know. I had to go back to the enclosure and I wanted him to stay and look after White in the hut – it wasn't safe to leave him alone even tied down with cord to the camp bed. But this was apparently another emergency to which the manual system did not apply.

He couldn't face it alone in the hut with that man tied to the bed. White was certainly not a pretty sight writhing about there, and his face – have you ever seen a man in the last stages of DT? I beg your pardon. I suppose you haven't. It isn't nice, and White was also seeing things, not nice either: not snakes you know as people do in novels when they get DT, but things which had happened to him, and things which he had done – they weren't nice either – and curious ordinary things distorted in a most unpleasant way. He was very much troubled by snipe: hundreds of them kept on rising out of the bed from beside him with that shrill "cheep! Cheep!" of theirs: he felt their soft little feathered bodies against his bare skin as they fluttered up from under him somewhere and flew out of the window. It threw him into paroxysms of fear, agonies: It made one, I admit, feel chilly round the heart to hear him pray one to stop it.

'And Robson was not a nice sight. I hate seeing a sane man break down with fear, mere abject fear. He just sat down at last on a cane-bottomed chair and cried like a baby. Well, that did him some good, but he wasn't fit to be left alone with White. I had to take White down to the enclosure, and I tied him to a post with coir rope near the table at which I sat there. There was nothing else to do. And Robson came too and sat there at my side through the night watching White, terrified but fascinated.

'Can you picture that enclosure to yourself down on the sandy shore with its great fence of rough poles cut in the jungle, lighted by a few flares, torches dipped in coconut oil: and the white man tied to a pole raving, writhing in the flickering light which just showed too Robson's white scared little face? And in the intervals of taking over oysters and settling disputes between Arabs and Somalis and Tamils and Moormen, I sat at the table writing a report (which had to go by runner next morning) on a proposal to introduce the teaching of French in "English schools" in towns. That wasn't a very good report. White gave us the whole history of his life between ten pm and four am in the morning. He didn't leave much to the imagination; a parson would have said that in that hour the memory of his sins came upon him – O, I beg your pardon. But really I think they did. I thought I had lived long enough out there to have heard without a shock anything that men can do and do – especially white men who have "gone under." But I hadn't: I couldn't stomach the story of White's life told by himself. It wasn't only that he had robbed and swindled himself through India up and down for fifteen years. That was bad enough for there wasn't a station where he hadn't swindled and bamboozled his fellow white men. But it was what he had done when he got away "among the natives" – to men, and women too, away from "civilisation", in the jungle villages and high up in the mountains. God! The cold, civilised, corrupted cruelty of it. I told you, I think, that his teeth were pointed and spaced out in his mouth.

'And his remorse was the most horrible thing, tied to that post there, writhing under the flickering light of the flare: the remorse of fear – fear of punishment, of what was coming of death, of the horrors, real horrors and the phantom horrors of madness.

'Often during the night there was nothing to be heard in the enclosure but his screams, curses, hoarse whispers of fear. We seemed alone there in the vast stillness of the sky: only now and then a little splash from the sea down the shore. And then would come a confused murmur from the sea and a little later perhaps the wailing voice of one man calling to another from boat to boat across the water "Abdulla! Abdulla!" and I would go out on to the shore. There were boats, ten fifteen, twenty, perhaps, coming in from the banks, sad, mysterious, in the moonlight, gliding in with the little splashings of the great round oars. Except for the slow moving of the oars one would have thought they were full of the dead, there was not a movement on board, until the boats touched the sand. Then the dark shadows, which lay like dead men about the boats, would leap into life – there would rise a sudden din of hoarse voices, shouting, calling, quarrelling. The boats swarmed with shadows running about, gesticulating, staggering under sacks of oysters, dropping one after the other over the boats' sides into the sea. The sea was full of them and soon the shore too, Arabs, Negroes, Tamils, bowed under the weight of the sacks. They came up dripping from the sea. They burst with a roar into the enclosure: they flung down their sacks of oysters with a crash. The place was full of swaying struggling forms: of men calling to one another in their different tongues: of the smell of the sea.

'And above everything one could hear the screams and prayers of the madman writhing at the post. They gathered about him, stared at him. The light of the flares fell on their dark faces, shining and dripping from the sea. They looked calm, impassive, stern. It shone too on the circle of eyes: one saw the whites of them all round him: they seemed to be judging him, weighing him: calm patient eyes of men who watched unastonished the procession of things. The Tamils' squat black figures nearly naked watched him silently, almost carelessly. The Arabs in their long dirty night-shirts, black-bearded, discussed him earnestly together with their guttural voices. Only an enormous negro, towering up to six feet six at least above the crowd, dressed in sacks and an enormous ulster, with ten copper coffee pots slung over his back and a pipe made of a whole coconut with an iron tube stuck in it in his hand, stood smiling mysteriously.

'And White thought they weren't real, that they were devils of Hell sent to plague and torture him. He cursed them, whispered at them, howled with fear. I had to explain to them that the *sahib* was not well, that the sun had touched him, that they must move away. They understood. They salaamed quietly, and moved away slowly, dignified.

'I don't know how many times this didn't happen during the night. But towards morning White began to grow very weak. He moaned perpetually. Then he began to be troubled by the flesh. As dawn showed grey in the east, he was suddenly shaken by convulsions horrible to see. He screamed for someone to bring him a woman, and, as he screamed, his head fell back: he was dead. I cut the cords quickly in a terror of haste, and covered the horror of the face. Robson was sitting in a heap in his chair. He was sobbing, his face in his hands.

'At that moment I was told I was wanted on the shore. I went quickly. The sea looked cold and grey under the faint light from the East. A cold little wind just ruffled the surface of the water. A solitary boat stood out black against the sky, just throbbing slowly up and down on the water close in shore. They had a dead Arab on board, he had died suddenly while diving, they wanted my permission to bring the body ashore. Four men waded out to the boat: the corpse was lifted out and placed upon their shoulders. They waded back slowly: the feet of the dead man stuck out, toes pointing up, very stark over the shoulders of the men in front. The body was laid on the sand. The bearded face of the dead man looked very calm, very dignified in the faint light. An Arab, his brother, sat down upon the sand near his head. He covered himself with sackcloth. I heard him weeping. It was very silent, very cold and still on the shore in the early dawn.

'A tall figure stepped forward, it was the Arab sheikh, the leader of the boat. He laid his hand on the head of the weeping man and spoke to him calmly, eloquently, compassionately. I didn't understand Arabic, but I could understand what he was saying. The dead man had lived, had worked, had died. He had died working, without suffering, as men should desire to die. He had left a son behind him. The speech went on calmly, eloquently, I heard continually the word *khallas* – all is over, finished. I watched the figures outlined against the grey sky – the long lean outline of the corpse with the toes sticking up so straight and stark, the crouching huddled figure of the weeping man and the tall upright sheikh standing by his side. They were motionless, sombre, mysterious, part of the grey sea, of the grey sky.

'Suddenly the dawn broke red in the sky. The sheikh stopped, motioned silently to the four men. They lifted the dead man on to their shoulders. They moved away down the shore by the side of the sea which began to stir under the cold wind. By their side walked the sheikh, his hand laid gently on the brother's arm. I watched them move away, silent, dignified. And over the shoulders of the men I saw the feet of the dead man with the toes sticking up straight and stark.

'Then I moved away too, to made arrangements for White's burial: it had to be done at once.'

*   *   *

There was silence in the smoking-room. I looked round. The Colonel had fallen asleep with his mouth open. The jobber tried to look bored, the archdeacon was, apparently, rather put out.

'It's too late, I think', said the archdeacon, 'to – Dear me, dear me, past one o'clock'. He got up. 'Don't you think you've chosen rather exceptional circumstances, out of the ordinary case?'

The Commissioner was looking into the few red coals that were all that was left of the fire.

'There's another Tamil proverb', he said: 'When the cat puts his head into a pot, he thinks all is darkness.'

Afterword to the 2005 Edition

Woolf's novel *The Village in the Jungle* sits with *Burmese Days* by George Orwell as the very best of the literature written by servants of the British Empire in the twentieth century. It is emphatically not about what the East means to white people; it does not fantasise about the jungle and the people who live there from a European perspective. It shows a remarkable, deep empathy for the hard lives of poor Sinhalese jungle dwellers and their psychology, and gives a devastating portrayal of the irrelevance of the colonial regime to their needs and world. Written after seven years serving as a colonial officer on the island of Ceylon (now Sri Lanka), it arose directly from the misgivings Woolf came to feel about the imperial enterprise.

Leonard Sidney Woolf was born in London in 1880 and educated at St Paul's School, though it was the five years at Trinity College, Cambridge that were the most formative in his life. There he established lasting friendships with Lytton Strachey, EM Forster and John Maynard Keynes. After he left Cambridge he applied to the Civil Service, hoping for a position with the Home Office. Instead, in 1904, he was sent to Ceylon as a cadet in the Ceylon Civil Service – the small group of white administrators who ruled the island.

Woolf's letters home (especially to Lytton Strachey), coupled with *Growing*, the volume of his autobiography that deals with this time, give a comprehensive and frank expression of his thoughts and feelings, and recall his experiences of the country and its inhabitants during his seven years there as well as his growing disillusionment with the British colonial system.

Colombo, when Woolf arrived by boat in mid-December 1904, was a capital city and seaport of fewer than five-hundred thousand people. He later wrote that in those days, 'which were before the days of the motor-car, Colombo was a real eastern city, swarming with human beings and flies, the streets full of flitting rickshaws and creaking bullock carts, hot and heavy with the complicated smells of men and beasts and dung and oil and food and fruit and spice'. Woolf went straight to the GOH, the Grand Orient Hotel, which was indeed both grand and oriental and a stone's throw from the magnificent harbour. Colombo had been a settlement since the eighth century, when Arab traders used it as a cinnamon port, and it would later be used by the Portuguese, Dutch and British. Although only a few Portuguese and Dutch buildings remain, the downtown area is still called the Fort from their days. In 1796 the British flushed out the Dutch and most of Colombo was built in their colonial image.

After Woolf disembarked, he spent two weeks at the *kachcheri* (office), signing letters for the colonial secretary. He then set out to take up his first appointment as cadet at the Jaffna *kachcheri*, about two-hundred and forty kilometres north of Colombo. He travelled by train to Anuradhapura, about half way, then by mail coach – 'an ordinary bullock cart in which the mail bags lay on the floor and the passengers lay on the mail bags' – to Elephant Pass, before boarding another train for the last few kilometres to the Jaffna Peninsula. Breaking his journey overnight at Anuradhapura, Woolf dined with the government agent. 'I was a very innocent, unconscious imperialist,' he later wrote. 'What is perhaps interesting in my experience during the next six years is that I saw from the inside British imperialism at its apogee, and that I gradually became fully aware of its nature and problems. In so far as anything is important in the story of my years in Ceylon, imperialism and the imperialist aspect of my life have importance and will claim attention.'

'One of the charms of the island is its infinite variety,' Woolf wrote in *Growing*. 'In the north, east and south-east you get the flat, dry, hot low country with a very small rainfall which comes mainly in a month or so of the north-east monsoon. It is a land of silent, sinister scrub jungle, or of great stretches of sand broken occasionally by clumps of low blackish shrubs, the vast dry lagoons in which, as you cross them under the blazing sun, you continually see in the thickening distance the mirage of water, a great non-existent lake sometimes surrounded by non-existent coconut or palmyra palms. This is a country of sand and sun, an enormous blue sky stretching away unbroken to an immensely distant horizon. Many people dislike the arid sterility of this kind of Asiatic low country. But I lived in it for many years . . . and it got into my heart and my bones.'

'Travelling through it by road, all you see is the unending solid wall of trees and undergrowth on either side of you. The green walls are high enough to prevent the slightest eddy of wind stirring the hot air. The jungle's almost completely silent. All the way up to Elephant Pass, I saw hardly any birds and no animals except once or twice the large grey *wanderu* monkey loping across the road or sitting in attitudes of profoundest despair upon the treetops.'

When Woolf arrived, the white community in Jaffna consisted of government officers, some ten missionaries and an ex-army officer 'with an appalling wife and an appalling son.' The Jaffna Peninsula, he said, was unlike any other part of the island. It was inhabited by Tamils, who were Hindus and 'generally darker and dourer than the Sinhalese. The Tamil crowd swarming on the station platforms, in the villages or in the Jaffna streets has a look and air of its own, much less animated (unless it is angry) and less gay than the Sinhalese in Colombo or Kandy or the Southern Province.'

Of John Penry Lewis, the government agent in Jaffna, Woolf wrote, 'he really took little interest in administration; he has the mind of an antiquarian, a historian or archaeologist'. After Woolf became Lewis's office assistant, he was given an increasing amount of responsibility, working up to eleven hours a day. He developed typhoid and went on to suffer from chronic malaria with intermittent exacerbations. Soon after, in February 1906, Woolf took up a special appointment as *koddu* superintendent at the Pearl Fishery in the Gulf of Mannar; the camp was always at Marichchukadi, one hundred and thirty kilometres as the crow flies from Jaffna. As well as the short story featured here, one of several published in 1921 as *Stories of the East*, Woolf wrote a detailed, informative and interesting account of the two months spent with the officials,

the Arabs who came down in their *dhows* from the Persian Gulf and the
Tamil and Moor divers from India. This was in addition to a host of
jewellers, merchants, traders, financiers and criminals. He was extremely
pleased to get away from Jaffna. 'Here for the first time I learnt the
profound happiness of complete solitude.'

Returning to Jaffna, Woolf found that the government agent was
often away on official responsibilities, leaving him completely in charge
of the province. 'The company of white *sahibs* in Jaffna formed a strange
society such as I had never known before and would never know again,'
he wrote. 'It was the produce of British imperialism in Asia.' Nonetheless,
Woolf was a hard administrative taskmaster, but innovative; he gained
the respect, and confidence of the local people by his fair evaluations. He
learnt Tamil during his period in Jaffna and, later, Sinhala while in
Kandy. This enabled him to understand and sympathise with both races.

Woolf took up duties in Kandy on 19 August 1907. 'I had again on me
that delicious feeling of setting out alone on a voyage into the unknown,'
he wrote, adding, 'I'm glad that I spent a year of my life at twenty-seven in
Kandy, for life there was unlike any that I had ever known elsewhere, but
I did not like it in the way that I liked Jaffna or Hambantota, and it did a
good deal to complete my education as an anti-imperialist.' In Woolf's
time, Kandy had a population of thirty thousand and was 'full of white
men'. Being a beauty spot, it entertained a perpetual stream of tourists
from Colombo. Although much more populated today, it still enjoys a
cool, hill-country climate, being four hundred and fifty metres above sea
level. The hills and mountains surrounding the town are clothed in the
luminous green of extensive tea estates. By the time he reached Kandy,
Woolf was developing a strong social conscience. Writing to Lytton
Strachey, he argued that the Europeanising of non-Europeans was a
mistake. 'The Kandyan grovels on the ground and touches your boots,
but has retained his independence and his manners. This letter reflects
my growing awareness of the problems of imperialism and my personal
relation to it.' Increasingly, Woolf was beginning to dislike the whole
system. 'I certainly, all through my life in Ceylon, enjoyed my position
and the flattery of being the great man and the father of the people. That

was why, as time went on, I became more and more ambivalent, politically schizophrenic, an anti-imperialist who enjoyed the fleshpots of imperialism, loved the subject peoples and their way of life, and knew from the inside how evil the system was beneath the surface for ordinary men and women.'

In addition to long working hours Woolf, when he was in Kandy, also played tennis, squash and hockey. His day typically ended at the Kandy Club – 'a symbol and centre of British imperialism' – for a drink, bridge, billiards and dinner. Perhaps Woolf's most exalted social responsibility during his stay in Kandy was entertaining the ex-empress Eugénie of France, showing her the *Dalada Maligawa*, which then housed, as it does today, Buddha's Tooth – one of the most sacred of Buddhist relics. Inviting Sir Hugh Clifford, the colonial secretary, to escort the empress, and then later organising an evening of Kandyan dancing at the King's Pavilion, Woolf somehow impressed Clifford.

Woolf's most unpleasant tasks in Kandy, and during his other postings, involved the prisons. One of his duties was to be present when anyone was flogged or hanged, and to certify that the sentence had been carried out. He was repulsed by corporal and capital punishment, writing that, 'the flogging of a man with a cat-o'-nine tails is the most disgusting and barbarous thing I have ever seen – it is worse than a hanging'. Although he believed that it was important that law and order were strictly maintained, Woolf observed that much of the British criminal law was an uncivilised method of punishing and deterring crime. Woolf's efficiency and organisational abilities after only a year in the post of the office assistant in Kandy convinced Clifford that he should recommend Woolf for the position of assistant government agent in Hambantota. Woolf was duly appointed, becoming the youngest AGA in the British Civil Service.

Woolf arrived in Hambantota as assistant government agent on 28 August 1908. He lived in the Residency, which was situated on a promontory jutting out into the sea. He was in charge of an area of two thousand six hundred square kilometres with a population of one hundred thousand. In those days, the eastern part of Hambantota District was taken up by an area known as Magampattu, which was almost entirely covered with jungle. In the region's extreme east was the Government Game Sanctuary, which had a resident game manager and some Westerners to look after it. The hunting of big game – elephant, buffalo, deer and leopard – was permitted in a small area to the west of the sanctuary, and during the game season princes, counts, barons and other dignitaries from all over the world came to enjoy the 'sport'. Woolf was responsible for issuing licences.

Hambantota was in the Magampattu and thirty kilometres to the east was Tissamaharama where there was major irrigation work. Rice was produced at Tissamaharama, and beyond Hambantota all along the coast were great lagoons, or *lewayas*, producing salt. 'Salt in my day was a government monopoly and it was my duty to arrange for the collecting, transport, storing and selling of the salt, a large scale complicated industry,' Woolf wrote. The lagoons are still there and salt is still a government monopoly, owned and run by the Ceylon Salt Corporation.

In Woolf's day, the only other Europeans in the area were the district judge and superintendent of police in Tangalla, and a Belgian Catholic missionary, Father Cooreman, who had a Sinhalese school in Hambantota. 'I learnt in Hambantota to like solitude and I do not think I ever felt what people call loneliness.' In a letter to Strachey, Woolf wrote, 'I disliked the European side of it. The white *sahib* side of it, the kind of second-rate . . . ' Woolf's obsession with work was stimulated by two considerations. 'I fell in love with the country, the people, and the way of life, which were entirely different from everything in London and Cambridge to which I had been born and bred. The second impulse . . . was a passion for efficiency.'

The sea here had a similarly strong impression on Woolf. 'All year round day and night,' he wrote, 'if you looked down that long two-mile line of sea and sand, you would see, unless it was very rough, continually at regular intervals a wave, not very high but unbroken, two miles long, lift itself up very slowly, wearily, prise itself, for a moment in sudden complete silence and then fall with a great thud upon the sand. The moment of complete silence followed by the great thud, the thunder of the wave, became part of the rhythm of my life.'

Working sixteen hours a day and being responsible for salt and rice production, education, combating cattle disease, judging local disputes, and looking after visiting dignitaries, Woolf made the area the most efficiently governed in the country. He was tireless, and spent his years in the district riding his horse, walking, travelling in a bullock cart and bicycling over the entire area. His severe work ethic didn't always make him popular, but he certainly achieved results and gained an enormous amount of respect.

Although he detested big-game hunting, Woolf developed a fascination with the area's wildlife and for the jungle. Sometimes alone, but often with Henry Engelbrecht – the park's first game warden – he had some alarming encounters in the Magampattu jungle (which encompasses Yala), once literally digging out a wounded leopard from a cave that Woolf luckily shot at point-blank range when it charged. The Sinhalese jungle life he witnessed in Hambantota enthralled him and continued to obsess him in England.

Woolf returned to England in 1911. Only two months after his return he began *The Village in the Jungle*, set in the Hanbantota region of southern Ceylon. He started writing in the middle of October 1911 and continued to work on the novel over the first half of 1912. EM Forster encouraged Woolf to offer it to his own publisher, Edward Arnold, and in November of that year the manuscript was accepted. Woolf wrote to Mr Arnold thanking him for the acceptance and asking him to mark the passages his reader had objected to, as revisions were required before publication. Woolf added that he would be pleased to give Arnold first refusal on his next book. In Woolf's collected letters Spotts notes that in a condescending reply, Arnold predicted poor sales and deprecated Woolf's wish to keep the copyright, dismissing the notion that foreign publishers would have any interest in the book. It bore the touching dedication to Virgina Stephen (who Leonard would marry in 1912) which it still bears: 'I've given you all the little, that I've to give; You've given me all, that for me is all there is; So now I just give back what you have given – If there is anything to give in this.'

The Village in the Jungle

The Village in the Jungle was published in 1913. Arnold soon revised his opinion as the first year's sales not only required a reprint but also a second edition. Arnold now wrote to Woolf that he had heard 'nothing but enthusiastic praise from everyone who had read it' and asked when he might expect another book from his talented author. By 1929 it had sold 2,149 copies and earned Woolf £63. It was later translated into Sinhalese, so that alongside the original English edition *The Village in the Jungle* has become an essential part of the literary culture of Sri Lanka.

In 1912 Leonard Woolf formally retired from the Colonial Service and four years later joined the Fabian Society, a forum for progressive reforming socialists. In 1917 he founded the Hogarth Press with his wife and their household became the accepted centre of the Bloomsbury group of writers, artists, critics and social reformers. His own writings were inevitably overshadowed by the writer acknowledged to have been 'one of the two great modern innovators of the novel in English.' His political works included *Socialism and Co-operation* (1921), *After the Deluge* (1931) and *Principia Politica* (1953), but it is his five-part autobiography – *Sowing* (1960), *Growing* (1961), *Beginning Again* (1964), *Downhill all the Way* (1967) and *The Journey not the Arrival Matters* (1969) – which continues to be admired and enjoy a wide readership. Leonard Woolf returned only once more to Ceylon, in 1960, nine years before he died.

Christopher Ondaatje
Author of *Woolf in Ceylon*
London 2005

About the Author

Leonard Sidney Woolf was born in London in 1880. Educated at St Paul's School, he then won a scholarship to Trinity College, Cambridge in 1899. In 1904 he joined the Civil Service in Ceylon, working there for several years as a government agent. On his return to England in May 1911 he married Virginia Stephen who was, like her husband, a central figure in the Bloomsbury Group. His first novel, *The Village in the Jungle*, was published in 1913 followed by *Wise Virgins* (1914). His other books include *Socialism and Co-operation* (1921), *After the Deluge* (1931), *Barbarians at the Gate* (1939) and *Principia Politica* (1953), and a five-volume memoir. He worked as literary editor of the *Nation* from 1923–30, as well as for the Hogarth Press, which he co-founded with Virginia in 1917. He died in 1969.

ELAND

61 Exmouth Market, London EC1R 4QL
Tel: 020 7833 0762   Fax: 020 7833 4434
Email: info@travelbooks.co.uk

Eland was started in 1982 to revive great travel books
that had fallen out of print. Although the list has diversified
into biography and fiction, it is united by a quest to define the
spirit of place. These are books for travellers, and for readers who aspire to
explore the world but who are also content to travel in their own minds.

Eland books open out our understanding of other
cultures, interpret the unknown and reveal different environments
as well as celebrating the humour and occasional horrors of travel. We take
immense trouble to select only the most readable
books and therefore many readers collect the entire series.

All our books are printed on fine, pliable, cream-coloured paper.
Most are still gathered in sections by our printer and sewn as well
as glued, almost unheard of for a paperback book these days.
This gives larger margins in the gutter, as well as
making the books stronger.

You will find a very brief description of all our books on the
following pages. Extracts from each and every one of them can be
read on our website, at www.travelbooks.co.uk. If you would
like a free copy of our catalogue, please telephone, email
or write to us (details above).

ELAND

'One of the very best travel lists' WILLIAM DALRYMPLE

Memoirs of a Bengal Civilian
JOHN BEAMES
*Sketches of nineteenth-century India
painted with the richness of Dickens*

Jigsaw
SYBILLE BEDFORD
*An intensely remembered autobiographical
novel about an inter-war childhood*

A Visit to Don Otavio
SYBILLE BEDFORD
*The hell of travel and the Eden of arrival
in post-war Mexico*

Journey into the Mind's Eye
LESLEY BLANCH
*An obsessive love affair with Russia and
one particular Russian*

Japanese Chronicles
NICOLAS BOUVIER
*Three decades of intimate experiences
throughout Japan*

The Way of the World
NICOLAS BOUVIER
Two men in a car from Serbia to Afghanistan

Persia: through writers' eyes
ED. DAVID BLOW
*Guidebooks for the mind: a selection
of the best travel writing on Iran*

The Devil Drives
FAWN BRODIE
*Biography of Sir Richard Burton,
explorer, linguist and pornographer*

Turkish Letters
OGIER DE BUSBECQ
*Eyewitness history at its best:
Istanbul during the reign of Suleyman
the Magnificent*

My Early Life
WINSTON CHURCHILL
*From North-West Frontier to Boer War
by the age of twenty-five*

Sicily: through writers' eyes
ED. HORATIO CLARE
*Guidebooks for the mind: a selection
of the best travel writing on Sicily*

A Square of Sky
JANINA DAVID
*A Jewish childhood in the Warsaw
ghetto and hiding from the Nazis*

Chantemesle
ROBIN FEDDEN
*A lyrical evocation of childhood
in Normandy*

Croatia: through writers' eyes
ED. FRANKOPAN, GOODING & LAVINGTON
*Guidebooks for the mind: a selection
of the best travel writing on Croatia*

Viva Mexico!
CHARLES FLANDRAU
A traveller's account of life in Mexico

Travels with Myself and Another
MARTHA GELLHORN
*Five journeys from hell by a great
war correspondent*

The Weather in Africa
MARTHA GELLHORN
*Three novellas set amongst the
white settlers of East Africa*

The Last Leopard
DAVID GILMOUR
*The biography of Giuseppe di Lampedusa,
author of* The Leopard

Walled Gardens
ANNABEL GOFF
An Anglo-Irish childhood

Africa Dances
GEOFFREY GORER
*The magic of indigenous culture
and the banality of colonisation*

Ask Sir James
MICHAELA REID
The life of Sir James Reid,
personal physician to Queen Victoria

A Funny Old Quist
EVAN ROGERS
A gamekeeper's passionate evocation
of a now-vanished English rural lifestyle

Meetings with Remarkable Muslims
ED. ROGERSON & BARING
A collection of contemporary travel
writing that celebrates cultural difference
and the Islamic world

Marrakesh: through writers' eyes
ED. ROGERSON & LAVINGTON
Guidebooks for the mind: a selection
of the best travel writing on Marrakesh

Turkish Aegean: through writers' eyes
ED. RUPERT SCOTT
Guidebooks for the mind: a selection
of the best travel writing on Turkey

Valse des Fleurs
SACHEVERELL SITWELL
A day in St Petersburg in 1868

Living Poor
MORITZ THOMSEN
An American's encounter with
poverty in Ecuador

Hermit of Peking
HUGH TREVOR-ROPER
The hidden life of the scholar
Sir Edmund Backhouse

The Law
ROGER VAILLAND
The harsh game of life played in
the taverns of southern Italy

Bangkok
ALEC WAUGH
The story of a city

The Road to Nab End
WILLIAM WOODRUFF
The best selling story of poverty and
survival in a Lancashire mill town

The Village in the Jungle
LEONARD WOOLF
A dark novel of native villagers struggling
to survive in colonial Ceylon

Death's Other Kingdom
GAMEL WOOLSEY
The tragic arrival of civil war in an
Andalucian village in 1936

The Ginger Tree
OSWALD WYND
A Scotswoman's love and survival
in early twentieth-century Japan

Poetry of Place series

London: Poetry of Place
ED. BARING & ROGERSON
A poetry collection like the city itself, full of
grief, irony and delight

Andalus: Poetry of Place
ED. TED GORTON
Moorish songs of love and wine

Venice: Poetry of Place
ED. HETTY MEYRIC HUGHES
Eavesdrop on the first remembered glimpses
of the city, and meditations on her history

Desert Air: Poetry of Place
ED. MUNRO & ROGERSON
On Arabia, deserts and the Orient of
the imagination

Istanbul: Poetry of Place
ED. ATES ORGA
Poetry from her long history, from paupers to
sultans, natives and visitors alike

The Ruins of Time
ED. ANTHONY THWAITE
Sized to fit any purse or pocket, this is just the
book to complement a picnic amongst the
ruins of time